Praise for *Inheriting Edith*

"Zoe Fishman's *Inheriting Edith* pairs struggling single mother and professional housecleaner Maggie with prickly, resentful, eighty-two-year-old Edith, thrown together in a Sag Harbor beach house after Edith's famous author daughter, Liza, takes her own life and bequeaths the house and her mother to Maggie, her former friend and employee. Fishman deftly explores the intricate territory of mother-daughter relationships as well as the haunting specter of an Alzheimer's diagnosis for famously independent Edith. Throw in winsome toddler Lucy, the hilarious meddling of best friend/yenta Esther and an intriguing potential suitor in the form of a local toy store owner, and you have a delicious literary chicken soup for the soul." —Mary Kay Andrews, *New York Times* bestselling author of *The Weekenders*

"A beautifully crafted story about second chances and life's big surprises. Warm spirited and emotionally rich, *Inheriting Edith* celebrates the fine line between friendship and family. These characters will tug at your heart."

—Jamie Brenner, author of *The Wedding Sisters*

"*Inheriting Edith* is a beautifully written story about what it means to remember and what it means to forget. Fishman masterfully portrays both a single mother and an older woman with Alzheimer's, as they are both struggling to come to terms with their pasts, their futures and each other. I loved this compelling and achingly real novel about friendship, family and second chances."

—Jillian Cantor, author of *Margot* and *The Hours Count*

"A heartbreaking story about life, love and friendship that you'll want to devour in one sitting."

—Erin Duffy, author of *Bond Girl* and *Lost Along the Way*

Also by Zoe Fishman

Driving Lessons
Saving Ruth
Balancing Acts

Inheriting Edith

A Novel

ZOE FISHMAN

wm

WILLIAM MORROW
An Imprint of HarperCollins*Publishers*

P.S.™ is a trademark of HarperCollins Publishers.

INHERITING EDITH. Copyright © 2016 by Zoe Fishman. All rights reserved. Printed in the United States of America. No part of this book may be used or reproduced in any manner whatsoever without written permission except in the case of brief quotations embodied in critical articles and reviews. For information address HarperCollins Publishers, 195 Broadway, New York, NY 10007.

HarperCollins books may be purchased for educational, business, or sales promotional use. For information please e-mail the Special Markets Department at SPsales@harpercollins.com.

FIRST EDITION

Designed by Diahann Sturge

Library of Congress Cataloging-in-Publication Data has been applied for.

ISBN 978-0-06-237874-3

16 17 18 19 20   OV/RRD   10 9 8 7 6 5 4 3

For my muses, Ari and Lev

ACKNOWLEDGMENTS

Thank you to my editor, Amanda Bergeron, whose encouragement and insight brought these characters to life. Thank you to my former agent, Mollie Glick, whose tenacity and honesty I will miss greatly, and to my current agent, Jess Regel, whose enthusiasm has meant so much.

Thank you to my husband, Ronen Shacham, who spent countless weekends covering for me as I worked on draft after draft. And to my mother and father, Sue and Ethan Fishman, and my brother Brenner Fishman, whose faith in me is a gift for which I am always grateful.

Thank you to Kathi Tobey, for your help in better understanding memory loss from the inside out.

And finally, thank you to my boys, Ari and Lev, for teaching me so much and making me a better writer in the process.

Inheriting Edith

CHAPTER 1

A beach house, thought Maggie, her head spinning like the revolving glass door that deposited her back onto Eighteenth Street. People headed home after work bumped and jostled along the sidewalk as she slipped in unsteadily.

"A house in Sag Harbor." Just the words *Sag Harbor* conjured up images of the kind of life she had never known. Sand dunes and waves; sea grass and farmers' markets; rich women with their sun-kissed faces stretched tight like rubber bands.

"Are you sure?" she had asked incredulously when the lawyer had told her upstairs.

"Yes, Miss Sheets," he had replied brightly. "Here it is, plain as day," he explained, tapping the will with his finger. "She wanted you to have it."

Maggie shook her head, still not believing him. They hadn't spoken in over four years. It made no sense.

"Sag Harbor is lovely, Miss Sheets. A beach town with a New York mentality."

"Oh, do you have a house there?" she asked, not really caring if he did.

"No, we have a place upstate. My wife hates sand."

Maggie had nodded absently, thinking that hating sand said a lot about a person. She had to hate sand on principle, because of the way it crept into every uneven ridge of a hardwood floor; collected in grainy, wet piles in the bathtub and settled in the rumpled ridges of bed sheets. It was impossible to clean. But to hate it as someone who didn't clean houses for a living, who probably employed someone just like Maggie to do it for her, that implied something else entirely.

"But back to you," he continued, "and Sag Harbor. The house comes with something."

"Something?" Maggie asked.

"Or someone, I should say." Maggie's stomach dropped. Of course.

"Her mother."

"Yes, yes—so you know Edith?"

"Know? No, I wouldn't say that. We met once."

"So you know that she had been living with Liza when she passed." *Passed*, thought Maggie. Liza had killed herself. *Passed* was not the right word, not even close.

"Yes, I know." Maggie looked down at her feet, thinking about Edith. What must it be like for her now, she wondered, in the aftermath of her daughter's death? Maggie hadn't exactly been a fan of Edith's—she had treated her like the help at the one lunch they'd shared, despite Liza's repeated attempts to clarify the fact that they were friends—but no mother deserved her child dying before she did. The lawyer clasped his hands in front of him on the desk.

"Edith has recently been diagnosed with early stage Alzheimer's," he announced.

"Oh no," said Maggie. "I had no idea. Liza and I . . . we hadn't spoken in some time."

"Yes, apparently the diagnosis was quite recent. Two months ago, to be exact."

Maggie rubbed her temples, overwhelmed. "I'm sorry, isn't there a family member better suited for this?" she asked. "I clean houses, Mr. Barnes. I don't— I've never cared for an elderly person. I don't have the first clue about it."

Maggie's mother had been dead a long time, and her father had begun a new life with new kids shortly thereafter. She'd never even seen either of them old, she realized, much less cared for them. She thought back to all of the times Liza had scolded her about her financial recklessness; her relationship decisions; her lack of ambition; the fact that she wore a denim jacket in February. Why would she choose her for this?

"No, I'm afraid not. Edith is the only remaining member of Liza's immediate family, and as an only child she had no siblings."

"And what if I don't take the house? What happens to it? And Edith?"

"The house goes on the market and Edith goes to an assisted living facility nearby," he answered.

"And Liza didn't want that."

"No."

Maggie wondered when Liza had written the will, and whether or not she knew that she was going to kill herself at the time. She felt a stab in her heart, imagining Liza sitting at her desk in her old apartment, making the decision to bequeath everything to Maggie of all people, snacking on her fluorescent orange peanut butter crackers, the crumbs of which always ended up everywhere, and sipping from one of her Diet Coke cans that always left impossible to erase rings in their wake.

"Liza, would it kill you to use a coaster?" she had asked once.

"Yes, it would kill me," Liza had replied, not looking up from the book she was reading on the couch as Maggie stopped mid-vacuum to point out the ring of condensation on her coffee table. Maggie's choice of words seemed so thoughtless now.

No mutual friend had called Maggie to alert her of Liza's death—there were none of those four years after their friendship had ceased to exist. Maggie had read about it online, scrolling through headlines in bed.

For days Maggie had wandered through her life like a visitor, her head like a tethered balloon, filled with memories. And then, the voicemail from the lawyer, telling her to come in, that he had news. She still couldn't believe it—any of it. Liza had known so many people. Why had she chosen Maggie for this? Maggie supposed it could be her way of apologizing, but it was so dramatic, so beyond what the situation called for. But who even knew if it was an apology at all?

Regardless of Liza's intentions, there was no denying what this offer meant. A paid mortgage and a monstrous stipend that would last far beyond the foreseeable future. Security for her daughter, Lucy. Cleaning houses to support herself was one thing—to support two and pay for childcare was quite another. It had been hard, since Lucy had been born, there was no denying it. Maggie thought about the beach; sand between her toes and Lucy giggling as she ran from the shoreline, the waves crashing behind her. It would be a nicer life there, for Lucy. Easier.

And there would be no more housecleaning, except for her own. She'd begun to resent her job lately. Scrubbing floors while she paid for someone else to watch Lucy didn't make sense. In terms of financial freedom, Liza's offer was akin to winning the lottery for Maggie.

And yet, the winnings included an uptight old lady who Maggie would have to play nursemaid to. It also meant uprooting their lives to live in a place where they knew no one; and more than that she would be submerging herself in the sadness and guilt Liza had left in her wake. Maggie didn't believe in ghosts, but the remorse she felt about her friend's death already felt like being haunted, even at a safe distance. Across the street, the light flashed *Don't Walk*, but Maggie, glancing both ways quickly, darted across the intersection anyway.

Maggie had met Liza ten years before, when she was twenty-eight. A lifetime ago, now. She had just begun working for the agency, just started to clean houses for a living, which on paper she knew seemed really sad for a college educated woman, but in reality paid her bills far better than her desk job ever had.

It was fancier even than she had initially thought, the agency she worked for, catering exclusively to rich people with deep pockets. Maggie enjoyed the work, much preferring hard labor to sitting in a chair all day, her ass growing as she indulged in the endless supply of stale leftover Danish and soggy pasta salad from the steady stream of meetings in the conference room across from her. Plus, there was tremendous satisfaction in knowing that even the wealthiest people were dirty behind closed doors.

She'd been excited to know she was going to the world-famous author Liza Brennan's Upper West Side penthouse. And it was just as she expected, with its built-in bookshelves crammed to bursting, its expensive artwork and French cotton bed sheets as soft as silk. There was nothing fussy about her apartment, but it looked expensive nevertheless. Liza had good taste. She bought the things Maggie would have bought, if she had had the means.

When she had first begun cleaning it—once a week on Thursday mornings—Liza would greet her and then leave, her laptop and papers peeking out of her navy leather satchel. Soon, though, she had asked if Maggie minded if she stayed—her focus was hopeless at coffee shops, she admitted—and Maggie said of course, she didn't mind, although truthfully she did. As a rule, she hated when her clients hung around, watching her every move, making sure she wasn't snooping or half-assing it. But Liza was different. She kept her eyes on her computer or the book she was reading without so much as glancing Maggie's way. It made her want to work harder, that trust. And she had.

"I could eat dinner off this floor," Liza had remarked, when Maggie bid her farewell, her small cart of cleaning supplies in tow. "Thank you." And then she would hand Maggie a fifty-dollar tip without so much as a flinch.

Maggie walked around the perimeter of Gramercy Park; the wrought-iron fence separating the plebeians like herself from its impeccably groomed grounds and residents. Was *plebeian* the right word? she wondered. Liza would have known.

A few months in, she and Liza began to talk. "What's your story?" Liza had asked one morning, startling Maggie, who was scrubbing Liza's sink in yellow gloves up to her elbows. Her hands were as dry as driftwood, with cuticles as flimsy as tissue paper. No way around it in her line of work, but the gloves helped.

"My story?" she had replied.

"Yeah, how'd you end up cleaning apartments? You don't exactly seem like the toilet scrubbing type."

Maggie wasn't one for sharing much of anything about herself, but there was something about Liza that made her feel at ease, something familiar. They became unlikely friends. Until they weren't.

Maggie hustled past the bodegas and the thrift shops; the wine bars and the bar bars; the Peruvian place; the Chinese restaurant; the nail shop where she had once had her eyebrows waxed into commas.

"Hey, Jose," greeted Maggie, her voice cracking.

He looked up from the tiny black and white television perched on the table beside him and nodded. Once July hit, Jose would emerge from the basement apartment he had owned for close to forty years and take up a daytime residence on their stoop. Sunup to sundown, he sat in his green folding chair and watched baseball in his shorts and V-neck T-shirt; his bald head and forearms were brown by the time September rolled around.

She took the four flights of stairs two at a time, panting as she got higher. At her door, finally, Maggie turned the key, only to have the chain abruptly stop it from opening.

"Mommy!" bellowed Lucy.

"Hey Miss S.," said Dahlia, unlocking the chain. Lucy sprang forward like an Olympic sprinter, attaching herself to Maggie's legs with unbridled glee. A delicate flower, she was not, her daughter. "Lucy's been real good. Had her snack, played with some puzzles—"

"Sesame!" Lucy shrieked, interrupting her.

"Yeah, we watched a little bit," admitted Dahlia.

"It's okay. She's a handful today. I get it." She pulled her wallet out of her bag and handed Dahlia her pay, noticing that she only had two twenties to last through the rest of the week.

"Thanks, Miss S." Dahlia folded the cash into a neat U and slid it into the back pocket of her shorts. "Bye Lucy."

"Bye Dawwa," replied Lucy. "Hug!"

Dahlia laughed and bent down. Lucy pulled her head close, like the Don of Avenue B, and then released it, pleased with the blessing she had bestowed and ready to move on to the next order of business.

As Dahlia slipped out the door, Lucy galloped around the apartment, neighing. Maggie noticed for the millionth time just how much she looked like her father. The blond curls; the brown eyes; the dimple that had gotten Maggie into trouble in the first place.

"How was hanging out with Dahlia?" asked Maggie. "Did you guys play horsey?" she asked, collapsing onto the couch in a sweaty heap as Lucy climbed onto her lap. Once settled, she drank from her sippy cup of milk in silence, crossing her chubby legs in contentment.

"You sad, Mommy?" she asked.

"Yeah, I'm sad."

"About that lady?"

"Yeah."

"Where she at again? She died?"

"Yes, baby, she died."

The morning after reading about Liza, Maggie's eyes had been red and swollen from her tears, so much so that she could barely open them. When Lucy had asked her what was wrong, Maggie had had no time to concoct a sensitive story about the circle of life.

"My friend died," she had told her, surprising herself with the word. She hadn't considered Liza a friend in a long time.

"What's 'died' means?" Lucy had asked.

"Gone."

"Oh."

She had patted Maggie on the hand and returned to her

favorite activity—lining up her parade of tiny plastic zoo animals—as Maggie stared blankly out of their lone window into her neighbor's empty kitchen, exhausted.

Maggie looked around the room now—the puzzles and crayons, the threadbare rug, the Ikea kitchen table and chairs she had bought when she was fresh out of college—and sighed. She looked at her hands, as dry as chalk.

She thought about Liza; what her advice would have been had someone else left Maggie their home and mother.

What's the problem here? Liza would have asked.

But the mother— Maggie would have argued.

So what about the mother? How hard can making sure an old lady takes her medication be? If you don't take this offer, you're an idiot. It's a once in a lifetime opportunity.

And then she would have moved on to another topic of conversation. Maggie could take her advice or not, it was up to her. That was how their relationship had worked, until it didn't.

So this was Liza's final piece of advice. *Take my house and mom, take Lucy out of that tiny apartment in that crazy city and start over.* Maggie didn't like being told what to do usually, but this was different. Since Lucy had been born, she had felt like she was drowning, slowly but surely, the water inching up all around her.

And so she would.

CHAPTER 2

Edith woke. Blinking in the darkness, she knew even before turning to the clock on her bedside table that it was 5:22 AM. Her body, stubborn old thing that it was, would not sleep a minute more. The world outside her bedroom windows was silent, but soon the birds would begin their inquisitive chirping; the bugs their interminable buzzing and the twenty-somethings their incessant shrieking and splashing in the pool next door. It was the middle of summer, but Edith wished it was the end.

Every year it was the same. Spring would arrive, timidly at first—a daffodil here, a crocus there, an unexpected sunburn across the bridge of her nose while she was out walking—and then, right behind it: people. So many of them, in their shiny cars filled to bursting with designer weekend bags and organic snacks; the women's tresses highlighted just so and the men's receding hairlines artfully disguised, their children spilling out like groomed monkeys. Edith despised them. Sag Harbor was her home year-round—through the sunshine and the snow, the open windows and the grumbling furnace—but these people, these were quite literally fair-weather friends.

Edith stretched carefully, wincing at the papier mâché–like stiffness of her eighty-two-year-old joints. It was hard, this aging thing, especially since her body had once been as limber as a rubber band. She had been a dancer when she was young; her body her instrument. Now it felt more like an old car, with a faulty transmission. The wrinkles that rippled out from the corners of her eyes and across her cheeks and forehead like the waves of a pond didn't bother her as much as the fact that her body just wouldn't move like it used to, stalling out when she least expected it. Bending over and getting up hurt now, and stairs were best avoided, but she wasn't going down without a fight. She made herself walk every morning, no matter how difficult it was. She was still the boss of it, thank you very much. And her mind, too, no matter what that fancy doctor in Manhattan said, in her condescending and nasally voice.

Irritating or not, she had scared her, and so Edith took her pills every morning before brushing her crisp white bob, donning her khaki Bermuda shorts and sleeveless chambray blouse, slipping into her sandals and climbing into her car to drive the short distance to the beach, where she strolled the shore for twenty-five minutes precisely. She loved the way her muscles responded to the soothing lap of the waves against her feet, unfurling like flags to remind her of their strength, and the way the sun hung hesitantly in the sky, groggy from a night's rest. It was her favorite time of the day.

After she had found Liza, Edith had foregone her morning ritual, instead hiding in the house with the lights dimmed and the shades drawn—an informal Shiva if there ever was one. She was the world's worst Jew, hadn't so much as thought about the religion her mother had tried to impress upon her as a child unless she saw a particularly inviting looking loaf of challah at the supermarket, but then, in the aftermath of such awfulness, it suddenly felt like second nature. There was no Rabbi, but the door was open and people who had known and loved Liza had come through, heaping gelatinous looking casseroles and lopsided cakes on the kitchen counters.

Normally, Edith was not one to dwell on her emotions, whatever they were, but this was a sadness that she had never felt before. If only she hadn't done this or said that to Liza; if only she hadn't been so judgmental and impatient; if only she'd been a different kind of mother altogether. Her mind raced back and forth, on a hamster wheel of guilt.

The lawyer had called and called, leaving message after message on the machine for the next two weeks, but Edith could not be bothered. He had had Liza cremated, as per the will that he had helped her draw up, and that was all that she needed from him as far as she was concerned. She wasn't ready to hash out the copious details of her daughter's life with anyone yet, much less a total stranger.

And then he had shown up, at her doorstep, his suit

wrinkled from the ride. Edith wished she hadn't answered
the door, but she was a practical woman, even in her grief,
and knew that she couldn't avoid her daughter's wishes forever. She had laughed in his face when he told her that the
cleaning lady had inherited the house, and that she and her
daughter would be moving in to look after her. The cleaning lady!

"Over my dead body," she had replied.

"I'm sorry, Edith, you don't really have a choice. Well,
you do, but it would involve moving out and relocating to
an assisted living facility. Liza has provided the necessary
funding for that. It was her house, after all." He laughed
awkwardly—a half laugh that sounded more like a cough.
As much as she wanted to wring his skinny little neck, it was
true.

"Mom, you can't live on your own anymore," Liza had
told her matter-of-factly after Edith had taken a tumble in
her pink tiled bathroom five years earlier; the same pink tiled
bathroom that Liza had grown up using.

And so, Edith had moved in with her daughter, kicking
and screaming, until she had realized that living there wasn't
all that bad. It had taken her a while to get used to what Liza
had called their tree house because of the open floors and
upside down layout, with the kitchen and living room on the
second floor, but soon she had fallen in love with its conflux
of light and air amongst the green leaves outside their windows. It soothed her.

She and Liza had developed a real friendship, or so Edith
had thought. Now it was clear that she had not been her

daughter's friend at all, but instead, a burden to be passed onto someone who had no other options. She felt like a fool.

Edith had wrestled with the lawyer's news for a day or two, sitting on the couch and thinking as her sadness turned into anger. How dare Liza insinuate that she was incapable? Edith had started over before, had overcome obstacles her daughter didn't even know about, and she could certainly do it again without unwanted help from a stranger.

There was no way in hell she was leaving. So she had forgotten things a few times. She was eighty-two years old for God's sake! She hadn't been sleeping well, that was it. Lack of sleep had always made her forgetful. As far as falling now and again, so what? She would wear one of those MedicAlert bracelets gladly if it meant keeping her independence.

And just who was Liza, thinking that her word was more credible than Edith's? Liza wasn't well; hadn't been well for years—the proof obvious. You didn't do what she did if you had your senses about you. She would contest the will, she decided. But figuring out how exactly would require time and money, and she certainly didn't want to leave this house, the house that was rightfully hers, while she did so. She would stay.

So here she was. The evening before, Edith had said hello when Maggie had arrived with her sleeping toddler in her arms. The movers were coming the next day, she had told her. Edith had nodded, showed Maggie Liza's bedroom, and retreated to her own, where she had holed up with a small glass of whiskey and a plate of cheese and crackers. She'd eaten on her bed and washed the dishes in her bathroom sink, feeling vaguely like a prisoner, but not minding it too terribly much. The alternative—engaging in forced conversation and pretending to not be furious—seemed unnecessarily exhausting.

Now, what if they were awake and wanted to talk to her? Before her coffee? Hopefully Maggie had some common sense. She'd certainly had enough sense to glom onto Liza anyway, and reap her friendship's rewards: no rent and money to cover whatever utilities and expenses cropped up for a good long while, if not forever. The only wrench in the works, at least from Maggie's perspective, Edith figured, was of course her. The crotchety old lady who didn't live in a shoe like the nursery rhyme suggested, but instead, came with the house, like a goddamn appliance or something. Edith was so mad at Liza that she could spit. You could do that, Edith had discovered—miss and despise someone at the same time.

The three bedrooms of the pagoda-style house were on the first level; the kitchen and dining and living rooms were on the second. On the outside, its red wood and white stone exterior peeked out from the dense, green foliage with a porch that wrapped around its second floor, hugging the floor to ceiling windows like a belt. There was a tiny guesthouse—more like a box, really—that Liza had used for her writing, and a pool, too, that she had sometimes swum laps in when she had been in one of her fitness phases.

Edith smoothed the white coverlet of her bed and surveyed her room. She had never been much for fuss: there was her bed, a study in crisp white linen; a bedside table upon which sat a bookmarked paperback mystery and a brass lamp; a blue velvet chair that looked inviting but wasn't; and a maple bureau, over which hung a small mirror. Attached to her bedroom was her bathroom, which boasted a long stainless steel rail around its perimeter, along with two smaller ones in the shower. Liza had had it updated for Edith, but Edith hated it. She felt like she was taking a shower in a subway station.

She closed the door behind her. This was her territory now, small as it was, and she would protect it. Besides, who knew what a two-year-old would do to her bedspread? She shuddered, imagining tiny strawberry jam handprints all over it.

In the hallway, she paused to listen, grateful for silence. Good, she was the only one awake. She ascended the stairs carefully, leaning on the banister with more weight than she cared to admit as the rising sun cast a purple light through the trees.

In the kitchen, Edith set about making her coffee, frowning slightly at the new snacks that sat at the corner of one of the long marble counters, wedged between the toaster and the wall. Graham crackers and tiny yellow goldfish; bananas and shiny red apples inside a green ceramic bowl. Her green ceramic bowl. She poked it, thinking, *Mine.*

As the coffee percolated, she willed her own inner child away, knowing that these types of thoughts, about the ownership of bowls, were infantile and useless. She had always been terrible at sharing. Edith startled suddenly, hearing footsteps creak up the stairs behind her.

"Good morning," a soft, clear voice announced.

Edith took a deep breath and turned to face Maggie, taking in her ragged tank top and ripped pants; the fact that she wore no bra. Liza had always swaddled herself in layers of colorful silk and chiffon, like a plump parrot, so it had been some time since Edith had seen the female form like this—in all of its honey-hued glory.

"Did you sleep well?" asked Maggie.

"Yes, thank you. And you?" The beep of the coffee machine shattered the tension, and Edith, grateful for something to do, held her red coffee mug up in an awkward salute.

"Very well, thanks," answered Maggie.

"And what about little— Forgive me, what's your daughter's name?"

"Lucy. Lucy had a bit of a tough night, what with it being a new place and all. She ended up in my bed. Practically pushed me out of it. She's a spreader." Maggie flung her arms over her head in demonstration. Edith knew she should smile, nod in understanding, but she didn't feel like it.

"You know, I'm happy to make the coffee for you, Edith. I can set it up the night before, no problem. Does it have a timer?" asked Maggie, examining it closely. "Oh yes, there it is. Just let me know when you wake u—"

"Why should you make the coffee for me?" barked Edith, cutting her off. "I'm perfectly capable of making a pot of coffee, Maggie."

"Suit yourself," said Maggie.

"I'm not sure what that ridiculous lawyer told you, but I don't need your help."

"Message received," said Maggie. She turned to face the cabinets. "Is the sugar in here?"

"Yes," answered Edith. "And the milk is in the refrigerator."

"Thanks," said Maggie. Edith glared at her back as she prepared her cup.

"So," she said, turning around.

"So," repeated Edith.

"If you're looking for a fight, you've got the wrong girl," said Maggie, before taking her first sip. "I'm just as surprised as you are that Liza chose me."

Edith raised her mug to her mouth and took a sip of her own, not knowing what to say.

"But she did, and I'm here, so I think we both just have to deal with it, Edith. And being rude isn't exactly a productive way of dealing with it."

"Excuse me?" asked Edith.

"Come on, Edith, I know you're angry about the situation. I would be, too, if I was in your shoes. But I am sincerely here to help you, you know. As best I can, anyway. We can stay out of each other's way until that kind of opportunity presents itself, if you like. But consider yourself warned— staying out of the way of a two-year-old is tough."

"Maggie, I don't appreciate being spoken to like this," said Edith. "Not at all."

"I mean no disrespect, believe me. I just thought it would be easier to put our cards on the table."

"I don't know what you're talking about," Edith replied.

"Okay, I get it. I'm not going to bully you into admitting your discomfort." Maggie walked over to the table and pulled out a chair. "I guess it'll just happen when it happens. Forget I said anything."

"Is that supposed to be some kind of a bad joke?" asked Edith.

"What?"

"Forget you said anything? Are you making a joke about my Alzheimer's?"

"Oh, God no, Edith, please, I would never. I meant it figuratively—"

Edith stormed past Maggie and down the stairs, a furtive smile on her face. Of course she knew that Maggie hadn't meant anything by saying that, but it felt good to scare her a little. Maggie had surprised her with her forwardness. Edith had been expecting a meek mouse, not a pit bull.

Downstairs, Edith grabbed her keys from the slim wooden table that hugged the wall in the narrow hallway.

"Mommy?" a small voice from Liza's bedroom called out. Edith froze, glancing at the clock.

Already she was twenty minutes behind schedule. Engaging with a toddler would set her back at least twenty more. Soon her normally deserted beach would be plastered with the yoga mats of those smug, supple people; its sand flying under the hooves of the gazelle-like runners she always made sure to avoid. Not to mention the brighter sun, which would pink up her skin like a boiled shrimp. She turned as quietly as she could towards the door and then, of course, dropped her keys, which landed in a loud, jangled mess at her feet.

"Mommy!" the voice demanded, now outraged by the injustice of being ignored.

Edith retrieved her keys and looked up, willing Maggie to hear her daughter, but knowing that she probably wouldn't. She could either ascend the stairs again and alert her to the fact that her child was awake or handle it herself. She walked towards the voice instead and gently pushed open the door, which was not entirely shut.

In the middle of a sea of rumpled white sheets was a very small girl swaddled head to toe in pink striped pajamas that zipped up the front. Her curly blond hair pointed north, south, east and west all at once. She regarded Edith coolly, as though a strange old lady appeared in her doorway every day.

"Good morning," greeted Edith formally. The girl blinked back at her. Edith had forgotten her name again. "Your mother is upstairs, getting breakfast ready," she continued. "I'm Edith."

"Edith," she repeated, tilting her head slightly. And then, "Woommay."

"Yes, that's very nice," replied Edith. "I have to be going now. Do you need help out of bed?" She moved towards her and extended her hand.

"Woommay," the child said again.

Maybe she's telling me her name, thought Edith, although it didn't sound familiar. She'd always had a hard time remembering names, even when she was young. If indeed it was her name, it was a strange one, but all of the names she heard these days were. Whenever she got her hair cut at the salon in town, she would thumb through magazines of celebrities toting children named things like Apple and Moon. It was absurd.

"Hello Woommay," she said now. "I'm Edith."

"No! Woommay!" the child yelled, switching from docile lamb to Bengal tiger cub in a matter of seconds, reminding her of Liza as a toddler in the process. Edith backed away slightly as Maggie appeared in the doorway.

"Lucy!" she reprimanded. "That's not how we speak to people. Apologize to Edith."

Lucy, thought Edith. Lucy's face crumpled like a Kleenex.

"Sorry Edith, she's just a little disoriented, I guess." Maggie scooped her out of the bed and held her on her hip. Lucy's lean, striped legs curled around her mother like parentheses.

"Oh no, that's quite alright. I understand."

"Woommay," Lucy whimpered again.

"Yes, this is Edith. Your new roommate." At the correct translation, Lucy's face unfolded into a spectacular smile, her brown eyes twinkling.

"Ah, roommate!" said Edith. *Roommate*. As though the three of them were sharing a dorm room in college.

"That's an impressive word, Lucy," she offered. Lucy nuzzled her face into Maggie's neck, pleased. "Well, I better get going," Edith continued.

"Of course, go ahead," said Maggie kindly, as though their kitchen confrontation had never happened.

"Bye woommay," said Lucy.

"Goodbye Lucy."

Edith nodded and saw her way out.

CHAPTER 3

Maggie lay in bed the next morning, eyes open as the early morning light dappled the sheets. She had awoken in the middle of the night from a dream about Liza, and hadn't been able to fall back asleep. They had been walking in Central Park together; Maggie's breath hanging in front of her in the cold air. Liza had been so real, so there—her infectious laugh ringing in Maggie's ears. Suddenly, Maggie had lost her balance and fallen forward, her heart in her stomach as the pavement rose up in front of her and then—bam! She had woken up.

In Liza's bed, of all places. It would have been the kind of thing she would have laughed with Liza about, irony of ironies. A haunted bed. Would have made for a great story to write, too, but Maggie's former hobby had been wrapped up in resentment for years, so much so that she had abandoned it altogether. She hadn't tried since Liza had died, though. Maybe it would be different now. Although, in her absence Liza was more present than ever in Maggie's new life.

She regretted coming at Edith so hard the day before, guns blazing at a harmless old lady, even if she was a curmudgeon. She was hurting, after all. Maggie needed to be more patient; more understanding—the way she was with Lucy. If she had to pretend to be Lucy's well-compensated nanny just to make it through the day without screaming, so be it.

Outside, birds greeted the day with warbles and trills. Maggie couldn't remember the last time she had awoken to anything but jackhammers, car horns and the sound of buses wheezing down the street below. It was disconcerting now, to be surrounded by nature, in a room that was as foreign as the new world outside her window. She pushed a pillow against the oak headboard and sat up, reclining against it with a yawn.

To her right was a bank of windows—three across the upper third of the wall and veiled by white wooden shades that Maggie had forgotten to close completely. Below them was a long, squat dresser—the furniture equivalent of a dachshund. Its surface was completely devoid of any mementos of Liza, as was the rest of the room. Maggie wondered who had come in and taken the photos and jewelry; the lotions and hair creams—all of the affectations that made a house a home. A cleaning lady, no doubt.

Maggie had had to do that once, rid an Upper East Side

apartment of all traces of its former inhabitant before it went on the market. She'd walked in to find dozens and dozens of empty boxes, ready to be filled and then shipped to a storage unit in Queens, where who knew what would happen to them. She'd taken the job because it paid a boatload, but she'd felt wrong about it, like she was betraying its former inhabitant.

"Just wrap everything up and fill each box to the brim," the man's niece had instructed her over the phone. "We don't want any of that crap."

But that was his life, she'd wanted to say to her. *You shouldn't call it crap.* Instead she just said, "Yes, yes, alright, of course," and did what she was told.

Maggie sat up. Directly across from the bed was the entrance to the marble sanctuary otherwise known as her personal bathroom. Everything, from the floor to the counter to the glass-encased shower to the freestanding bathtub, gleamed expectantly, accentuated by the kind of lighting that magically erased wrinkles and dark circles. She would have to use the expensive cleaner, the kind that didn't scratch but practically burned her nose hairs off with its smell, to keep it looking good. Most people didn't understand Maggie's compulsion to clean, but it made her feel good; like she had accomplished something.

Her father had been that way with their lawn. Every Sunday, from sunup to supper, he would weed his immaculate flower beds, mow his green rectangle in perfectly straight lines and edge its perimeter like a barber giving a buzz cut.

The best yard on the block, he would say proudly, standing in the middle of their sidewalk as he mopped his sweaty brow with a washcloth. Once Maggie had said, *No, what about the Hendersons'?* and he had swatted her behind, right there in the open, where everyone could see.

Maggie wondered if he had a yard now, if he still took the same painstaking care of it. He was much older, would be, what? Seventy-three? Less than ten years younger than Edith.

It had been almost fifteen years since they had spoken, since he had remarried not even a year after her mother had died, without so much as asking Maggie to meet his betrothed beforehand. It had been her first year after college graduation and she'd been living in New York when he had told her.

"Didn't want you to have to buy a ticket home, Mag," he had explained, as though that was a totally normal way to handle things. "It was just a justice of the peace thing anyway."

He'd wanted to come up, to bring his new wife and stepdaughter with him, but Maggie had told him he didn't have to bother. Soon after, she had gotten a cell phone to which he didn't have the number. She didn't want to speak to him ever again, this sham of a father who had traded her and the memory of her mother in for shinier and newer models as soon as the opportunity had presented itself. Whenever people asked—which wasn't often since Maggie wasn't so great at making or keeping friends; they were too much work—she told them that he was dead.

Maggie willed her mind to return to the present, to continue her appraisal of her new surroundings. In the left hand corner was a cream, pleasingly lumpy chair and a half with a matching footstool. A slim lamp stood beside it, along with a small, round table that needed dusting. Maggie imagined Liza there, in a silk robe and matching nightgown, her lime green glasses slightly unbalanced across the bridge of her nose.

Lucy began to babble in her crib next door.

"Lucy, Mommy, Lucy, Mommy, Birds!"

"Mommy!" Lucy demanded, growing louder. Maggie threw the covers off, swung her legs over the side of the bed and stood up. She opened Lucy's door slowly. Inside the dark room, her crib creaked as she sat up to greet her.

"Mommy!" she yelled happily, as Maggie's heart soared. It still surprised her, the unabashed affection she felt for Lucy. It wasn't her nature; she was much more guarded usually, but being a mother had changed her.

"Hi, baby girl, how did you sleep?" she asked, walking over to the window to open the blinds.

Maggie had helped the movers disassemble the bed that had occupied the room upon their arrival the day before, instructing them to move it into the garage to make room for Lucy's crib and dresser, after asking Edith for permission to do so.

"Move it into the garage?" Edith had echoed skeptically. "Where will we park?"

"I thought we could just lean it against one of the walls."

"The mattress, too?"

"Sure, unless you—"

"What is this, a junkyard? Why don't we put the toilet on the front lawn while we're at it?"

"Edith, I really don't think a mattress in the garage is comparable to a commode on the front yard. I could try to sell it—"

"Do whatever you like, Maggie," Edith barked, clearly not meaning it at all before she turned on her heel and left.

And so Maggie, in an attempt to keep the peace, had moved the bed to the other wall. She would move or sell it later, when Edith wasn't quite so riled up. Though Edith seemed to exist in a permanent state of riled up.

With a crib, bed, and all of Lucy's toys, books and animals in their myriad baskets and bins, the room was practically as crowded as their former apartment had been. A woman of Edith's age, not to mention her temperament, couldn't have tiny cars and zoo animals underfoot, and so Lucy's belongings were almost all here, save for one lone basket she had placed upstairs. Lucy needed a bookcase, Maggie thought. That would free up some space.

"Mommy, Mommy, Mommy. Breakfuss!" She held out her arms and Maggie scooped her up, relishing her shampoo scented hair, and the warmth of her arms and legs as they wrapped around her neck and waist.

"Good morning, Luce. What would you like for breakfast?"

As Lucy rattled off her wish list, Maggie unzipped her

pajamas, changed her diaper and pulled a T-shirt over her head before depositing her on the floor. She scrambled for the door and began to ascend the stairs when Maggie looked down at her bedraggled tank top, her right breast threatening to escape.

"Luce, wait a sec. Just let me change." Maggie grabbed her and carried her back to her room, throwing her on the bed with one arm while she grabbed a bra with the other.

"Why you putting a bwa on?" demanded Lucy. "Where you going?"

"Nowhere, baby, I just need to look a little more presentable for Edith."

"Edif?"

"Yes, Edith. Our new roommate."

"Ahhh, our woommay. Yahs." Lucy nodded knowingly. "I need bwa?"

"No honey, you're fine." Maggie slid a new shirt over her head and then wriggled into a pair of cutoffs. "Okay, all set, let's go."

"Let's go!" yelled Lucy, crawling off the bed carefully. She ran ahead, up the stairs. Maggie followed her, pausing to notice that Edith's bedroom door was a sliver ajar. She peeked inside. Her bed was made—its white coverlet as pristine as freshly fallen snow.

When they reached the top, Lucy ran into the loft-like space, which included the kitchen, the dining area and the living room. Morning light filtered through the floor to ceiling windows that encircled them.

"Good morning," greeted Edith, perched primly on a bar stool at the kitchen counter and sipping her coffee. Maggie jumped.

"Good morning, Edith," she replied. "Lucy, can you say good morning to Edith?"

"Good morning!" Lucy shouted. On cue, she ran to her bin and pulled out her favorite, and most ear-splitting, toy: a Day-Glo yellow bird that sang "Rockin' Robin" at the touch of a button.

"How did you sleep?" Maggie asked with an apologetic smile, determined to start over.

"Very well, thanks. But I'm certainly awake now." She glanced towards Lucy with a frown.

Maggie went about preparing her coffee, concentrating on keeping her mouth shut. *She's only two and a half, Edith, what do you want? Beethoven's Fifth?*

"What do you two have planned for the day?" asked Edith.

"We'll probably go into town. I really want to get Lucy some sort of a bookcase for her room."

"Unless you want to spend a fortune, I wouldn't look for that in town, Maggie." Edith smoothed some nonexistent wrinkles in her khaki Bermudas. "Nothing but rich Manhattanites there, robbing you blind. You're better off driving around and looking for a yard sale."

"That's a good idea. Is summer a good time of year to find them?" Maggie sat down at the dining room table. Lucy ran to her, climbing into her lap and threatening to spill her mug of steaming coffee all over the table's expertly weathered expanse.

"Sure, people always have things to sell. It's worth the savings, too. Just because you have money now doesn't mean you should squander it, you know." Liza's money, she meant. Maggie was the least likely person on the planet to squander anything. She reused Ziploc bags, for God's sake.

"Right," she replied coldly.

"Alright, I'm going for my walk," said Edith.

"Edith, I want to apologize for yesterday," Maggie announced. "I shouldn't have been so abrasive. You're going through a lot, I know."

"Yes. Well, thank you. I accept your apology. I'll see you."

Maggie watched her exit, her spine straight as a ruler in her refusal to take responsibility for her own behavior in return. She stuck her tongue out at the back of Edith's head as she descended the stairs.

Lucy looked up.

"Breakfuss?" she asked.

"JUST ONE MORE minute, honey," Maggie yelled to Lucy from inside the car.

She had been hunched over the car seat, trying desperately to latch it in place for twenty minutes, and now was sweating profusely in the late July humidity, as well as being on the verge of losing her mind from Lucy's incessant whining. For all she knew, she had unrolled every spool of toilet paper in the house.

A bead of sweat rolled off Maggie's nose and landed with a splat on the gray fabric of Lucy's seat just as she felt the clasp miraculously catch.

"Oh, thank you, Jesus!" she exclaimed.

"Mommy, what?" yelled Lucy.

"Nothing, honey."

"What?"

"Nothing!"

The other latch followed quickly and then, with the pull of a strap, she was done.

She stood up, her lower back creaking like a trap door as she did so, to proudly survey her work. Sometimes she wondered what life would have been like with Lucy's father, Lyle. Would he handle the things she didn't want to do, like installing this car seat? She thought of him, sprawled on her couch watching the U.S. Open and drinking green glass bottles of beer as she cooked dinner and thought not.

Not that she had ever asked him to help with anything. That wasn't her style.

"Lucy baby, let's go!"

She closed the car door and went back inside the house to retrieve her daughter. As suspected, the entire first floor was covered in toilet paper. She gathered it quickly, rolling it into a giant ball in her hands.

"Mommy, where we going?"

"Into town," Maggie replied, cramming it into her bathroom's waste bin, walking out and then returning to retrieve it. She'd throw it in the kitchen bin, under the sink. It felt so lazy to her, a filled waste bin out in the open, for anyone to see. The things she had learned about clients from emptying their bathroom bins—the list was infinite.

"I need my poise," Lucy declared, running into her room to get it. Seconds later, she emerged with a tiny pink quilted bag hanging from her wrist.

Maggie ran upstairs to dispose of the toilet paper and threw a spare diaper, some wipes and a Ziploc of goldfish crackers into her purse. Before Lucy, Maggie had been the kind of person who hadn't even owned a wallet, who left the house with her license and debit card rubber banded together and shoved into her back pocket. Now she prepared for the apocalypse every time she stepped outside.

"Mommy, you wet," accused Lucy.

"Yes, it's called sweat."

"Mommy, ewwww."

With Maggie behind the wheel, finally, they passed a small stretch of sand and surf on their right.

"Beach!" exclaimed Lucy. "Water!"

"Yes! We'll go soon," Maggie promised, rolling down the windows to breathe in the trees and earth and salt and sunlight.

She pulled into an empty spot on the main drag. There were antique stores and clothing boutiques, tasteful havens for expensive beach gear with eighty-dollar sweatshirts in their windows. Why anyone, especially women, would be interested in having the word *Sag* emblazoned across their chest was beyond her, but she guessed it was a status thing. Once out of the car, she and Lucy ambled along, Lucy's chubby hand gripping hers sweetly.

"Mommy! Toys!" she exclaimed, eyeing a storefront filled

with lifelike baby dolls and plush stuffed animals, pull toys in vibrant reds, yellows, greens and blues and a train set that weaved delicately in and out of the organized chaos.

"No touching, just looking!" Maggie called after Lucy as she ran inside.

Every surface was crammed with plastic limbs, handles and shapes that begged to be pulled from the shelves. *How was she ever going to get Lucy out of here?* Maggie wondered. Bribery, most likely in the form of a purchase, would have to be involved.

"Hi," said a male voice on the other side of a Thomas the Tank Engine display.

"Hi," replied Maggie to the voice. His head appeared around its side, like a giraffe's.

"Welcome to Siggy's Toys."

His hair was shaved in the way that men with good sense shaved their heads when a large portion of their hair packed up and left. Nice hazel eyes, a broad nose and acceptable lips. Could have been a little fuller, but at least he had something to work with. Maggie couldn't remember the last time she had sized up a pair of lips. She hadn't been with a man since Lucy had been conceived.

He stepped out to reveal the rest of himself—somewhere in that gray area between short and tall, and sturdy with just a hint of paunch. Cute. He extended a pleasantly ropy forearm to shake Lucy's hand, and she accepted coyly by gripping the ends of his fingers in response. *No ring,* thought Maggie, and then immediately chided herself for being such a cliché.

"I'm Sam," he said.

"Not Siggy?" asked Maggie.

"That's my dad," he replied, smiling again. "Left the place to me when he passed."

"I'm sorry," said Maggie. "I really should never try to be clever, I'm terrible at it." Sam waved his hand in dismissal.

"Please, no offense taken. And you are?"

"Maggie. And this is Lucy." She looked down, but Lucy had escaped. "Was Lucy, I mean."

"Nice to meet you. You guys looking for anything in particular?"

"No, just killing time. We're new in town, so we're exploring the neighborhood. Although there's no way Lucy is going to leave without something."

"I'll watch her closely. Make sure nothing gets slipped into that tiny pink pocketbook. Like a marble or something."

"Or a lone checker," Maggie added.

"Or a thimble. Thimbles are all the rage with toddlers these days."

"But only vintage thimbles," said Maggie.

"Yes, the newer models just don't have the same kind of character."

He smiled at her again. Maggie smiled back, realizing that they were flirting. What a relief, to know that she could still do it, could still follow the rhythm of a conversation and laugh at the right moments. Like riding a bike.

"Mommy!" yelled Lucy, interrupting them.

"One second," Maggie said to Sam. He nodded and turned to straighten a dinosaur figurine on the shelf behind him as Maggie walked briskly towards her daughter's voice.

Here I am, she thought, *flirting with someone I don't know from Adam, with my daughter not even in my field of vision, probably trapped under an avalanche of Barbies, barely breathing. Mom of the year.*

Nearly out of breath, she found Lucy, who was not trapped under anything of the sort. Instead, she was draped in a hot pink feather boa, wearing a purple tutu over her shorts with a silver tiara perched sideways on her head.

"Mommy, isn't I beauteeful?" she asked, giving a little twirl for effect.

"The most beauteeful," Maggie replied. "And the smartest. Smartest is better than prettiest any day of the week." Lucy gave her a blank stare. "Sorry, sorry. I just want to be sure you know that."

There was so much pressure nowadays to make sure your daughter didn't derive all of her self-worth from her sense of beauty. You couldn't even tell a little girl she was pretty for fear of getting your retinas burned off by her parents' scornful side eyes.

Oh, who the hell knew how to raise a kid anyway? thought Maggie. All of the conflicting philosophies would drive you crazy. You just did the best you could and hoped that you produced a kind, thoughtful and considerate human being that could survive on her own. She watched Lucy, digging through the dress-up bin with her mouth set in a determined line, no doubt searching for just the right sparkling accessory to complete her look, and sighed.

"Mommy, help."

"What are you looking for?" asked Maggie. "A bracelet or a necklace?"

"No. An alligator."

"An alligator? I'm not sure you're going to find that here, honey." Lucy stopped digging and looked up at her, perplexed.

"Why?"

"Well, this doesn't seem to be the place where alligators live. This bin is for dress-up clothes." Lucy's lip began to tremble.

"But whyyy?"

"Lucy honey, really, it's not a big deal. I'm sure we can find an alligator somewhere else in the store. Maybe over there, by the puzzles."

"Whyyy?" Lucy started to cry, reduced to tears by the store's organization. Maggie moved towards her to disrobe her princess costume as quickly as she could and get them both out of there in one piece.

"Mommmyyy, no, no, no!!! My tiara!! Noooo!!!" Lucy screamed at the top of her lungs as Maggie attempted to remove it from her head.

"Lucy, this is not ours, we have to give it back to the store," said Maggie firmly, trying to unwind its teeth from one of Lucy's curls.

"Mommyyy! Noooo!!! Peeaazz nooo!"

Maggie's face blazed as she finally wrenched it free. The front door's bells jangled. Great, people were here right at Lucy's moment of absolute combustion. She flipped the crown over in her hand, searching for a price tag. Should she buy this to make her daughter stop screaming or teach her that sometimes in life you didn't get what you wanted? Below her, Lucy had thrown herself on her back, like an overturned beetle—her limbs flailing. The crown was six dollars. She would teach her a life lesson later.

"Lucy, would you like the tiara? To take it home and wear it whenever you want?" On cue, Lucy's crying ceased. She sat up, as though surprised to find herself rolling around on the floor.

"Yes," she replied, victorious. Immediately, Maggie regretted caving in. Too late now, though. Retracting her offer could lead to the destruction of the entire store—Siggy's empire brought to its knees by one enraged toddler.

"Fine, we'll buy it. Come on, let's go."

Lucy jumped up and skipped ahead of her towards the register. Maggie followed, flinching ever so slightly with disappointment to find a woman there, smiling sweetly.

"Is that all for you today?" she asked, as Lucy hugged Maggie's calf and kissed her knee.

"Thank you, Mommy," she said sweetly, looking up at her with devotion as though her meltdown had never happened.

Maggie handed the crown over to her queen, scanning the store for Sam as discreetly as possible, but he was nowhere to be found. *For the best*, she told herself.

"Yes, that's it. Thank you."

CHAPTER 4

Edith slowed down slightly. Was that them? To her left on Main Street, Maggie and Lucy ambled along, the little girl wearing a silver tiara that shined brightly in the nearly noon sun. Should she honk hello? No, no, she was running late. She ducked down in her seat and drove past them, feeling only slightly guilty. She would see them later—she had to see them now, too?

The thickening humidity had turned the air into peanut butter. They wouldn't be able to eat outside as she had hoped. Esther's hair would never stand for it, and she would tell Edith so from the moment she stepped out of her chauffeured car. She would set them up at the dining room table and hope that Maggie got the picture—that this was a private lunch between friends, and a ladylike lunch at that. There was no room for the dried smears of hummus that always followed in Lucy's wake. Not to mention Maggie, who seemed averse to utensils on principle, and scavenged her daughter's leftovers like a prisoner of war.

She pulled up the driveway, anxious to get started. There was no time for a shower unfortunately, but a washcloth, some perfume, a change of clothes and some lipstick should do the trick. She just had to slice the block of cheddar and set out the crackers and then she could pop down to get herself ready. She opened the car door and eased herself out gingerly, while looping the two plastic bags over her thin wrist. Slowly, she made her way up the porch steps to the door.

"Jesus, Mary and Joseph," grumbled Edith. Maggie had locked it. She set her bags down and fumbled in her pocket for her keys. She wiggled it until it blessedly opened, the wood sighing as she pulled the door towards her.

In the kitchen, Edith's grumbling continued. There was no room in the refrigerator for any of her things. She unwrapped the block of cheddar cheese and placed it on the cutting board, willing her lip not to tremble. She would not cry.

She sliced the cheese into orange rectangles and fanned them around the perimeter of one of her good china plates before depositing a handful of Ritz crackers in the center. She had ten minutes to get ready. Esther was never late. Never.

Down the stairs she went. *Get it together now, Edith*, she warned herself. *Don't make a big show for Esther.* Every day now, she found herself teetering on the brink of a crying jag, and had to force herself back from the ledge. What good did crying do anyone? She would allow herself to lament her fate, but she wouldn't burden others with her misery. And by others, of course, she meant Esther. There was no one else.

Standing naked in her bathroom, she ran a soapy washcloth under her arms before spraying a liberal dose of perfume in the air and letting it rain down on her. She stepped into her favorite dress, the one with the subtle pattern of rosebuds set against a cream background, cinched her matching belt and slipped on her sandals. In the mirror she smoothed her bob, brushed her teeth and then swiped her lips with her signature crimson shade—the same one she had been wearing for over sixty years. If she had learned anything from her dancing days, it was that a signature something was the key to people remembering you.

Esther would agree. She was never without her amethyst hairpin—the lavender had sparkled beautifully against first her raven tresses and now, her white. Outside, the gravel crunched, signaling her arrival. Edith smoothed her dress and opened the front door to greet her.

The Lincoln Town Car idled, as though it was waiting at the foot of a red carpet. Vinnie, Esther's driver, got out.

"Good morning, Mrs. Brennan," he said, tipping his cap. "You're looking ravishing today."

Edith blushed. Vinnie had a way with words. Esther had told her proudly that he used to be in the mafia, and you could tell. He had a certain swagger that hinted at such a past, even as a fifty-something-year-old Town Car driver for a little old lady. Then again, Esther could also have been exaggerating for conversation's sake; a trait that Edith had gotten used to over the course of their sixty-four year friendship.

Vinnie opened the door and Esther extended her bejeweled hand for him to take. It wasn't easy getting in and out of cars at eighty-two, Esther would be the first one to tell you that. Esther stood, smiling at Edith. She had her hair done every Tuesday without fail, and it waved back from her fully made up face like cotton candy, the amethyst pin twinkling against her scalp. Beneath this grand presentation, she always wore cotton housedresses in a never-ending array of colors and patterns, or what Edith called her *shmatas*.

"I should spend so much time on this face and worry about the outfit, too?" she would say unapologetically. "You're lucky I'm wearing anything underneath it, Edith," she'd add, cackling as Edith blushed.

"Edith, get me out of this heat already, my face is melting!" she squawked now. "Vinnie, see you in two hours." She patted his hand and approached Edith slowly. "These shoes cost me three dollars in Chinatown," she announced proudly, shuffling past Edith and through the door. Edith looked down to see Esther's fuchsia toenails peeking through the mesh overlay of a pair of white rubber slippers. Despite the fact that Esther lived with her daughter, Barbie, who had more money than she knew what to do with, Esther still loved a bargain.

Esther paused in the foyer to ogle herself in the mirror. She loved the sun, and so every part of her that peeked out from her *shmata*—her forearms, the V of her chest, her legs from the knee down and her feet—glistened like a honey-baked ham.

"For God's sake, Edith, turn down the thermostat in here! What is this, the Depression?" she asked, fiddling with her hair for a moment before turning towards Edith. "You're looking well, Edith. Do you eat, for God's sake?"

"Yes, I eat, Esther," replied Edith, pleased by the comment. She had lost weight lately; she could tell by the way her clothes fit.

"Where's the girl?" Esther peeked around the corner of Liza's bedroom. *Maggie's bedroom*, Edith reminded herself.

"This room is neat as a pin. You could do worse than landing a cleaning lady as a roommate. What about the baby's room?" Esther shuffled down the hall, the plastic soles of her shoes wheezing beneath her weight. "Aw, would you look at this? I remember when my Barbie was this age." She turned to face Edith with her hands on her hips.

"Edith, you know, having these two here is a blessing. You need to take the stick out of your ass and realize that Liza had your best interest at heart when she left this place to her. What would you do, rattling around this place all by yourself? You'd go nuts, that's what. Now, what's for lunch? I'm starving."

"AND SO I said to her, I said, 'Just a little off the sides, not that hatchet job you did last time, Melanie,'" explained Esther.

"Edith, you're not listening to me," said Esther, before crunching into a mouthful of lettuce. Edith had forgotten to buy pre-made sandwiches at the store, much to her—and

Esther's—horror. She'd had to improvise on the spot with a wilting head of lettuce and some of Maggie's vegetables, which they ate begrudgingly now.

"I'm listening, Esther," replied Edith. But she wasn't really. She was dwelling on the fact that she had forgotten the very thing she had gone to the store for in the first place. It worried her.

"This salad dressing tastes like glue," said Esther. "But of course I'll eat it, because God forbid I should refuse a calorie. Really, it's an illness, Edith. Food is placed in front of me and I have to consume it. Like a cow in a field. Anyway! What's doing, Edith? You seem sad."

"Me? I'm not sad," said Edith, studying her plate.

"You miss her." Esther covered Edith's hand with her own. "And who can blame you? She was such a dynamic person. Such creativity! It was inspiring."

Edith nodded, feeling her throat constrict. She was so grateful that Esther let her indulge like this—let her talk about Liza with her, even if it was Esther that did the majority of the talking. Edith wasn't much for expressing her emotions, at least in a direct way. She'd rather bang around some pots and pans in the kitchen under the guise of making dinner than actually admit to her frustration. But Esther was the opposite. Esther could talk feelings all day, every day. She would have been a great psychologist, Edith often thought. Not that she's ever been to one, but she imagined that's what they did—poked and prodded at your hard shell until somehow you ended up on your back, your tender underbelly exposed. Liza had been going to a woman named

Phyllis for years, but had stopped abruptly, a few months before she died.

"Phyllis doesn't get me anymore, Mom," she had said to Edith, when she had inquired about what had happened; why Liza had stopped going into the city to see her shrink. Edith had bit her tongue for once, not wanting to start an argument. Now she wondered guiltily if an argument had been exactly what Liza had needed.

The door opened downstairs, and what sounded like a small herd of cattle came bounding in. Esther raised her eyebrow at Edith.

"That's them," whispered Edith.

"Good God, Edith, you're nervous! It's a young woman and her two-year-old, not the Gestapo for chrissake. Lighten up, already!"

Edith had the sudden urge to bang a cast-iron skillet against the top of Esther's head. What did she know about lightening up? She lived in a luxury suite in her daughter's McMansion, complete with live-in maid and personal chef. She had a lot of nerve, judging Edith.

"Mommy, hungry," Lucy's high-pitched voice demanded, coming up the stairs towards them. Edith really should have told Maggie about her lunch with Esther, she thought now. This was going to be a disaster.

"What would you like me to make you?" asked Maggie, sounding tired. Lucy stood before them suddenly, dangling a tiny pink pocketbook from her chubby forearm.

"Well, hello there," cooed Esther.

Edith was taken aback. She would never have pinned

Esther as a baby talker. She had one grandson, Ryan, but she talked to him like he was an old Jewish man trapped in a nine-year-old boy's body. Which he was really, from what Edith could tell. He and Esther had debated the pros and cons of the bialy and talked Jacuzzi heat settings for a good hour the last time Edith had been out to lunch with the two of them.

"Oh hello," said Maggie. "Sorry to interrupt."

She was so thin, Edith noticed. Like she spent all of her time feeding her daughter and none feeding herself. No wonder she ravaged the remains of Lucy's meals. That was probably all she ate, Edith surmised. And she was pretty, really, in a very angular, natural way. Not like Liz Taylor pretty by any means, but interesting pretty, like Katharine Hepburn. A very unkempt Katharine Hepburn, that was.

Maggie's hair was pulled back into a messy ponytail, and her gray T-shirt hung on her like an empty pillowcase. And those shorts! In Edith's opinion, denim cutoffs for a woman past the age of fifteen were unacceptable, no matter how nice the legs. And Maggie's legs weren't her best feature, either. She had, and Edith had only noticed this because she called so much attention to them in shorts and flip-flops, cankles.

"Nonsense!" said Esther. She extended her hand, like the Queen. "I'm Esther, honey. And you must be Maggie."

"That's me," she replied. "And this is Lucy. Lucy, can you say hello to Esther?" Lucy hid behind her mother's leg, suddenly shy.

"It's okay, Lucy," said Esther. "I wrote the book on playing hard to get. You take your time, get to know me before you show me your smile. I bet you don't have any teeth anyway."

"I do have teef!" yelled Lucy, indignant.

"Really? Let me see." Lucy opened her mouth wide, revealing two perfect rows of tiny white pearls. "Ohhhh, those are beautiful," said Esther. "You must be very proud of those."

Edith was annoyed. Why did Esther feel the need to charm everyone? Couldn't she just, for once, say *nice to meet you* like a normal person when introduced instead of overwhelming the moment with her shtick? Lucy beamed at Esther. In the week since they'd arrived, Lucy hadn't so much as given Edith a giggle.

"Hello Lucy," she said, wishing she had a lollipop to give her.

"Hi Edif." Lucy sighed dramatically. "I'm hungry, Mommy," she reminded her.

"Hello Maggie," said Edith. She pushed her chair back before she stood, motioning for Esther to do the same. Esther ignored her.

"Where are you going? You're not even finished with your lunch," said Maggie. "Please stay. I can't promise that we'll be particularly pleasant company." She pointed to Lucy, who was swaying slightly in front of Esther, entranced by her vivacity. "But we'll try our best. Won't we, Lucy?"

"Hungry," she replied.

"Okay, I'll make you a grilled cheese, how does that sound?"

"Good," replied Lucy. She trotted over to her basket and

pulled out a gaggle of small plastic zoo animals. Slowly, she lined them up, talking softly to them in her own language.

Liza used to play like that, Edith remembered. Never with dolls, she hadn't liked them, but with Tinkertoys and plastic army figurines, murmuring quietly to them for hours as she arranged them this way and that. There had always been something different about Liza, a creative quality that Edith had wanted to cultivate. She herself had gravitated towards dance from the time she could walk, but her mother had never encouraged her, only begrudgingly signed her up for lessons when she could no longer take Edith's begging. Even when Edith had gone on to show real talent as a young woman, she had only sent a letter expressing halfhearted congratulations, a single sentence buried in her news from home.

It had hurt Edith, her mother's disregard, and so when Liza had declared that she was a writer at age eleven, Edith had gone out and bought her daughter a typewriter.

"The thing about writers is that they write," she'd explained to Liza as she set it up in her room. "So get cooking." Liza's subsequent success was the thing Edith was most proud of in her life, even though really it had nothing to do with her. But she'd made a point to nurture her daughter's talent; to water it like a plant until it bloomed. And boy, had it ever.

"So, how do you like Sag Harbor, Maggie?" asked Esther. "Quite a change from the big city."

"It certainly is," agreed Maggie. "But it's beautiful here,

really and truly." She spread butter on the outsides of Lucy's sandwich and dropped it into the hot pan.

"You used to clean Liza's apartment?" Esther asked, going right for the jugular. She wore her nosiness proudly, like a badge.

"Yes, that's true." Maggie pushed a stray strand of hair out of her eyes. "That's how we met."

"But you became friends?" continued Esther.

"Yes. Very good friends."

"You know, I understand that. I consider Marie a friend."

"Who's Marie?" asked Maggie.

"She cleans Barbie's house. She's lovely. And really gets in there. Mops the baseboards even. That's someone who has your best interests at heart."

"Esther, don't be ridiculous. That's not a friend, that's your maid," said Edith.

"Lucy, lunch is almost ready. Come over to the table," said Maggie. Lucy looked up from her animals.

"Grilled cheese?" she inquired.

"Yes ma'am. Come on over here and I'll strap you into your chair."

"Where'd you live in the city?" asked Esther as Maggie finished buckling Lucy in and sat down herself.

"We were in the East Village."

"Oh," said Esther, taking a sip of her soda through her straw. "Isn't that dangerous?"

"Not really. NYU has turned it into Disney World. I'm an old lady there."

"Get out of here!" said Esther. "You can't be older than twenty-eight," she told Maggie, who smiled gratefully in return.

"Esther, bless you, but twenty-eight was almost ten years ago now."

"No!" said Esther. *Wasn't that just like Esther?* thought Edith, jealous. One compliment and the conversation was back on track.

"Did you live there at any point?" asked Maggie, stealing a bite of Lucy's sandwich.

"Sure we did. Edith and I both did. Isn't that right, Edith?" Edith smiled.

"Of course. That was over sixty years ago now, can you believe that Esther?"

"No. Well, who am I kidding? I considered putting a diaper on this morning for the car ride over. Yes, I can believe it actually."

"Esther!" scolded Edith. "Really!"

"We lived on the Upper West Side, Maggie," Esther explained. "Oy, that apartment was a tenement if there ever was one. Like Kosovo or something. And there were what? Six of us in a two bedroom, Edith?"

"Two bedroom? Try a one bedroom. I think poor Helen was in a sleeping bag on the kitchen floor."

"What were you doing?" asked Maggie.

"We were dancers on Broadway," replied Esther proudly.

"Get out!" exclaimed Maggie. "*Broadway,* Broadway?"

"The one and only," replied Esther.

"And Esther sang a little, too. She has an amazing voice,"

said Edith. "People used to call her Ethel. You know, like Ethel Merman?" Esther waved her hand dismissively.

"Oh please. They only made that comparison because we were both Jewish and had big mouths. Although, I was a hell of a swimmer, too. But Edith! Edith had it all. Those girl next door looks and a waist no bigger than twenty-four inches around. And boy oh boy, could she dance!"

"Now, Esther, let's not get carried away," said Edith. "I was an adequate dancer. Good enough, but never a star."

"Oh, for God's sake, Edith, you are a piece of work. You think anybody can dance on Broadway? Give me a break with this adequate business. She always pulls this crap," Esther explained to Maggie. "It's ridiculous." Edith rolled her eyes.

"Surely you had to be better than average, Edith," Maggie acknowledged.

"Did you hear that, Lucy? Edith is a dancer!"

"Dance?" asked Lucy suspiciously.

"I know it's hard to believe," answered Edith. She knew she came off as a killjoy, but she was only telling the truth. She'd been good, but not great. Not once had she been given a solo. The proof was in the pudding.

"Which productions were you in?" asked Maggie.

"*South Pacific, Guys and Dolls, The Pajama Game, Wonderful Town*," Esther rattled off. "Am I forgetting anything, Edith?"

"*Top Banana* and *Wish You Were Here*."

"Oh God, *Wish You Were Here*, of course. With the swimming pool. What a disaster."

It had been a long time since Edith had thought of those

days, the long hours rehearsing, the ice packs on her feet, the cigarettes and the booze. The walks home from the theater in the freezing cold, her teeth chattering in the threadbare peacoat she had bought at a thrift store for fifty cents.

Esther's phone rang, jolting everyone out of the moment.

"That's Vinnie," said Esther. "My driver," she explained to Maggie as she hoisted herself out of her chair slowly. "Hard to believe this body used to dance across the stage, right?" She straightened up, suddenly holding her hands out in front of her. "Still got my jazz hands, though!" Lucy clapped delightedly at the sight of Esther's splayed palms, her fingers like explanation points.

"Nice to meet you, Esther," said Maggie, standing up to say goodbye.

"The pleasure was mine," replied Esther.

"Bye Estah!" exclaimed Lucy.

"Goodbye darling." She pinched her cheek. "Edith, walk me out, will you?"

"Of course." She followed Esther down the stairs.

"Edith, those are nice girls up there," said Esther, once they were alone outside together. "Who cares why they're here, just that they're here."

Edith frowned. "Easy for you to say, Esther. You're going home to your own private suite, with your daughter who's still alive."

"True. But life dealt you this deck, whether it was fair or not, and I think you came up with a pretty good hand. Teach her something, this Maggie. How to dress, for one. Dungaree cutoffs at almost forty?" She shook her head. "She needs you as much as you need her." Vinnie came around to open her door, the sunlight bouncing off the black plastic strip of his cap like a spotlight.

"Stay well, Esther," called Edith after her.

"You too, doll," she replied.

CHAPTER 5

Maggie closed Lucy's door softly. Inside, Lucy chatted and sang quietly in her crib, slowly winding herself down. She tiptoed past Edith's closed door, towards her own bedroom.

"It wasn't a nap, I was resting my eyes," Edith had retorted the day before when Maggie had made the mistake of inquiring, the words shooting out of her mouth like flames.

What was so wrong with taking a nap? Maggie wanted to know. She would kill for a nap. But no matter how tired she was, how sleepless her night before had been, her brain would just not shut off. There were so many things to do—vegetables to cube or laundry to wash or clothes to fold or floors to sweep or kitchen counters to disinfect or her own legs to shave. It was bad, Maggie knew, but no matter how much she willed herself to stop thinking, just for five minutes in a row, she couldn't.

But now, here in Sag Harbor, things were different. She had the time now, to retrain her brain. Maggie pulled back her covers and crawled inside her bed. *Sleep*, she told herself. *You're tired.*

Her bed was gigantic. King size. So big that she would wake up in the morning and forget where she was. All she could see stretching out on either side of her was its white expanse, like snow.

In New York, sometimes Liza would sleep for days. The first time, Maggie hadn't known, opening Liza's bedroom door tentatively to peek in when she was there to clean.

"Don't come in here," Liza had warned, her voice scratchy and deep. "Everything but this room." Maggie had lingered, concerned. "Maggie, I mean it. Get out."

The next week, when Maggie met her for coffee, Liza hadn't mentioned it, but Maggie had asked anyway.

"Are you okay?"

"Of course I'm okay. Do I not seem okay?" she had barked back.

"Last week, when I came over—"

"Every once in a while I have a couple of dark days, Maggie. It's an artist thing."

"An artist thing or a depression thing?"

"A little of both."

Maggie's mother had been depressed; Maggie knew the

drill. She, too, would disappear into the depths of her bed for a week or two, leaving her and her father to fend for themselves.

"Don't worry about your mother, she's on her period," her father used to offer as explanation. For the longest time, until Maggie had started menstruating herself, she thought a period was a concrete object. Something her mother literally sat on.

Maggie sat up. Through the sliding glass doors she could see the guesthouse. Just four walls, a window and a door, enough for Liza's desk and chair, and maybe a few personal items from the size of it. Maggie wondered if Liza's existence had been erased there, too, all of her books and manuscripts packed up and sent who knew where.

Stealthily, she pushed back her blanket, stood, slipped into her flip-flops and out the French doors to the back porch. She felt like a teenager, sneaking out while her parents slept to smoke cigarettes in the woods. Lucy, she thought automatically. What would she do when Lucy started smelling like smoke and rolling her eyes at everything Maggie said? Standing on the porch with a yellow butterfly fluttering around her head, Maggie considered her fate.

She made her way down the two steps to the gravel path, getting trapped in a sticky spiderweb along the way. She needed to clean this porch, arm herself with a serious broom and hack away at all of its corners and nooks. Tomorrow. Or maybe later, with Lucy.

Quickly, she skipped over the stones, afraid to make too much noise. She felt guilty, barging into Liza's sacred place without Edith's permission, but technically, she didn't need it. It belonged to her now, too. At the door, she brushed away another nest of webs encasing its knob like a knitted cozy. With a twist, it opened—a porthole into the past, a past where Liza was alive and well.

Maggie sat on the edge of a daybed that hugged the wall, moving one of at least a dozen throw pillows in varying shades and patterns to do so. Beneath her, the bed's colorful quilt could have been straight from a bazaar in India, and probably was. Liza had been a voracious world traveler. Then again, who knew? She easily could have overpaid for it in Manhattan. Schlepping a blanket back from India did not sound like Liza. *Schlepping* was a Liza word, though.

The white walls were primarily devoted to the room's windows, which didn't leave a lot of space for paintings or photos. Behind her desk, Liza had managed to squeeze in a Matisse reproduction, which filled the corner with its rich reds and blues. A well-worn Persian rug in muted brown and gold woven through with bits of maroon covered most of the dark wooden floor and below the windows on the wall opposite the desk, deep shelves were built into the wall for books and Liza's yellowed manuscript drafts, their editorial sticky notes jutting out like neon spikes.

She looked at Liza's cherrywood desk from her seat on the bed. A layer of dust, at least two inches thick, covered it like gauze, and Maggie fought the urge to clean. She stood up and crossed over to it, lowering herself into its chair.

Liza had deliberated over this chair for months—What was the best to buy? Which one would support her back properly? Was it worth the astronomical price tag or was she just being a sucker?—before dragging Maggie with her to an enormous office supply warehouse in Queens. They had sat, spun and reclined in chair after chair as the winter sun set and the salesmen became more and more exasperated. Finally, Liza had decided to buy herself this one, "the Lamborghini of office chairs" she had called it. Maggie gave it a halfhearted spin now, coming to a stop in front of Liza's laptop.

She reached her hand out, hovering over the surface of it for a moment before retracting it back into her lap. No, it wasn't right to snoop through Liza's files. Not now, maybe not ever. When her mother had died, Maggie had dug through her bedside table and bureau, hoping for a diary even though her mother was not the diary keeping kind, desperate for some sort of insight. There had been nothing, though. She was a mystery to Maggie still.

Pencils stood at attention in a ceramic jar, their pink erasers crisp and untouched, save for one that was worn down practically to its nub. Maggie pulled it out, surprised to find its exterior ravaged by teeth indentations. She placed it back in the jar. The rest of the surface was bare, except for a black stone paperweight, a green ceramic coaster and a box of Kleenex. No papers, no clips, no notebooks.

Outside, Maggie heard the crunch of gravel. Liza? She held her breath, terrified, and then immediately felt silly. Edith. The steps came closer. She should have told Edith she was coming back here; asserted herself. The crunching stopped outside the door.

And then, blessedly, it resumed. Maggie exhaled and crept to the window. Edith moved slowly down the path towards the pool, which sat below the rest of the yard. She descended the stairs and then was out of sight, shielded by the greenery that surrounded it. Quickly, Maggie grabbed her things and darted out, running over the rocks at breakneck speed. She slid the screen door back and then shut it behind her, her heart thumping wildly in her chest.

CHAPTER 6

Edith sat on the pool steps half submerged, like a mermaid. She stretched her legs out in front of her, relishing the ease with which they moved in the water. Overhead, the sun's afternoon rays baked her head and shoulders and Edith wished she had applied more sunscreen.

Edith inched further down, so that her feet were firmly planted on the pool's floor. She stood, the water up to her hips, and made her way to the far wall, which was shaded. Once there, she turned, her elbows resting on the wooden deck behind her.

The guesthouse stared back at her, causing her stomach to churn just as it had that day. Its events came to her in the pop and sizzle of ancient camera flashes from her dancing days on Broadway. Pop—there was Liza on the daybed.

Flash—Edith yelling her name with no response, her hand trembling as she touched her cold face.

Edith turned back around, facing a wall of fir trees. Maybe it was a blessing that her memory was in peril. All of the sadness, all of her secrets and regrets—poof! Gone. Like magic. But no, Edith didn't want that. That was the core of who she was. Without them, she'd be hollowed out, a corn husk of a human being.

Just beyond their property was the neighbor's pool, which played constant host to renters, always young and always loud, throughout the summer. Edith hated them. She scissor-kicked twice to the pool's opposite side and stood, holding its edge as she extended her leg up and down, an exercise that was as familiar as her own face in the mirror. For now, anyway.

"Mom, they're just kids," Liza would say to her when she complained about the noise next door. "You were a kid once, right?"

She had been a kid once, that was true. And not a goody-goody, either. Not by a long shot. Still, these summer idiots wore their sense of entitlement proudly, like a medal. She had never felt entitled to anything in her life.

Edith stopped abruptly. That was enough exercise for the day. Slowly, she made her way back to the pool steps, up and onto the deck, dripping. She grabbed her towel and wrapped it around herself, slipped her feet into her sandals, looking down at them with pity. Her poor, beaten-up, bunion feet—mementos of her past life.

She crunched along the gravel path, stopping in front of

the guesthouse warily. Liza's writing had socked Edith in the gut the first time she had allowed herself to read her words; to understand the way her daughter saw the world. She had expected to be quietly entertained at best, but instead was in awe. Liza was the kind of artist Edith had wanted to be before the limit of her talent had presented itself.

She climbed the three steps and opened the door. It was so quiet. When Liza had worked here, the entire place had hummed like an air conditioner.

"Mom, I'm headed out to work," Liza would say as Edith prepared for her walk, a steaming mug of coffee and something sweet, usually a cookie, peeking out of the breast pocket of her pajamas.

Edith perched on the edge of the daybed. It was getting harder to see Liza's face—how it was in person and not how it looked in photos—or hear her voice; the Long Island meets London cadence of her speech. Edith's plan was to reread all four of her novels, but instead they sat on her bedside table, untouched. Every time she reached for one, she just felt so tired. Too tired.

She pulled her towel tighter around herself, realizing that she was dripping pool water everywhere, and stood up to face Liza's desk. Slowly, she circled it before forcing herself into its chair.

Liza's laptop. Should she? She should. She yanked it open and the screen sprang to life, revealing a photo of Liza, tan and smiling against the magnificent crystal blue water and white stucco of Greece.

"Mom, can you believe it?" Liza had asked, her eyes shining as she dangled the email print-out in front of her like a First Place ribbon. "A free trip to Greece!"

Edith had been so happy for her in that moment—in so many moments of her daughter's career. To reap that much joy from what you did, that was something. Especially since there were no kids for Liza. And no love that she spoke about, either. Ever.

Someone had accompanied her daughter on that Greece trip and many others. There was someplace where Liza spent the night sometimes, too. And once, when she was leaving for her walk, Edith had seen a pocketbook that was not Liza's draped over the banister.

She had looked at it, and then back to the closed door of Liza's room, and then back to the bag, fitting the pieces of the puzzle together. But she had never mentioned it to Liza. She couldn't, not because she had anything against the fact that her daughter was a homosexual; she had known plenty of them in New York, but because she was waiting for Liza to tell her first. But Liza never did.

She supposed that was because she was a bad mother. The kind of mother you were scared of confiding in lest you be judged. Edith was ashamed of herself for being that person, ashamed that she had done nothing to reassure Liza otherwise. That yes, she would most certainly judge an unflattering outfit or idiotic right wing political pundit, but she would never judge Liza's sexuality. She had come close to confronting Liza once, after a particularly enjoyable evening together sipping Scotch and watching old movies on the couch, but at the last second she had choked. Why, she couldn't say exactly. Now it was one of her biggest regrets, not asking. Maybe if she had been the kind of mother Liza could confide in, things would have turned out differently.

Edith pulled open a drawer, searching for a pair of Liza's glasses. She had had several because she was always forgetting where she had left them—all boasting large, rectangular lenses behind thick, brightly colored frames. They weren't Edith's taste, but they worked on Liza, with her salt and pepper short hair and delicate features. A pair greeted her now, their mulberry frames gleaming. She put them on, and Liza's face came more into focus on the screen.

Edith put her finger to the monitor, tracing Liza's nose and jaw lightly. When the lawyer had told her that Liza was leaving the house, and her, to this Maggie that Edith had only met once over a hurried lunch in Manhattan, she had assumed that she had been a lover of Liza's. Now, upon meeting Maggie and Lucy, she wasn't so sure. Maggie didn't seem like a lesbian, but what did Edith know really? She took off Liza's glasses and placed them back in the drawer carefully before shutting it.

She adjusted her towel again and walked out the door, closing it behind her firmly. And then, without remembering the steps separating her from the ground below, she fell.

Reflexively, she shielded her face with her hands as it was happening, and was relieved in the first moments afterward to not feel or see any blood seeping down her brow or from her nose. That was a good sign, at least. Heart racing from a mixture of fright and embarrassment, she wiggled both sets of toes hopefully, and moved her knees against the rocks. Good, those were working.

Okay Edith, keep breathing, she told herself. *On the count of three, you're going to get up. One, two, three.* She pushed up on her hands, willing her body to follow, only to be met with blinding pain that shot up her right arm like a volt of electricity and pierced like a dagger.

"Liza!" Edith yelled, collapsing back onto the ground in shock.

CHAPTER 7

Want to swimming!" declared Lucy as Maggie rolled her up the driveway. She was getting heavy now, this baby of hers.

"Alright," Maggie agreed, stopping at the foot of the porch stairs and catching her breath. Sweat pooled in her bra and covered her face like a mask. "Get inside and we'll change." She unbuckled her daughter, who sprang out of the stroller like a jack-in-the-box.

Inside the house, Maggie pulled Lucy's sundress over her head and changed her into her suit.

"I'm going!" yelled Lucy, taking off down the hall.

"No, no you're not!" Maggie yelled back, topless as she searched frantically for her own suit. Where had she put it?

The unmistakable sound of a door opening forced her upright from her position crouched over the crowded bureau
drawer with a start.

"Lucy!" No answer. "Lucy! Damnit!"

Maggie pulled her T-shirt back over her head and ran out
the open back door, adrenaline and terror coursing through
her veins.

"Mommy!" Lucy cried, realizing all of Maggie's fears in
one instant. She tore down the porch steps after her daughter, convinced she was drowning.

"Mommy!" she cried again. To her great relief, Lucy was
just ahead of her on the path, near the guesthouse.

"Mommy, Edif fell."

"What?" asked Maggie, confused. "Edith fell? Where?"

"There." She pointed to the guesthouse. Maggie followed
the arc of Lucy's chubby finger to Edith, sprawled on the
ground like a gunshot victim, with her head turned towards
them.

"Edith!" Maggie ran to her, yanking Lucy along. She knelt
down to Edith's face level and gingerly placed her hand on
her arm. "Edith, can you hear me?"

"Where's Liza?" Edith asked accusingly, her blue eyes
blazing. Maggie sat back on her heels.

"Who are you and where is Liza? I want Liza."

"Do you have a boo-boo?" asked Lucy, kneeling down on
the gravel inches from Edith's face. The fire in Edith's eyes
dimmed slightly as she regarded the little girl.

"Yes," she answered.

"Mommy, she has a boo-boo," Lucy sat up and reported.

"I know, Lu. Let's help her, okay?" Maggie willed herself back from the brink of hysteria.

"Edith, Liza isn't here, but I am, and I'm going to help you," she said with confidence.

"I want Liza," replied Edith, but this time her tone was less confrontational.

"We help you," declared Lucy.

"Lucy, you go sit on the porch steps, okay? Make sure the coast is clear when Edith and I are ready to move."

"What coast is clear means?" asked Lucy, skeptical.

"It means, make sure that no one is coming. It's a very important job. A very helpful job." Lucy nodded. She liked being helpful.

"Okay." She ran to the steps. "Coast is clear!" she yelled.

"Very good. Now stay there and make sure it stays that way, okay, Lu?"

"Okay." Maggie turned back to face Edith. "Hi Edith," she said, hoping that Edith's disorientation had passed.

"Who are you? Where's Liza? I want to get up, goddamnit!" She pushed on her forearms and then grimaced in pain.

"I'm Maggie, and that's my little girl, Lucy. I'm going to help you up, Edith, but first I need to know where the pain is. Is it your arms that hurt?"

"My hand," Edith whimpered. "I think I've broken my hand."

"Your hand? Which one? Your right or left?"

"This one works," replied Edith, wiggling the left one.

"So here's what I'm going to do, Edith. Give me your good hand. I'm going to pull you up. Can you do that?"

"Are you going to hurt me?" asked Edith.

"That's not the plan," said Maggie. "If anything hurts in the midst of all this, you let me know, okay? We'll stop, and I'll call an ambulance."

"No, no ambulance!" yelled Edith. Lucy looked up from the pile of leaves she was carefully assembling.

"Okay, no ambulance. Whatever you like, Edith." Lucy went back to her leaves.

"Is Liza on her way?" Edith asked. Maggie took a deep breath. She would play along, she had to.

"Yes, she's on her way." Maggie kneeled in front of Edith and grabbed her hand, marveling at the impossible delicateness of her fingers and wrist. "Okay, on the count of three, I'm going to pull you. You come up onto your knees as I pull, okay?"

"Okay." Lucy, sensing the possibility of entertainment, abandoned her station to get a better look.

"Alright Edith, here we go. One, two, three!" Maggie lifted, pulled and promptly fell backwards, taking Edith with her.

"You did it!" yelled Lucy, dancing a celebratory jig. "Hooray, Mommy! Hooray!"

"Now what?" asked Edith.

"Shit," said Maggie. "That's not how I was planning for that to go. Are you on your knees? Are your knees okay?"

"Yes."

"Okay, now I'm going to sit up and you're going to come with me. Here we go." Maggie rolled up slowly, hugging Edith to her.

"We did it!" heaved Maggie, as she embraced Edith—both of them upright at last, Edith's arms hanging limply at her sides like a belligerent teenager's.

"We're still not standing," said Edith.

"Yes, I'm aware of that, Edith." Maggie took a deep breath. "I'm going to stand up first by myself and then I'll pull you."

Edith gave her a look.

"No, this time it will work. I'm ready, I promise." Maggie stood up, her lower back screeching in protest. "I'm going to take your hand and pull you up on the count of thr—"

"No more counting!" interrupted Edith. "I'm ready." Maggie pulled with all of the strength she had left and finally, Edith was on her feet.

"Oh!" she said. "That was fast."

"Okay," said Maggie, relieved to have her upright. "Let's get you inside and into some clothes."

"I need something for the pain," Edith confessed, as Maggie took her arm and led her towards the house. "My hand is killing me." Maggie looked down and winced. Edith's hand was already swelling to balloon-like proportions.

"Oh my," said Maggie. Her mind raced. Four o'clock on a Sunday. No doctor's office open, she was sure. "Edith, I'm afraid I have to take you to the emergency room. Your hand, it—"

"No!" yelled Edith. "No hospital, Celeste. I'm not ready."

"But Edith, your hand looks like it may be broken. We need an X-ray."

"No, Celeste, please." Edith began to cry.

"Okay," she agreed. "Okay. We'll put you to bed now, but first thing tomorrow, we're going to the doctor. Deal?"

"Mommy, Edif okay?" asked Lucy, guarding her leaf pile carefully as they ascended the stairs.

"Yes, Edith is okay, but she hurt her hand," Maggie explained.

"Ah yes, a boo-boo," Lucy remembered.

"Thank you, Celeste," said Edith, leaning on Maggie for support as they ascended the steps to the porch.

MAGGIE SAT CROSS-LEGGED on the couch, holding a glass of whiskey, her reflection in the window an unwelcome companion. She turned off the lamp.

She'd been convincing herself that she'd never taken care of anyone other than Lucy before, but it wasn't true. Kneeling on the ground next to Edith this afternoon, memories had surfaced like lily pads in the pond of her subconscious, about her mother.

What did any little girl know about depression, especially back when she had been a kid? All Maggie had known was that her mother slept a lot. Maggie had tried to take care of herself, tried to make her own meals—she was fine with peanut butter and jelly three times a day—but her father wouldn't have it. "I'm going to teach you how to cook," he had declared, taking the butter knife from her hand. And so, along with him because he hadn't a clue either, they had jumped back and forth through the pages of *The Joy of Cooking*, sometimes not sitting down to dinner until nine or ten o'clock. "Why eat peanut butter and jelly when you can make chicken cacciatore?" he had asked, lifting the fork to his mouth appreciatively as Maggie chewed her first bite apprehensively.

Being the best at whatever she did made her father happy, she had discovered early on. She could cook gourmet dinners, make straight A's and score soccer goals; none of that was particularly hard. *But how could she make things better for her mother?* she had wondered. She wasn't sure.

And then one morning, watching television alone while her father busied himself with the lawn, a commercial for Mr. Clean flashed across the screen. Maggie could still see it now, all these years later—his bald head gleaming like a lightbulb, the family smiling and laughing in their spotless kitchen. *She would clean*, she thought. She pushed a stepstool over to the sink and began with the pile of dirty dishes. When that was finished she had grabbed the broom and swept the crumbs and grass blades off the floor, careful to guide them into the dustpan and into the trash. When her mother had shuffled in, the smile on her face was like a thousand suns.

Maggie rested her glass on a coaster and rubbed her eyes. How irresponsible she had been, not calling Edith's neurologist right away. But that lawyer, he'd made Maggie think that she had all the time in the world.

She would call the neurologist tomorrow, first thing—set

up an appointment to talk and drive into the city to meet her. Well, not first thing. First thing, she would take Edith to get an X-ray, to find out just how bad the damage to her hand was. Her right hand, on top of everything else. The hand she did everything with. Not only would Maggie have to serve as her memory now, but her literal limb, as well.

Maggie had no idea how Alzheimer's even played out. How quickly did it accelerate? Would Edith be a vegetable within the year? Mopping the floor or taking care of a toddler was not the same thing as taking care of an old woman. Tonight, helping Edith out of her swimsuit and into her pajamas, she had seen all the proof she needed. The breasts like oblong water balloons; the loose skin pooling around every joint; the shock of gray pubic hair; the road map of sunspots and veins covering every inch of Edith's skin.

And who was Celeste? Maggie wondered. Edith had called her by that name when she'd suggested an ambulance. She wished she knew more about Edith than she did, wished Liza had at least left her some sort of family tree to consult, but she'd left her nothing in the way of explanation, not about anything.

Maggie drained the rest of her drink, placed it back on the coaster and stretched out on the couch, hoping for sleep.

CHAPTER 8

"Well, Edith, it looks like you've got two broken fingers on your hands." The doctor smacked the X-ray onto the light board with a practiced flourish. "Or hand, rather."

He smiled, revealing a perfectly aligned set of blinding white teeth. Edith wondered why no one had teeth that looked like teeth anymore. She did not smile back. Well, this was just great, she thought. Her dominant hand, shot to hell.

"Do I have to wear a cast?" she asked, not liking the thought of being trapped in itchy papier mâché for God knew how long.

"Not a cast, but a splint. We'll tape your ring and pointer fingers together on top of it."

"Like a finger gurney?" Edith did not like the idea of dragging around two dead fingers with her.

"I suppose you could call it that," said the doctor. "Although, you can take it on and off as needed. Better to keep it on more often than not, though, so your fingers have time to heal. I assume you will be helping her as she recovers?" The doctor shifted his focus to Maggie, who sat against the wall with Lucy in her lap.

"Yes, we live with Edith," said Maggie.

"Very good," said the doctor. "So Edith, your daughter here will help you with getting the splint on and—"

"She's not my daughter," said Edith sternly.

"Oh? Okay then, my apologies. I just assumed. At any rate, she'll help you with the splint and of course the other tasks you'll have difficulty performing for a while."

"How long is a while?" asked Maggie.

"Eight weeks at least."

"Eight weeks?"

"Yes, at the least, I'm afraid. It could very well be longer, because of your age."

"My age," repeated Edith.

"Yes, and then there's the physical therapy, too," he added.

"Physical therapy for my fingers?" asked Edith. "That's the most ridiculous thing I've ever heard. Do you have a tiny finger treadmill somewhere back there? A minuscule finger wading pool, too?" She shook her head. "I can't believe this. You people could squeeze money out of a lime."

"Edith, we want your fingers to work again. They've been pretty badly damaged, after all, and at your a—"

"Mention my age one more time, Doctor, and expect an earful." The doctor's smile disappeared momentarily. Good, she had scared him a little. "All due respect," she added.

"Right. Fair enough, but even the youngest finger break patients go to therapy. It's part of the process."

"Great," said Edith. "Will I be able to drive with the splint on?"

"It's not recommended, I'm afraid. You're not going to be able to grasp the wheel efficiently."

"Christ," mumbled Edith. She was going to have to rely on Maggie for everything.

"So, let's get those fingers wrapped up, Edith. I'll write you a pain prescription and then you're free to go. For now, anyway. Unfortunately you'll be seeing me a few more times before this is all over and done with."

Edith sighed. She didn't know if she could endure those teeth again.

"Do you want me to run in and fill your prescription?" asked Maggie. "Might be easier." She looked over her shoulder and into the backseat, where Lucy slept. "Don't worry, she won't wake up."

"Okay," complied Edith. The dull ache of pain in her fingers had started to pulse threateningly.

"Would you like anything else? A magazine? Some candy? A soda?" Maggie asked.

"No thank you," replied Edith. Maggie undid her seat belt and opened the door.

"Actually, on second thought, perhaps I will take one of those trashy magazines. You know, about celebrities? And some licorice. The black kind. With a Coke." *Why not?* thought Edith.

"Sure, no problem. Although, black licorice?" Maggie wrinkled her nose.

"Yes, it's a controversial choice, I know. Go on now, chop chop."

Maggie grinned, stunning Edith for a moment with her prettiness. Hers was a face that was better in motion. She left the keys in the ignition and shut the door.

That morning, Edith had woken up surprised by her hand, which had swollen to the size of a catcher's mitt. She remembered falling, and she remembered Maggie helping her up and into bed, but the smaller details were fuzzy, like static on the television. She had felt like this once before, the morning after Liza told her that she had found her wandering almost clear to East Hampton when she was supposed to be walking the beach. Part of her wanted to ask Maggie what exactly had happened, but she was afraid of the answer.

Suddenly, there was a knock on Edith's lowered window. Her heart jumped. She turned around to find Murray Gold peering at her as though she was an animal at the zoo.

"Edith, is that you?" asked Murray.

"Yes, I suppose it is," answered Edith glumly.

"I thought so! I was walkin' outta' the drugstore and who do I see? Edith Brennan of all people. With a baby in tow, no less!"

Murray was the yenta to end all yentas. "The King of Sag Harbor" is how he had introduced himself to Edith when she had moved in. Liza had dragged her to the Fourth of July fireworks, and he had zeroed in on Edith like a moth to a menorah's flame. Edith nodded now, in response.

"This your grandkid?" he asked, digging. He knew perfectly well that she had no grandchildren.

"No." Edith willed Maggie to walk out and save her from this interrogation. She had lain very low since Liza had died, and for good reason. She hated manufactured sympathy.

"Listen Edith, I'm so sorry about Liza." Murray leaned in and Edith could smell the onion on his breath. "She was the real deal. They don't make 'em like her anymore."

"What does 'the real deal' mean, Murray?" asked Edith stonily.

"It means what it means, Edith. She was the total package. And very kind, always." *Unlike you*, he added silently with his arched eyebrow. "At any rate, I'm sorry the world lost her. And I'm sorry you lost her. Shame how she went, too. You know, my great-aunt Sylvia went the same way. Threw herself off a bridge."

Edith felt a tidal wave of nausea rising in her. Nobody had brought up Liza's suicide with her, nobody except Esther, which was acceptable. She was family.

Just then, Maggie exited briskly, headed for the car.

"Hello," she said to Murray absently. "Edith, is everything okay? You look upset."

"I'm fine," Edith muttered.

"Hello, I'm Murray," he bellowed, despite the fact that

Maggie was less than a foot away. "The King of Sag Harbor, they call me. Pleased to meet you. And you are?"

"Maggie. Maggie Sheets."

"I was just telling Edith about what a shame it is that Liza is gone. My great-aunt Syl—"

"Fuck your great-aunt Sylvia," said Edith suddenly, causing Maggie to gasp.

"Now, Edith, is that really necessary?" asked Murray. "I was just—"

"Murray, I think you should be on your way now," interjected Maggie, following Edith's lead.

"But—"

"Goodbye Murray," Maggie declared emphatically. She jogged to the driver's side and opened her door, starting the ignition and rolling Edith's window up as he continued to stand there, rooted to the spot.

"Mommy, Edith said 'fuck,'" Lucy announced gleefully, awake.

"Edith, you okay?" she asked, driving away.

"That fool of a man had the nerve to bring up Liza's suicide with me," she explained. "He had no right. I barely know him." Edith's throbbing fingers sent currents of pain up her arm.

"That's horrible, Edith. I'm sorry," offered Maggie. "What an ass." Edith nodded, grateful for the support.

"Could I have my pills please, Maggie?" she asked, as they pulled back onto the road.

"Oh, of course, sorry, Edith. The bag is right here, on the console. Can you access it with your left hand?"

Edith grabbed it and placed it between her legs, using them as a means of stability. It was so strange, using her left hand to do things her right always did. And time consuming. Just pulling the package out of the bag took far longer than she would have liked.

"Oh, for Christ's sake, a package *in* a package?" The blue and white paper bag in which her pills resided lay limply on her lap.

"Here. Let me pull over and help you," offered Maggie.

"No, I've got it," said Edith. "I can do it myself." She pulled at the paper to no avail, beads of sweat forming on her brow. The car jerked to a stop and Edith looked up to find them parked at a gas station.

"Edith, please," pleaded Maggie. "Stop pretending like you don't need help. Enough."

"I don't need your help."

"You don't? You're going to gnaw through that bag with your teeth to get to your pills, I suppose? And don't give me that look, like what I'm saying makes no sense. Not to mention what happened yesterday, after your fall." Maggie's voice was rising, almost to a bona fide yell.

"What happened yesterday?" Edith countered.

"You asked for Liza," Maggie explained, lowering her voice. "You thought she was still alive. You didn't know who I was. And you called me Celeste."

"I called you Celeste?" asked Edith, incredulous. She hadn't uttered that name, hadn't so much as given her a second thought, in years.

"Edith, you're in trouble. I'm here because, for God knows

what reason, Liza wanted me to take care of you. It was her wish. I'm here to carry it out, come hell or high water."

"Well, it's not like you're not being paid handsomely for it," Edith retorted. "A house, a pile of money, a car—I'd say you won the damn lottery."

"If this is winning the lottery, I'm selling my ticket back. You, Edith, are no prize."

Edith recoiled, as though she'd been slapped. Gingerly, Maggie removed the paper bag from Edith's hand and handed a pill to Edith. Edith placed it on her tongue and reached for her soda.

"I'm sorry. It's a lot, Edith, this arrangement. And for you, too, I get that, but man. Cut me a break and make it easier for both of us. I want to make things easier for you. Please."

"Thank you for what you did back there, with that old idiot," said Edith.

"My pleasure," Maggie replied. "I'd have run over his foot if I could have. I hate nudniks, too."

"I'm very angry at her, you know," Edith confessed, staring out beyond the parking lot to the shoreline in the distance.

"At who? Liza?"

"Yes. She left me with no choices."

"I can see why that would make you angry," offered Maggie. "I'd be angry, too, if I was you, being left to a cleaning lady."

"You're not just a cleaning lady," muttered Edith.

"Listen, I'm not ashamed of it. I'm very good at it, actually."

"I know that Liza cared about you. That you were her friend. She spoke of you quite fondly. I remember a lot still, just so you know. The past is clear. It's the present that gives me trouble sometimes."

"I can help you out with that part," said Maggie. "You can let me know what you're comfortable with, help-wise, and we can just take it day by day. I certainly don't want to crowd you, Edith. That's not who I am."

"Who are you?" asked Edith.

"Someone who appreciates space, I guess."

"Me, too," said Edith, gazing out the window as she waited for the pill to take effect. "Will you look at that?"

"What?"

Edith pointed at a blue heron mere centimeters away. It regarded them both coolly, as still as a statue on its impossibly spindly legs.

"Oh," whispered Maggie. "How elegant."

"Isn't it?" agreed Edith. They sat in silence as the heron turned its long, powerful neck first, and then the rest of its body, picking its way up onto the curb and through the grass of the empty lot deliberately.

"Do you believe in reincarnation?" asked Edith quietly.

"No. That's a bit too woo-woo for me," answered Maggie.

"Me, too, although lately I've warmed to the idea." Her hand was hurting far less now, Edith was relieved to note. "Gives me a little peace, to think that Liza might still be around."

"What in the world would Liza come back as?" asked Maggie.

"A cat," answered Edith emphatically. "A plump tabby cat."

"That sounds about right." Maggie laughed. "We should keep our eyes peeled for one."

She started the car and Edith turned to look out the window as they drove towards home. The familiar smell of burgers and hot dogs on backyard grills in the salty air tickled her nose. Her pain was gone. In its place was a lovely feeling, as though her insides were bobbing in a warm, freshwater lake.

Edith had been high only once in her life, when she was dancing in New York. Some of her cast mates were passing what she had thought was a cigarette around backstage one night, after the show, and Edith had taken a drag, not knowing that what she was smoking was not a cigarette at all. After inhaling, she had coughed violently.

"Honey, honey!" the most beautiful of the male dancers had exclaimed, coming around to pat Edith gently on the back. "Easy on that joint now! You don't want to lose one of those pretty little lungs, do you?" Edith had composed herself, mortified by her naiveté. He had smiled at her, as seductive and sinuous as a panther.

The joint was passed around again, and as it made its way back to Edith, she had panicked. She couldn't leave the circle. She didn't want to insult its members, and besides, it felt good to be accepted by them. On the other hand, she wasn't the type of girl that smoked grass. And what would it do to her? Make her strip naked and run through Times Square? She had heard stories.

"Hold it like this, honey, between your thumb and index

finger. Easier to get a good toke that way," advised her new friend, as she grasped it awkwardly. The dancer adjusted her grip and smiled at her, the whites of his eyes dyed red.

Later she would find herself up to her elbows in French fries at a diner with Esther, whom she had pulled out of bed as soon as she'd returned home, stricken with paranoia and thinking about things she did not like to think about.

"It's just a little grass, Edith," Esther had said, dipping a fry daintily into Edith's pool of ketchup. "Get those away from me. One more and I'll split my leotard. And don't look so stricken for God's sake, Edith. You're a nice Jewish girl from Ohio that accidentally took a toke because you wanted the queens to like you. It's a story a million years old. Don't sweat it."

Edith had nodded in between bites. Esther was right, as usual.

EDITH ASCENDED THE stairs slowly. Her stomach growled loudly. She was ravenous. Through the screen of the sliding glass door, Edith saw Maggie sitting at the wooden patio table, her phone wedged between her shoulder and her ear.

Under the tape of the splint, Edith's fingers looked like malformed fingerling potatoes—swollen, crooked and purple. She had always liked her hands—her thin fingers and oval nail beds. Another vanity down the drain with age, terrific. Slowly, she stood up and walked towards Maggie. At the screen door, she hesitated, not wanting to eavesdrop but realizing that she was anyway.

"Okay, so we'll come in next Wednesday. Eleven o'clock. Thank you, Dr. Bloom. See you then."

Edith abandoned her post by the screen as quietly as she could, only to walk directly into a giant plastic elephant that immediately erupted into song.

"Edith, are you okay?" Maggie called. "Can I help you with something?"

"I'm fine," said Edith. She regained her composure and walked to the refrigerator at a brisk clip. "Just hungry."

"Can I help you with anything?" asked Maggie again. "I'm happy to make you a sandwich."

"I can certainly make my own sand—" Edith began, before remembering their agreement. Maggie was right, it would be easier if she did it for her. "Right. Okay. Thank you."

Maggie nodded and walked to the fridge. Edith, not knowing what to do with herself, sat down at the table to wait.

"I was on the phone with your neurologist, Dr. Bloom, just now," Maggie explained, her back to Edith as she retrieved the cheese, turkey and bread. "Mayonnaise? Mustard?" she asked.

"Neither," answered Edith glumly.

"She seems nice," Maggie added. "You and I are going into the city to see her next week. On Wednesday."

"I don't like her," said Edith. "She's hoity-toity."

"Really? How? You sure you don't want any condiments on this thing? It won't be too dry?"

"I've been making my own sandwiches for eighty-two years. I'm sure." It was one thing to be cared for, but another to be patronized. Of course Edith knew what she wanted on her own damn sandwich.

"Fair enough. Sorry." She cut Edith's sandwich down the middle and placed it in front of Edith. "Why is she hoity-toity?"

"She has an attitude, what do you want me to tell you?" Edith took a bite.

"I was checking her out online. She has a great reputation. She's one of the top five neurologists in Manhattan."

"Top, schmop," said Edith. She took another bite, even though her appetite was gone.

"Do you want me to find a different doctor?" asked Maggie.

"No. They're all the same." Edith pushed her plate away. "I didn't remember the last time, either," she announced.

"The last time what?"

"The last time I had an episode or what have you. Liza had to tell me after the fact."

"What happened?"

"I got lost on my walk. A runner found me wandering on the side of the road. Thank God I always pin my license to the inside of my waistband or who knows where I'd be. Canada, I suppose."

"You pin your license to your waistband?" asked Maggie.

"Of course. 'Carry a purse and you're asking for trouble,' my mother always warned me."

"Good advice," agreed Maggie. "Albeit slightly paranoid perhaps."

"Liza took me to see Dr. Bloom shortly thereafter."

"And that's when she was hoity-toity?"

"She ran a lot of ridiculous tests on me, asking me what year it was, who was the President, things like that, followed by an MRI—after which she sat us down and told me that my brain was turning into Swiss cheese. It was a delightful day."

"No, she didn't say that," argued Maggie.

"She may as well have. No bedside manner whatsoever." Edith's shoulders, usually as erect as a Manhattan skyscraper, slumped.

"Yeah, that's hard to come by. The doctor who delivered Lucy clearly had other places to be. Rushed me through delivery like I was wasting his time."

"It's criminal. But what can we do? They don't teach manners in med school I guess." Edith sighed. "The father, was he with you in the delivery room?"

"No. Just me."

Edith nodded sympathetically. "So why housecleaning?" she asked, wanting to change the subject. "You don't seem the housecleaning type."

"Me?" Maggie shrugged. "Why not? It paid really well and I'm good at it."

"That's it?"

"I graduated with an English degree and worked in publishing for a bit, but it wasn't for me," Maggie explained.

"Why not?" asked Edith.

"The hours, the pay, the schmoozing—I didn't enjoy it. And then my mother died."

"Oh no," said Edith. "I'm so sorry."

"Nothing to be sorry for. But it did change my perspective on things. Wasting time being unhappy doing something just to prove that I could endure it seemed ridiculous suddenly. The housecleaning thing, it just kind of fell in my lap. I was making an appointment for my boss, to have his apartment cleaned, and the cleaning lady, the one I was booking, made just about my entire weekly salary for three hours of scrubbing floors and changing sheets. It was crazy. And so I thought, why shouldn't I take a stab at it?. I've always been very good at it. Anyway, the next day, on my lunch break, I took the subway up to the agency and asked if they were hiring," Maggie explained. "They were, so after lunch, I quit, but not before pocketing a fat stack of Post-its from the supply closet on my way out."

"I like Post-its, too," said Edith. "But what about your father? What did he think about your decision?"

"What he would have thought didn't matter to me," Maggie replied.

"Oh, sorry," said Edith, recognizing herself in Maggie's sudden defiance.

"He remarried less than a year later," said Maggie. "Found himself an entirely new life."

"That's terrible," said Edith.

"You know, my mother, she was depressed," volunteered Maggie, switching gears. Edith went along. She understood not wanting to talk about things.

"Was she bipolar, like Liza?"

"No," said Maggie. "She was always down. None of those wild up periods like Liza had."

"Liza was always like that, even as a little girl," said Edith. "She was either the life of the party, with more kids around than I could count, or alone in her room for weeks on end. I'll never forget asking her where they all were, when the house had been deserted for a week or two. 'Liza,' I'd asked her, 'where are all of your fans?' 'They wear me out,' she said. Can you believe that, coming from a six-year-old?" Edith shook her head. "I thought she was just moody."

"God, when she was up she was so much fun," said Maggie. "Once, she had a book thing out in San Francisco and somehow convinced me to go with her. First class seats, a five star hotel—the whole nine yards. And the food we ate! It was the best weekend of my life."

"She really knew how to do it," agreed Edith. "Once we took a helicopter into the city for one of her book parties. Landed on the roof, champagne glasses in hand. It was really something." Edith laughed. "What did she think of Lucy?"

"She never met her, actually," replied Maggie. "Liza and I, we had a falling-out before she was born."

"A breakup?" asked Edith, feeling brave.

"Breakup as in a romantic breakup? Oh no, we were never like that. I'm straight."

"Oh."

"I remember feeling insulted in the beginning almost, though, that Liza wasn't interested in me. My ego knows no bounds, apparently."

"What did you fall out about then?"

"Just things," said Maggie, standing up and clearing their plates. It was obvious to Edith that she didn't want to talk about that, either. She had more in common with Maggie than she had imagined. Edith had her own things, too.

"I think I'll go rest for a bit," said Edith.

"Of course, go ahead," replied Maggie. "As long as it's not a nap."

"It's not a nap," Edith declared, smiling.

She turned to go but then stopped, turning around.

"You're not so bad, Maggie," she offered shyly.

"Thanks, Edith. You either."

CHAPTER 9

Maggie sat back on her heels, the pungent smell of bleach stinging her nostrils. She couldn't sleep and so here she was, at four in the morning, scrubbing her bathroom floor, tile by tile. Whoever had been cleaning this place had done a shit job.

She began scrubbing again, her brow furrowed. Yesterday, at the beach, she had been burying Lucy in the sand when a dad on the towel next to them had beat his hands on his chest like a gorilla, slung his daughter over his shoulder and bounded to the water's edge with the kind of vigor that Maggie couldn't channel even on her best day. It was testosterone in all of its glory, and for the first time in her two and a half years, Lucy was visibly intrigued.

"What's that?" she had asked, pointing to the water,

where the girl ran shrieking into the waves and away from her father, who was pretending to be an elephant.

"That's a little girl and her dad," Maggie explained.

"What's Dad?"

"Dad is . . . Dad is her friend." Maggie's father certainly hadn't been her friend, but she didn't know what else to say. *Teacher? Traitor?* Those words were better suited to Maggie's experience.

"Fwiend?" asked Lucy, skeptical. "Where mine?"

"Where's your what?"

"My fwiend?"

"You have lots of friends. Me, Edith, Esther—"

"Jose. Dawwa," Lucy called out, brightening up as her list lengthened.

"That's right, Jose and Dahlia," Maggie repeated, able to breathe again.

"Keep digging, Mommy," she instructed, satisfied by her explanation.

Friend wasn't applicable to Lucy's father, Lyle, either. He was a nonentity in Lucy's life, a nothing. When he had announced that he was moving to Portland, despite their years of being together, not together and then together again, Lyle hadn't even asked Maggie what she thought about the idea, much less invited her to join him. The only thing left to do was have sex one last time. Voilà: Lucy.

What she had told those who had asked was that Lyle had opted out of fatherhood. He had offered to pay for the abortion, she told them.

But that was not the truth. The truth was that she hadn't told him at all.

The decision had been an easy one at the time, mostly because she knew he would have reacted in exactly the way she pretended he had. It was easier to just move on with him none the wiser, she had figured, but now she worried. To lie to Lucy in order to save herself the hassle of inviting him back into their lives was a selfish choice. Lucy should know. And Lyle. He should know, too, she supposed.

Maggie didn't even know how she would go about it. She hadn't spoken to him in over three years. To resurface now with news of his daughter seemed ridiculous, like a plotline out of a soap opera. She hoisted herself up off her aching knees, finished with the floor and dumped the dirty water out of the bucket and into the toilet.

Sag Harbor was like a giant wooden spoon, stirring everything dormant up inside of her. Her parents, Liza, Lyle. She hadn't written in a long time, had sworn it off, but out here with so much noise in her brain, she longed to make sense of it the only way she knew how. She sprayed a mist of cleaner onto the mirror and attacked it with a paper towel.

"I'd love to have a look if you're ever interested in feedback," Liza had offered one rainy afternoon in the city, over coffee.

They had been talking about books and Liza's career, when Maggie had surprised herself by bringing up the short stories she'd been writing all of her life. It wasn't like her to talk about them. It was even less like her to share them, but for some reason, with Liza she felt safe. In so many ways she was like the mother Maggie had never had: supportive, curious, complimentary. In other ways, though, she was the same: depressed, complicated and honest. She was just familiar enough to make Maggie comfortable admitting to such a private part of herself. So she had.

To her great surprise, Liza had liked Maggie's work. She became a mentor of sorts—offering advice; encouraging Maggie to push herself further. Eventually, Liza's enthusiasm had become too much for Maggie, too overwhelming and too reminiscent of her own father's pushiness. What was so wrong with having a hobby? Why did people feel the need to wring the enjoyment out of everything in the name of success?

Maggie had backed out of their arrangement, telling Liza to lay off, that she wasn't interested in taking a class or launching a career—it was just therapeutic for her, her writing. A release. Liza hadn't understood and Maggie had felt patronized by the tone she began to use with her.

"There's no tone, Maggie," Liza had claimed when Maggie brought it up, using the very tone that she had been speaking of. Maggie stopped cleaning for Liza and soon after, she met Lyle. Their friendship had faded away, like a Polaroid left out in the sun.

Maggie plunged the toilet wand into the bowl, scrubbing its sides. She'd been at a bookstore with Lyle, meandering around in a post-coital Sunday haze when she'd seen it a year and a half later: Liza's new book on the front table. *The Insomniac Detective*, it was called. Maggie couldn't believe it.

Her insomniac detective, from one of her stories. She'd stood there, facing the display with her stomach in her shoes; her fists clenched by her sides, not believing it. She had bought the book and taken it home with her, relieved to find that the similarity ended with the concept. Her detective had been a reclusive young woman in Buffalo, while Liza's was a middle-aged man in 1950s Hollywood. She was still angry, though. Liza had stolen from her outright, like a common thief.

For weeks Maggie had endured the bubbling cauldron of resentment and anger swirling inside her, until finally she broke.

"You've got a lot of nerve!" she'd barked at Liza when she answered the phone, not recognizing her own shaky voice.

"Maggie, how nice to hear from you!" she had said, using that same tone.

"You stole my idea," Maggie had declared, wishing she had confronted Liza in person so she could see her big fat lying face.

"Maggie. Calm down. Please. You yourself said you had no interest in doing anything with your talent, despite my repeated attempts to convince you otherwise. I didn't steal your idea, I was simply inspired by it. I couldn't just let that detective wither on the vine!" And then she'd had the audacity to laugh, an evil cackle that rung in Maggie's ears still. "Did you read it? My detective is nothing like yours. He's a man, first of all."

Maggie had sat silently seething on the other end. Somehow Liza would see her way to an apology. She had to.

"Maggie, is this about money?" she had asked instead.

Maggie had hung up, pushed to the brink of disbelief.

"Sue her," Lyle had suggested, when Maggie had explained her predicament.

"All anyone seems to care about is compensation! What about the betrayal of a friendship! What about the fact that stealing is wrong?" she'd yelled.

Lyle had told her she was being dramatic.

That had been the end of it, until now. Now, she lived in Liza's house, was taking care of her mother. In the end, Maggie had accepted the very compensation she had scorned. She didn't feel vindicated, either. She felt confused.

Maggie rinsed out the bucket in the tub and placed it upside down inside of it to dry. She washed her hands in the sink, dried them on the towel and crawled back into bed.

On cue, Lucy began to cry.

CHAPTER 10

In the distance, the train approached steadily. Edith fiddled with the buttons on the placket of her camel coat. It was spring, and although still cold, the sun made Edith hopeful. Soon, the snow would melt completely and in its place, flowers would bloom.

All around her, her fellow commuters did their anticipatory boarding jigs as the train got closer. Cigarettes were extinguished beneath heels; bag straps were readjusted; crumbs were hurriedly brushed from lapels. Edith wondered where they were going, but only for a moment. Her mind was too busy with thoughts of her own destination.

She stepped back as the train whooshed into the station, her heart beating so quickly that she feared she would have a heart attack right there on the platform. How would she explain that to John, she wondered, who had no reason to think she was anywhere but the supermarket on what was, to him, a normal Wednesday morning?

The doors opened and Edith, in a panic, turned to leave. This wasn't right, she couldn't go through with it. The crowd surged however—somehow the smattering of people on the platform had multiplied in number and strength—and despite her best efforts to escape, Edith was pushed forward and into the car.

"No, no!" she screamed, as the door sealed shut. "I'm not ready!"

Edith jolted awake, tangled in her sheets. She willed herself to slow her breathing as she unwound the blankets from around her legs and pushed her pillow back to its rightful place.

It was those pills she was taking. They had been giving her crazy dreams—the kind of dreams she didn't need; drudging up old memories that were better left alone. Slowly, she sat up and brought her injured hand to her lap.

"So? How was it? Did your fingers do the walking?" asked Esther. The four of them—Edith, Esther, Maggie and Lucy sat around a table in a sun-soaked corner of the restaurant after Edith's first therapy appointment.

"What does that mean, did my fingers do the walking?" asked Edith, annoyed and in pain. She needed a pill desperately, but she didn't want to take one on an empty stomach. They had been sitting for ten minutes and nothing, not even a bread basket. She was in no mood to be teased.

"That was the tagline to a Yellow Pages commercial, back when we were young," Esther explained. "Touchy, touchy."

"Do the Yellow Pages still exist?" asked Maggie. "There's really no need for them, what with the internet. And then of course, from an eco perspective, they may as well be a bomb."

"Yes, it's a lot of paper," Esther agreed. "But I'm fairly certain they still print them. Not everyone has a computer, you know."

"That's tru—"

"Can we stop talking about this ridiculous topic?" hissed Edith.

Lucy looked up from the crayons and paper the hostess had given her. Art supplies were readily available here, Edith noted, but not food. Esther motioned for the waitress, whose forearms were completely covered in tattoos.

"Excuse me, could we get a basket of bread please, and some menus? My friend here is dying of hunger." The waitress looked at Edith, alarmed, as if Esther was being literal.

"Sure, of course, sorry about that."

She ran to the hostess stand—*Quick, quick, there's an old lady dying at Table Four!* Edith imagined her saying—and returned with their menus. Moments later, as if by magic, a deep basket of aromatic, warm bread arrived and was placed directly in front of Edith. She pulled out a piece and laid it on her plate before passing the basket around.

"Oh, for God's sake, Edith, eat your damn bread already," remarked Esther, rolling her eyes. "There's no need to wait for us. Go on—take a bite so you can be a human again."

"Edif, ees good?" asked Lucy. Edith nodded, her mouth full.

"Thank God," said Esther. "Next time, do us a favor and bring a snack."

"I'm sorry," said Edith, taking a sip of her water. "You can stop with the ribbing now, Esther. You're no prize, either, when you're hungry."

"Once Liza and I waited forty-five minutes to even be approached by a waiter," said Maggie. "Liza completely ripped him a new one, and the management, too. I was mortified, but then we ended up with a free lunch, so—"

"Were the two of you ever involved?" interrupted Esther. Edith choked on her water.

"Involved?"

"Sure, you know, romantically involved," said Esther.

"Esther, that's none of your business!" said Edith.

"Oh Edith, please, I'm just curious. Don't be such a prude!"

"Esther, keep your voice down. I mean it."

Lucy began to whimper, sensing the tension.

"Fine, Edith. Have it your way. Where's the waiter, anyway? I need a drink."

"I told Edith the other day, we were never romantically involved," answered Maggie. "I wasn't her type, anyway."

"Yes, you're right," agreed Esther, nodding. "I always saw Liza with more of an intellectual type—funky glasses, blazers, fancy sneakers. Like that famous photographer who went belly-up and was in all of the papers, what was her name?"

"Esther, that's enough!" barked Edith. "I won't have you surmising on who or what Liza was attracted to when she's not even here to defend or support herself. Her libido is not up for debate, do you understand me?"

Esther held her hands up in front of her in surrender just as the waiter appeared with a grilled cheese sandwich and a small mountain of French fries for a delighted Lucy. As Maggie helped her get settled, another one swooped in behind him with the rest of their orders and the conversation was blissfully, as far as Edith was concerned, over. If anything could shut Esther up, it was food.

Unsteadily, Edith cut into her omelet with her left hand and took a tentative bite. It was good. Probably better than the regular eggs from the regular chickens she bought at the regular store, but she couldn't be sure.

It wasn't right of Esther to ask about Liza that way, Edith thought. It wasn't for her to know.

"So, what else?" asked Esther, pretending as if Edith's outburst had never happened. She dabbed at her mouth with her white cloth napkin. "Edith, tell us more about physical therapy."

"Yes please, Edith," added Maggie, tearing the crust off Lucy's other half of her sandwich as she fidgeted impatiently. "Did you have to lift finger weights?"

"No," answered Edith brusquely, still sulking.

"No wonder you're in pain," Esther said. "Hey Edith, remember Madame Elise? What a piece of work she was!" Maggie looked at Esther and then back at Edith.

"Who is Madame Elise?"

"Madame Elise was our merciless ballet teacher," Esther explained.

"She was merciless," Edith agreed, the memory snapping her out of her funk. "I'd leave her class feeling like someone had beaten me up. But I liked her. She was very talented, Esther, that's an inarguable fact." Esther rolled her eyes.

"Of course you liked her, Edith, you were her pet. She couldn't stand me, but I guess there's no surprise there. I'm many things, but a ballerina is not, nor ever was, one of them."

"I was not her pet," said Edith, even though she had always thought she might be.

"Oh, go on!" exclaimed Esther. "You were. Any routine, any move that the rest of us couldn't get, ole Edith would nail. She was forever in the front of the room, demonstrating."

That was true, thought Edith.

"So what's this business about you not being good?" asked Maggie. "Sounds like you were, Edith."

"I was a quick study," she replied. "But I wasn't a star. Not like Liza." Maggie bristled, her body vibrating slightly in distaste as she shifted in her chair.

"What?" asked Edith, noticing.

"What?" Maggie replied, uncomfortable to have been called out.

"She wasn't a star?" Edith dared her. Esther leaned forward and clasped her hands in front of her on the table like a spectator at a tennis match.

"No, I mean, of course she was, her books sold millions of copies, but she wasn't perfect," Maggie replied.

"Did I say she was perfect?" asked Edith. "You don't have to be perfect to be a star, you have to have the right blend of talent and drive. Liza had that in spades. What she lacked was an imagination, thought. At least in terms of concept."

"What do you mean?" asked Esther.

"Yes, what do you mean?" Maggie echoed.

"She didn't have the capacity to make something up outright. Her plots were always culled from other people's gardens, she told me," explained Edith. "Her first novel, the carpenter with Parkinson's? That was her father. And I was so angry, too, when I first read it. 'You can't just steal someone else's life, Liza,' I told her. She laughed me off, talking about artistic license and all of that, claiming that that's what all writers did. Maybe they do, what do I know?"

Lucy put her arms up over her head and twisted her hands impatiently.

"Get down!" she demanded. "All done!"

"One second, honey, I'm having a conversation," Maggie pleaded.

"I've always thought that our Broadway days would make a wonderful novel, but I'm a terrible writer," said Esther. "And so is Edith. I wanted to ask Liza to help us out, but Edith wouldn't let me. Said I was a nudnik."

"I didn't like the idea of giving my story away!" exclaimed Edith defensively. "Besides, you think she had time for two old ladies?"

She returned to her omelet, picking at it carefully with her fork and secretly wishing that she had taken Esther's advice. She had been so naïve, taking her memories for granted.

"Mommy, I'm done," Lucy declared emphatically. "Get down."

Maggie unlatched Lucy from her high chair and Lucy, free at last, ran from the table towards the door.

"Meet you in the front," called Maggie over her shoulder as she ran after her.

The waitress appeared to clear the table. Edith watched her balance their plates on her forearm; collect their used silverware and glasses.

"Edith, look—I'm sorry," offered Esther, once she had settled the check. She reached over, covering Edith's disfigured hand with her own. "I didn't mean to upset you today."

"Well, you did," said Edith. "Asking Maggie whether they were involved and then making me feel guilty about not sharing our story? That's a lot for one lunch."

"I'm a lot, what can I say?" said Esther. "But you're right. I'm sorry."

Edith pushed herself up, her right hand smarting as she gripped the arm of her chair for support. "Apology accepted."

"One more thing and then I'll shut up, I swear, Edith," said Esther, behind her. Edith took a deep breath. Esther never knew when to stop.

"What about Maggie helping you out?"

"Helping me out with what?"

"With, you know, your memories. All of them, not just the dancing ones. You could tell her your stories and she could write them down. Me, I don't have the patience, but what else is she doing?"

"She's a maid, Esther, not a writer," Edith argued, even

as she remembered Maggie telling her that she had been an English major.

"What's so hard about writing down what someone is saying?"

"What about your memories? Don't you want them preserved, too?" asked Edith.

"Not now. But you, with the Alzheimer's. It's perfect. Good exercise for your brain, too."

"Esther, goddamnit, enough already!" Edith hissed.

"Fine."

"Hello Esther," greeted a male voice, just as they were at the front door. Edith and Esther looked up, surprised, as Lucy sprinted towards them, with Maggie following.

"Toys!" she cried, elated.

"Lucy, please," said Maggie.

"No, Mommy. Toys!"

"Sam!" cried Esther. "Aren't you a sight for sore eyes!" She extracted herself from Edith and went to hug him, practically toppling over in the process. "How's your mother?"

"Good, good."

"Thank God," added Esther.

"Thank God," repeated Sam dutifully.

A teenaged girl slunk up behind him, her face hiding behind a dense curtain of dark, curly hair. *Shoulders back*, Edith thought to herself. If she had a dollar for every time she had said those same words to Liza, she would be a millionaire.

"Edith, Maggie, Lucy—this is Sam. He owns Siggy's Toy Shop in town."

"Yes, we've met," said Maggie, her voice cracking slightly.

Edith looked at Sam. She had seen him before, but hadn't known his name. He was cute. On the short side with a bit of a nose, but cute. His eyes were nice—brown, sparkly, honest. Nice arms, and hands that looked like they fixed things. No ring.

"Maggie, right?" he asked. Edith could practically feel the current of matchmaking electricity coursing through Esther as she sized up the situation.

"And you're Lucy?" Lucy nodded.

"This is my daughter, Olive." He motioned to her like a game show host unveiling a speedboat.

"Hello Olive," everyone said in unison.

"Hello," she mumbled back.

"Olive is fifteen," Sam explained apologetically. "And she babysits! Don't you, Olive?"

"Yes, Dad."

She tucked a curtain of hair behind her ear to reveal herself. Her father's eyes but not his nose (thank goodness, thought Edith) and pink lips in a perfectly shaped heart. She was a little chubby, yes, but that would fade with time. Or not, Edith reminded herself, thinking of Liza. Eventually, Liza had owned her size, and it had suited her, sometimes beautifully. Edith had never told her that, but she should have, she realized now.

"Hello Lucy," said Olive, suddenly animated.

"Hello," Lucy whispered back. Outside, through the glass doors, Edith and Esther watched Vinnie pull up.

"That's my driver," said Esther. "Edith, Lucy, Olive? Will you help me to my car?"

"You need three people to help you to your car?" asked Edith. "I can handle it, Esther—"

"Edith. Yes. I need three people." She widened her eyes and clenched her jaw. Oh, of course, realized Edith. A setup.

"Right, sorry. Okay, let's go. Olive, if you could just keep an eye on Lucy outside. Do you mind?"

"No, that's fine."

Olive looked at her father and then at Maggie knowingly, before sighing resignedly. She held the door open for Esther and Edith and then scooped Lucy's tiny hand into her own, leading her out into the warm afternoon air.

CHAPTER 11

Maggie perched on Lucy's dinosaur stool beside the tub as her daughter plunged a plastic shark in and out of the bubbles, singing to herself.

Ever since their lunch, ever since Edith had said what she had said about Liza not being an ideas person, something had happened to Maggie. She felt lighter, like a large chunk of the resentment she'd hung on to these last few years had dislodged itself, plunging permanently into the abyss. Knowing that she hadn't been the only one, that Liza had felt entitled to everyone's story, had helped. It hadn't been a calculated betrayal at all. It changed things somehow, knowing that.

"Mommy, I blow bubbles!" Lucy announced.

"Oh yeah? Let me see."

Sam had asked her to dinner when everyone else had

trooped out to the parking lot under Esther's direction. She had said yes, surprising herself, but with the caveat that he bring takeout over tonight, instead of going out. With Lucy and Edith asleep downstairs, it would feel less like a date and more like a meal with someone she wasn't responsible for feeding—a treat.

At least Lucy would be asleep. Maggie wasn't entirely sure what Edith would be doing, which was another reason why she didn't want to leave. Sam had offered Olive's baby-sitting services, but given Edith's questionable state, Maggie was uncomfortable with the idea.

"Okay bee, ready to get out?" Maggie asked Lucy.

"No!" yelled Lucy. "Not ready!"

Maggie took a deep breath, summoning her patience. Lucy had to be in bed and asleep, and she had to change into something with a significantly smaller number of noticeable stains in less than thirty minutes.

"But your fingers are prunes!" Maggie exclaimed. She picked up one of Lucy's knuckle-less hands to show her. "See? That means it's time to get out, remember?" Lucy looked down at her fingers and then back up at Maggie, concerned.

"Okay," she agreed.

In her bedroom, Maggie sang to Lucy as she toweled her off and zipped her into her purple pajamas.

"Row, row, row your boat, gently down the stream—"

"Mommy, no singing," Lucy said, cutting her off. Sadly, it seemed that Lucy had finally realized that Maggie did not have the voice of an angel, but rather the voice of a thirty-seven-year-old former smoker who could not hold a tune.

"Fine, I'll stop. But I like singing for you. It makes me happy." Lucy considered this as Maggie ran a comb through her wet curls.

"Sorry Mommy, no."

Maggie looked at the clock. Twenty-one minutes before Sam was due to arrive.

"Say goo-night to Edif," Lucy stated.

"Yes, let's do that," Maggie agreed. Lucy climbed off the bed carefully and trotted to Edith's door. Edith sat in her armchair, with one of Liza's books open in her lap, her eyes closed.

"Goo-night, Edif," said Lucy expectantly. Edith woke with a start.

"Good night, Lucy," she replied. "Have a nice sleep."

"Mommy, I want to hug Edif," said Lucy.

"Okay. Edith, would that be alright?" Edith barely had a chance to nod her assent before Lucy was running at her full speed.

"Watch out for her hand, Luce," warned Maggie. Lucy hurled herself up and into Edith's lap, grabbing her around the neck and pulling her close as though she'd never see her again.

"Good night, sweet girl," she murmured into her neck, surprising Maggie with her unexpected softness. But that's what toddlers were capable of when they were at their best, melting polar ice caps with their cuteness.

Afterward, Maggie carried Lucy to her room. Two books and seventeen minutes later, Maggie closed the door softly behind her. She had four minutes to spare.

Please let him be late, she thought, running upstairs quickly to pour herself a glass of wine before he arrived. She needed to relax, be more like her former, pre-mom self—the unimpressed wise guy with the nice ass who was always game for a good time. Men had been attracted to that Maggie. As the single mother whose world didn't exist beyond the endless needs of Lucy, and now her eighty-two-year-old inheritance, she wasn't sure who she was.

Car wheels crunched through the gravel driveway, signaling Sam's arrival. She took a gigantic gulp, refilled the glass to the top and sprinted to her room, where she rested it on top of her dresser and brushed her teeth quickly before answering the door. She had to get to it before he had a chance to ring the bell and inadvertently wake Lucy.

"Hi," she said, wrenching it open forcefully, almost knocking him back.

"Sorry, I— Lucy's asleep and—"

"Say no more. I would have thrown myself in front of a train to keep Olive asleep at that age." The faint smell of soap hung in the humid August air and fireflies hovered around them, turning on and off like tiny lightbulbs.

"I didn't have a chance to change yet. Come in, come in."

"You look great to me," he replied. Maggie laughed—a little too loudly—in response. God, she was so out of practice.

"Just give me five minutes and I'm good to go."

"Sure, no problem, I'll just head upstairs and get things ready." He held up a bulging bag. "Hope you're hungry. I sort of went nuts at the store. Never shop on an empty stomach they say, but where's the fun in that? Hey, is Edith here?"

"She's in her room. Not sure if she's asleep or no—"

"I'm here," interjected Edith, from inside her room. Maggie's cheeks warmed, feeling self-conscious.

"Oh good, I just brought her a little something. Some chocolate. Go on and get ready, I'll just say hello and then make myself comfortable."

In her room, Maggie took another generous sip of her wine and surveyed her closet. She had nothing even remotely sexy to wear. Her entire wardrobe was a utilitarian, monochromatic testament to her mothering career. Shapeless gray T-shirts; beat up jeans and sweatpants; a blue button-down; a lone black dress for death and wedding purposes. She pulled each hanger forward, hoping to find something less depressing hanging behind it, but there was no such luck.

She hadn't always dressed like this, although she certainly had never been a show pony, either. But there had been V-necks at least. Tight jeans. Where had they all gone? Had she thrown them out in one of her frenzied closet cleaning rampages? She would do that every few months in the city, go through her apartment and toss anything that hadn't been worn or utilized in the last six months. Slash and burn. Shit, she remembered. She had.

Oh well, what could she do? She chose the button-down and her cleanest cutoffs and hoped for the best. As she buttoned her shirt, she considered the bra she was currently wearing—a sad, grayish beige number with one of its underwires just at the brink of breaking free. It wouldn't do. She selected a black bra from the drawer instead. Off went her cotton briefs, as well. She'd wear the lace boy short things. Just for herself, of course.

She brushed her straight hair and wrapped it into a bun on top of her head, pinning it with a tortoiseshell barrette. A swipe of her lip balm later, and she was as ready as she was going to be, plus just buzzed enough to pull off relaxed. She closed her door and ascended the short flight of stairs.

"You okay with paper plates?" asked Sam, standing guard over his bounty.

"More than okay. I do draw the line at silverware, though," said Maggie, sliding open the drawer. "Once I ate a plastic fork tong in a moment of ravenous overexcitement."

"Good God, you must have teeth of steel!" Sam remarked, his back to her as he put the final plates away. "I hope it was a worthy bite."

"You know what, I can't remember what it was." Maggie cocked her head. "For some reason a gyro memory is coming back to me, but shame on me if I was eating it with a fork, right?"

"I'm afraid your plastic consumption was just punishment." Sam leaned against the table and smiled. Maggie felt warm suddenly, the good kind of tingly warm. What would it be like to hug him? she wondered.

"Hey, would you like some wine?" asked Maggie, noticing that he didn't have a glass and wanting to refill her own.

"No thanks, I'm good," he replied. "I'm training for this triathlon thing. It seems highly unlikely that I'll survive it, but fingers crossed." He patted the slight swell of his stomach.

"Ah, so you're training now?" asked Maggie, her interest in him waning. She was winded just climbing stairs. They would never work.

"Yep. Six days a week I'm torturing myself in spandex."

"That's—" Maggie searched for the word. "That's impressive."

"Eh, not really. I was just tired of feeling like crap. Anyway, sorry, I know it's sort of a buzzkill," he added apologetically.

"No, no, not at all," lied Maggie.

"Maggie, please don't enjoy your wine any less on my account. Seriously."

"No, it's okay. I'll just have water. Can I get you some?" Maggie moved towards the cabinet that housed the glasses, feeling as though she had been unplugged.

"Don't be ridiculous, Maggie. Enjoy it."

"You're sure?"

"Positive." Maggie poured herself another glass, figuring she had nothing to lose.

"Let's talk about something else now," said Sam. "Please?"

"Yes, let's. But first, let's see what you brought. I'm starving."

Out from the bags came prosciutto and melon, crackers and hummus, cornichons and olives ripe with brine. Fried chicken and coleslaw, a potato salad and collard greens. Even a tiny loaf of corn bread. They amassed their treasure on the table like two delirious pirates.

"This is awesome, Sam," declared Maggie. "You know what you're doing."

"Thanks. I may not be drinking at the moment, but I am most certainly eating."

"Shall I start?" asked Maggie.

Sam nodded, and they were off, taking and passing, oohing and ahhing over the myriad tastes. *For someone that wasn't drinking, he was fun*, thought Maggie. But it was impossible not to feel self-conscious about her own consumption in his presence. And who needed that? Especially her, with the stress she was under. It was a shame really, she thought, crunching into a drumstick.

"So what's it like living with Edith?" asked Sam quietly.

"It's okay." Maggie shook her head at her nonanswer. "Sorry, I sound like an idiot. Thinking of the right word, though, it's hard. Unpredictable maybe?"

"Oh yeah? How so?"

"Her ups and downs are tough to navigate through. On one hand, at least legally, I'm supposed to be taking care of her, but on the other, she's a mostly completely capable and fiercely independent woman. Bridging that gap is tough."

"I'm sure. And with a two-year-old, too, no less." Sam helped himself to another piece of chicken.

"Yes. And I don't think she likes me very much, either, so that doesn't help."

"Who? Edith or Lucy?"

"Edith. Lucy is contractually obligated to like me."

"Yeah, don't be so sure about that. Once they hit teenagerdom all bets are off."

"Great."

"I don't know Edith at all really, but Esther I've known for years," he said in between bites. "She likes you. That's all you need, really."

"Oh yeah?"

"Definitely. A blessing from Esther in this town is worth more than a block of prime beachside real estate as far as I'm concerned. Edith will come around, don't worry."

"So what's it like, running a toy store?" asked Maggie. "Did you always want to take over for your dad?"

"Oh God, no." He laughed. "I majored in philosophy in college. Thought I wanted to go on to get my PhD originally, but then, well—life got in the way."

"How?"

"Well, I met Olive's mom here, fell in love. And then Olive happened. Pursuing a PhD with a family to support didn't seem particularly wise. My father had been after me for years to help him out in the store and so I caved, finally. But you know, it's been great, it really has. Surpassed my expectations by miles. Turns out I really like people. Plus, having Olive grow up there was pretty cool."

"I bet. Lucy would flip, having Siggy's as her own personal playroom."

"Yeah, it was great. When we first started out, my wife and I would just bring her to the store, set her up in one of those play yard things while we worked." He pushed his plate away with a sad smile. "It was a pretty wonderful time."

"Sounds pretty magical," agreed Maggie. She thought of Lucy's infancy, which had been anything but. The two of them had been trapped in her tiny apartment in the dead of winter—Lucy colicky and inconsolable; Maggie exhausted and drenched in her own breast milk.

"But all good things must end, as they say. Isn't that what they say? I don't even know," said Sam.

"I assume you're talking about your marriage?"

"Divorced," he offered. "Three years ago now. It's for the best of course, but man, it did a number on me. This triathlon thing I'm doing—it's partly because of that. To, you know, try to pull myself out of the muck." That Maggie understood.

"Slots are still available," offered Sam, grinning.

"No way."

"What about you? Where were you before Sag Harbor?"

"New York City," Maggie answered.

"Of course, duh. That's how you knew Liza, right?"

"Right."

"How did you guys meet?"

"I cleaned her apartment." Sam nodded the way polite people always did when she told them what she did for a living. The *Oh, that's nice, why in the world would anyone be a housecleaner?* nod. "Initially, anyway. We became friends through writing," Maggie explained.

"Oh yeah? You write?" Maggie hadn't spoken about her writing since she'd stopped, but learning what she had about Liza had loosened her resolve on that front, too.

"Just short stories," she answered now, testing the words on her tongue.

"About what?" Sam asked.

"Anything, really. Whatever strikes me as interesting. I do a lot of thinking when I'm cleaning, actually. Something about the quiet and physicality of the process—it's ideal. Or it was a long time ago. I haven't written in years."

"Why?"

"Oh, you know, life. Motherhood. Stuff."

Sam nodded. "Did Liza read your work?"

"She did," Maggie answered. "She was a wonderful editor, really." It was true, she had been. "Man, that was delicious. Really, really good. I'm too full to move," she said, pushing her plate forward.

"Too full for peach cobbler and ice cream?"

"Stop it. You brought dessert, too? You think everybody is doing a triathlon or something?"

"Let's go for a walk to the beach," said Sam. "Stretch our legs. Then we can come back and justify pigging out."

"Oh, I don't know. I have Lucy downstairs, and Edith . . ."

"Just a short one, I promise. Does Lucy usually wake up?"

"No." Maggie chewed the inside of her cheek. The odds of Lucy waking were slim to none, it was true. "Okay. A short one."

They trampled down the stairs and out into the night air.

"Damn, it feels good out here," said Sam. He let out an appreciative whistle.

"It really does," agreed Maggie. It was just the right amount of cool, with a slight breeze that smelled of the ocean and honeysuckle. Crickets chirped in the grass and the sky looked bruised—almost dark but not quite yet. The moon bobbed in the moving clouds above them, like a cork in the water. She was happy, she realized. Relaxed.

"Supposed to rain tomorrow," said Sam.

"Rain," sighed Maggie. "It used to mean books and toast in bed."

"Not anymore, huh?"

"With Lucy? No way."

"You should bring her by the store. We have story time tomorrow. Good reason to get out of the house, plus you can get a break."

"Story time, that sounds nice. Oh wait, no. Tomorrow we're taking Edith to a doctor's appointment in the city," she remembered.

"Edith okay?" They made a left onto the road that led to the beach.

"Just a checkup," Maggie lied. Edith would have her head if she told people about her diagnosis. She knew her well enough by now.

"She hurt her hand, she was telling me tonight."

"Yes, she fell and broke two of her fingers," said Maggie. "But her therapy is here, in town."

"That's what they say about old age—that your bones just snap."

Up ahead, waves lapped gently against the shore, the moon now center stage, its white light illuminating the sand. Tomorrow's chaos loomed large, but it was tomorrow, Maggie reminded herself. This was tonight. Tonight, the air felt like it was kissing her and the water beckoned seductively. She felt young; free; open.

"How long have we been gone?" she asked.

"About twenty minutes," answered Sam, looking at his phone.

"Let's go swimming," said Maggie, surprising herself.

"Like swimming, swimming? We don't have our suits."

"So? I won't peek if you don't." Maggie began to jog towards the water.

"I can't promise that!" yelled Sam behind her.

Maggie didn't answer. She unbuttoned her shirt as she jogged, her feet now in the grainy sand. At the water's edge she dropped it, slipped off her flip-flops and unbuttoned her shorts, the excitement at behaving in a way she hadn't for so long flushing her cheeks. She unsnapped her bra and at the last moment, decided to keep her underwear on, grateful that she had chosen her least matronly pair.

"Don't look!" she cried, running into the waves at breakneck speed, not caring that she could feel her thighs rubbing against one another; her breasts flopping. If he looked, he looked. She wasn't going to sleep with him anyway, she had decided.

She dove in, relishing the coolness cocooning her, closing her eyes to its salty sting. She stayed under, holding her breath, feeling grateful. The air; the water; the sand between her toes; the moon—they belonged to her now, because of Liza. It was a gift, all of it.

Maggie had made a mistake with her, she realized, by choosing to express her anger over an innocuous plot point instead of her hurt over the dissolution of her trust. It had been easier, though, to be angry. It always was.

Finally, she surfaced, taking a giant breath of air in, her wet hair blanketing her neck and shoulders.

"It feels incredible in here," she yelled to Sam, who was a few feet away.

"Amazing," he agreed. "A little cold maybe, but amazing."

Maggie dove down again, twisting around and around like a corkscrew, enjoying her weightlessness. It hadn't been about the stupid detective at all. Maggie wished for Liza; for the opportunity to tell her that. She surfaced again, and to her disbelief, realized that she was crying.

Sam floated on his back, his toes poking out of the water like tentacles.

"I can't believe she killed herself," she announced. He continued to float, oblivious with his ears submerged.

"I don't care about the stupid book. That's not what it was about," she sobbed. "I wish I could have figured that out before she died."

He looked over, sensing that she was speaking to him. With a splash, he righted himself.

"What?" He faced her, concerned. Maggie went under again, for just a second, to compose herself.

"I said that we should probably go now," she said once she had resurfaced.

"Oh, okay. Sure."

Maggie nodded and swam towards the shore.

CHAPTER 12

Edith leaned her head against the dirty window of the train and closed her eyes. Beside her, Lucy slept, her small feet clad in their pink and blue sneakers resting on her thigh. Her tousled mane of blond curls lay on Maggie's lap; her beloved stuffed monkey was clutched to her breast. A thin purple blanket covered her. Maggie's eyes were closed, too, her arm draped protectively around her daughter as their fellow passengers clambered onto the train in a cloud of perfume and food, anxiously jockeying for seats.

Edith had been so nervous, from the moment she had awoken, that she had considered taking one of her pain pills just to calm herself down. But asking Maggie to drag a groggy senior and an absolutely electric toddler around Manhattan in the rain seemed like a recipe for a nervous breakdown, and so Edith had abstained.

There had been no way around bringing Lucy with them, which Maggie had apologized for profusely. Edith understood—she couldn't just leave her baby with someone she didn't know. She'd mentioned Sam as a possibility, but Maggie had dismissed that idea very quickly. Edith supposed their date had not gone well. She had tried to stay up, to eavesdrop as Esther had commanded her to, but it had been no use. She had fallen asleep right in the chair.

Edith had a new respect for Maggie, watching her as a single mother in the wilds of Manhattan. From the moment they had set off on their considerable journey—Maggie laden with two giant bags like a pack mule and pushing a stroller filled with twenty-five pounds of child—it had been non-stop. *Mommy, what's that? Mommy, I'm hungry. Edith, we going to doctor? Mommy, I pooped. Pretzel, I want pretzel!* and on and on and on. By the time the three of them had arrived at Dr. Bloom's office, they had looked like war torn refugees, Edith had been sure.

The good news was that, as a result of the chaos, Edith's nerves hadn't had a chance to flourish further. It had been more a matter of actually arriving to the appointment alive. The people, the pace, the smells and the sounds of the street had almost eaten her whole. It had changed so much since she had lived there—so much cleaner and brighter and bigger— but the rhythm was the same. That remarkable, nonstop rhythm—the endless, staccato beat of a drum in her ears.

In the waiting room, Edith had tried not to stare at her peers, but failed miserably. There was an old, old man who looked to be about as stable as a dandelion, sitting in the corner, his mouth hanging open with a steady spool of drool leaking out. His caretaker—his daughter, Edith thought— looked as though she had been run over by a Mack truck, as flat and lifeless as a pancake in her cat hair covered black polar fleece vest despite the fact that it was a good eighty-five degrees out. Edith had looked at Maggie, wondering if it was all she could do not to run screaming out of the office in fear about her future, but she was busy bribing Lucy's silence with something on her phone.

There were also two women, one older than she and one around her own age, she surmised, who were thankfully less unkempt. Both of them appeared to be with their husbands. This had reassured Edith slightly. Here were people in her position, functioning fairly well, engaged and aware. That was something to hold on to.

An African American nurse had appeared suddenly, dressed in purple scrubs with her hair braided and pulled into a bun the size of a soccer ball on top of her head.

"Edith Brennan?" she had announced, and Edith had tensed, not wanting any of those people to know her name but then remembering that nobody would. There, a perk of the Alzheimer's waiting room. She had found one.

SHE GAZED OUT into the darkness of the train tunnel. The conductor came over the loudspeaker, announcing the various destinations along their route home. The names were familiar, but she supposed that one day, possibly soon, they wouldn't be. That her brain would start shutting down like a skyscraper's electricity, floor by floor, until the whole thing went dark.

The doctor had said as much, as the four of them had sat in her office, going over Edith's examination results. She hadn't been able to remember the third word the doctor, who was still hoity-toity as far as Edith was concerned, with her stiletto heels, had rattled off to her moments before, as part of some asinine list.

The Alzheimer's was progressing slowly, apparently. Edith didn't think progression of any kind was good news, but to say that she had been surprised to hear it would have been a lie. She was forgetting things all of the time now, like how to fasten her sandals. Just that morning, she had stared at them for ten minutes before surrendering to flats. She had even started making lists—people's names, her address, her phone number—just in case.

The train began to move, and Maggie stirred.

"Oh, thank God, she's asleep," she murmured to Edith. "What a day."

Edith turned from the window. "It certainly was."

"Only a month gone and all of my urban mothering muscles have gone slack." She rubbed her eyes.

"I wouldn't say that," said Edith. "You looked like a pro out there."

"Oh yeah?"

"Sure. I was certainly impressed."

"Thanks, Edith." Maggie smiled at her.

"I don't know how you do it, all by yourself. I couldn't have, certainly. John was a big help."

"Yes, well," said Maggie, shrugging, "it is hard, that's true. And some days I worry that it's hurting Lucy, but you know, her father and I—we didn't love each other. It wasn't a good relationship. That's not good for a kid, I know that much from personal experience."

"Your parents didn't get along?"

"No. They tolerated each other. That was about it."

"You could sense that?"

"Kids know everything. They have this emotional intuition that we lose, I think, as we get older; more cynical."

"Liza always did. She knew I was having a bad day before I did."

"Yeah?"

"Yes, she was very astute. I think that's what made her a good writer."

"What was it like, mothering Liza?" asked Maggie, as the train began to move.

"It was a challenge. She was stubborn." Maggie raised her eyebrows. "Like me, yes, but also not like me. Emotional intelligence has never been my thing. I'm a very logical sort of person. We clashed quite a bit."

"Was Liza more like her father?"

"Yes. He had a natural empathy about him. Much kinder than me. More accepting. And quiet."

"I wouldn't call Liza quiet," said Maggie.

"Privately, she was, though. In public she had this larger than life persona, but in private she was much more of an introvert, don't you think?" asked Edith.

"Yes, that's true. I wonder, though, if that was the depression."

"Is Lucy like you, do you think?"

"Hard to tell," answered Maggie. "I can't remember myself this pure, this untouched by experience. Maybe." The train rolled to its first stop and passengers scampered down the aisle, anxious to disembark. "Did you ever worry, as a mother, that you were screwing Liza up?"

"You kidding? All of the time." Edith paused before continuing. "I've been thinking about Liza's childhood so much since—well, since she died. What I could have done differently to make her a happier person. I made a point to give her her space, but I should have asked more questions I think. Then maybe that would have opened up more of a dialogue between us. With a different mother, maybe she would still be here," said Edith.

"Oh Edith, you can't think like that," said Maggie. "Depression is a chemical disease. I'm not sure you could have done anything really, to make her happier. That was up to her."

"I suppose that's true," answered Edith. "Technically, at least."

"My mom was depressed, I told you that, right?" asked Maggie.

"Did you?" Edith looked at her blankly for a moment.

"Oh yes, you did. You cleaned for her, that's how you got started. I remember now," said Edith, her words tumbling out in a rush of gratefulness at having been able to recall the memory.

"No amount of scouring or scrubbing I did would have had any long term impact on her happiness, I figured that out eventually. But the temporary fix, it felt good. To see her smile," Maggie explained, her voice gravelly with emotion.

"I know. Once I brought Liza a kitten in the hopes of seeing her smile, when she was living in the city."

"Did it work?" asked Maggie.

"Yes and no. She refused to take it in, said she wasn't a cat person, but we got a good laugh out of it. And I got her out of her bed. So, mission accomplished I guess. Had to bring the cat back home and take care of it myself for the next decade, but that was okay. She was a good cat."

"See? You were a good mom," said Maggie.

"I don't know if I was, really," said Edith. "But I did try my best, I know that. I loved her so much." She looked out the window at the scenery whizzing by, remembering the way the kitten shivered in her hands as they waited for Liza to answer the door.

She didn't want to forget about the kitten; about anything. Maybe Esther had been right. Maybe she should get her past down on paper. It was a daunting task, that was true, but what if Maggie was game to help her, as Esther had suggested? Edith turned back around to face Maggie, whose eyes were closed, her head rocking slightly with the train's movement.

"Maggie?" she asked. Her eyes opened.

"Yes?"

"How long do you think I have?"

"Have what?"

"Have before my brain turns to oatmeal?"

"Oh Edith, I wish you wouldn't say that."

"Too bad, I'm saying it."

Maggie sat up. "Dr. Bloom said it was progressing slowly, so I guess we don't really know."

"I'm going to start writing then," Edith declared. "Esther was right. I should. Before I forget everything. Will you help me?"

"Me?" asked Maggie. "Help you write? I mean, sure, if that's what you want."

"I do. That's what I want." Edith smiled, feeling relieved. "We could set a time, meet every day. Maybe I could talk, and you could transcribe?"

"Sure, we can try that out." Edith nodded, thinking of everything she wanted to say. There was so much.

"We'll start tomorrow," decided Edith. She reached across Lucy with her left hand.

"What's this?" asked Maggie.

"Let's shake on it."

"A contractual shake? Okay." Maggie grasped her hand gently.

"Eraser!" Edith cried as they unlatched their fingers, startling Lucy, who shifted slightly in her sleep.

Eraser. The third word. Take that, Dr. Bloom.

CHAPTER 13

Maggie sat, tipped back in Liza's chair with her bare feet perched on the desk's edge, going over her notes. Edith had given her permission to use the guesthouse to write, as part of their partnership. It was strange, to be here, facing down copies of the very book that had robbed her of her desire to write in the first place, but it also made sense in a circle of life kind of way, Maggie had decided.

She took a sip of her now lukewarm coffee and glanced at Liza's laptop, which she had removed to make room for her own. It sat, blinking, on the stack of hardback books that snaked up from the floor and around the back leg of the desk like ivy. A few days prior Maggie had opened it, feeling like her progress had earned her the right. She'd been hoping to uncover some sort of clue about Liza's demise, but there was nothing—just manuscripts and photos; speeches and contracts; the occasional recipe. But what was Maggie expecting? A desktop folder labeled "Suicide Letter"? Never in a million years would Liza be that transparent.

Maggie pressed play on her recorder and Edith's voice, speaking about her childhood in Cincinnati, filled the small room. She spoke so lucidly, as though every memory was just near the surface. It was hard for Maggie to believe, listening to her talk about playing by the river; her dance classes; her mother's lemon cake and her father's dress shoes, that Edith's brain was in jeopardy. Then again, Maggie had read somewhere, googling in bed before she fell asleep, that the earlier memories were the last to go. Maggie had been considering urging Edith to start over in the present and work her way back, but it seemed cruel somehow, to interrupt her rhythm.

Her phone buzzed. She pulled it out of her pocket, disappointed. It was only a stupid spam email. For a week now, she'd been hoping to hear from Sam.

They'd made plans to go out again, still damp at her front door, but he'd virtually disappeared. Although she'd initially convinced herself that it wasn't a match, he had grown on her in his absence. It was nice to have a companion, romantic or not. She glanced at the time. Lucy would be up any minute.

Birds chirped to greet the morning as Maggie crunched back through the pathway towards the main house. *Companion*. God, she sounded old. No wonder he wasn't interested.

Inside, Maggie heard murmuring coming from Lucy's room. She leaned against the wall and listened.

"And who is this?" asked Edith.

"Piggy," replied Lucy.

"Good morning, Piggy," said Edith.

"Give her a kiss and hug," Lucy instructed. There was the faint sound of Edith complying.

"And who is this?" she asked next.

"Giraffe."

"Good morning, Giraffe."

"Give her a kiss and hug."

"Mommy!" yelled Lucy, the moment her head rounded the doorway.

"Good morning, bee. Are you having fun with Edith?" Edith smiled at Maggie, looking pleased.

"Yes, wif my animals."

"How nice." Lucy nodded. "Should we go eat breakfast?"

"Okay," she agreed.

"Morning Edith," greeted Maggie, as she hoisted Lucy out of the crib.

"Morning. Writing?"

"Yes, a little. Same time, same place this afternoon?" Lucy took Maggie's hand and began pulling her out of the room, towards the stairs.

"One minute, Lucy, I'm talking to Edith."

"This morning, I have something," answered Edith, furrowing her brow and avoiding eye contact. "But I can't remember what. I'll check my list."

"Okay. See you upstairs. Come on, Lucy, let's eat."

"I have physical therapy," declared Edith breathlessly behind her later, as Maggie scrambled eggs at the stove.

"Ah, okay."

"And Esther is coming with Vinnie to take me." Maggie dumped the bowl of egg yolks and milk into the frying pan.

"Yoo-hoo, Esther's Limo Service," Esther yelled from below, letting herself in.

"Speak of the devil," said Maggie.

"Oh, for God's sake, Esther," said Edith. "She's so early."

"I know I'm early," called Esther, making her way up the stairs. "But I was up at the crack and knew you three would be, too. So why not?" At the top, she revealed herself—a vision in head to toe chartreuse.

"No chance losing you in a crowd," greeted Edith, sipping her coffee at the table.

Maggie smiled to herself as she fixed her own cup. The four of them—Esther, Edith, Lucy and herself—were beginning to feel like a unit. It felt good. Comforting.

"And you're wearing that?" asked Esther. Edith looked down to survey her blue linen sheath.

"What's wrong with it?"

"Nothing a scarf or a broach wouldn't fix. A little pizazz would do wonders for you, Edith. Is there coffee for me? And where's Miss Lucy?"

"Esthah's here?" asked Lucy, looking up from the castle she was assembling.

"Yes, she's here to take Edith to the doctor," explained Maggie. Lucy shook her head with a wry smile—an exact mirror of Maggie.

"Hello Esthah!"

"Hello Lucy. Hello Maggie," said Esther. "You're looking fit."

"Me?"

"Tan! You look nice with some color—like a whole different person." She placed her gigantic purse on the table with an impressive thud.

"My God, Esther, what do you carry in that thing?" asked Edith. "Bricks?"

"What do you like in your coffee, Esther? Milk, sugar?"

"Both and lots of it, thanks. So listen, Maggie, you're taking Edith to her therapy today."

"I can't with Lucy, Esther. It would be a disaster."

"She's right, Esther," agreed Edith. "There's nothing there for a two-year-old to do."

"That's why you're leaving her here," said Esther. "With me."

"Sorry, I don't follow," said Maggie, handing Esther her coffee.

"You're leaving Lucy here with me. You'll go to therapy with Edith and then after, you're going shopping."

"Shopping?"

"Yes, you and Edith are invited to my Barbie's party, which is, without exaggeration, the event of the summer. It's the Sunday before Labor Day, every year. All of the movers and shakers are invited," she disclosed to Maggie, as though telling her a secret. "Barbie doesn't socialize with anyone less. There's a band, catering, open bar—the works. Even a sushi station. It's fabulous."

Esther reached into the vast depths of her handbag and pulled out two off-white envelopes.

"I was going to mail these, but I figured, why waste stamps? I'm seeing you anyway," she explained, handing them over.

"Thank you, Esther," said Maggie. "I do love a sushi station, it's true."

"It's an off-white party."

"An off-white party?" asked Maggie.

"Yes, all of the guests wear off-white. It's much more suitable to Barbie's coloring," replied Esther in total seriousness. "True white washes her out." Edith rolled her eyes. "You'll both need something new to wear. Barbie is very serious about her dress code."

"Esther, I don't need to go shopping, I have a cream colored cardigan," declared Edith.

"A cardigan! What, are we going to synagogue? You need a dress. Enough with the cardigan."

"Esther, I don't know, with Lucy I—"

"Vinnie and I will stay back with Lucy, have a little fun of our own. Right, Miss Lucy?"

"Yes!" Lucy cried, erupting into an impromptu jig of delight.

"Maggie, don't look so concerned," said Esther. "I have a grandson that I practically raised. Besides, this will be good practice for the party. You can't bring her, you know. Adults only."

"I don't know, Esther, I've never used a sitter out here before," said Maggie.

"So use Sam's daughter. He practically threw her babysit-ting availability at you, at the restaurant that day. Take the help and treat yourself to a night out for a change. What's her name? Pickle?"

"It's Olive," barked Edith. "Even I can remember that."

"Oh, I don't know about Olive babysitting. She's so young."

"She's not that young," countered Edith. "Besides, you put her to bed, hand Olive the television remote and leave. Lucy will never know the difference. Anyway, just an idea, Maggie. Feel free to ignore me. God knows everyone else does."

Maggie smiled halfheartedly. The idea of a night out alone with an open bar and passed hors d'oeuvres was not a terrible one, that was true.

"You sure you and Vinnie can handle her for a few hours?" asked Maggie. "It's not too much?"

"Go on." Esther waved them off. "Buy yourself something special."

"I'm going to the loo," Edith announced. "Then we'll go, okay?"

"Go, go," said Esther. "Just call up when you're ready and Maggie will come down, right, Maggie?" Maggie nodded her agreement. There was no arguing with Esther when she had her mind set on something, apparently. "Good. Send Vinnie in on your way out."

"So how is she?" asked Esther quietly, when Edith was out of range. "She told me about the two of you working together—that's great news. For both of you."

"It is," Maggie agreed.

"So important for Edith, with the Alzheimer's. Not that she talks to me about it. God forbid she talk about her feelings."

"Has she always been that way?"

"Since the day we met."

"Was Edith the one to tell you about the diagnosis?"

"No," answered Esther. "Liza called me the day Edith went missing, but the truth is that I noticed before then that things weren't right with her. She was forgetting simple things—words, dates, things like that—long before she got lost at the beach." She reached out and took Maggie's hand. "It's terrible, what's happening to her. You're going to take care of my Edith, aren't you?" She looked Maggie right in the eye, daring her to waver.

"Yes, of course, Esther."

"Very good. I'm still furious with Liza for leaving the way she did but what can I do? Mental illness is a disease and everybody knew she was nuts, God rest her soul." She pretended to spit. "Puh, puh. No disrespect to the dead, of course." She patted Maggie's hand. "You're a good girl, Maggie."

"And me! I'm a good girl, too!" yelled Lucy, who had sidled over from her blocks somewhere in the middle of their conversation.

"Yes, you too, dear," agreed Esther.

"NINETY-TWO DOLLARS FOR a T-shirt?" muttered Edith, fingering the soft cotton fabric. "Are people crazy?" Maggie laughed in commiseration.

"I know, I think it's ridiculous, too," she whispered, avoiding the stare of the overly eager saleswoman. "Maybe the fibers are laced with gold."

"Really, we should leave," said Edith. "My cardigan is more than suitable. Esther is too much sometimes."

"I dunno, maybe it would be fun to buy ourselves something a little extravagant," suggested Maggie, although boutique shopping was far from her forte. Normally she was a "wear it until the elastic went slack as a limp spaghetti noodle" kind of person, but rummaging through her closet in preparation for her date with Sam had been depressing. "I can't remember the last time I did anything for myself, now that I think about it." Edith smirked, unconvinced.

"Come on, let's go to the back. Maybe there's a sale rack," Maggie suggested, motioning to Edith to lead the way.

"Can I help you with anything?" the saleswoman chirped at them as they walked by.

"No," answered Edith plainly, her eyes trained on the far wall. Maggie stifled a laugh, enjoying her moxie.

"Oh Edith, look," said Maggie. "A cream sheath."

"I don't wear dresses," said Edith, wrinkling her nose as Maggie removed it from the rack, admiring it as she held it against herself.

"I meant for me."

"Oh." Edith cocked her head. "It is nice, now that I see it in the light. And you have the figure for it. Although, I think I'd like to see you in something long. Delicate on top with more of a flowing skirt."

"A flowing skirt?" asked Maggie. "That's not me. I like my legs."

Edith shrugged.

"What? Is there something wrong with my legs?"

"It's just, you've got such a lovely chest. Play up your best feature is what I always say," explained Edith.

Maggie put the dress back on the rack, the hanger clattering with the force of her embarrassment.

"No, nothing, forget it," said Edith. "I shouldn't have said anything."

"You're right, you shouldn't have," said Maggie. "What business of yours is it what I do with my legs?"

"You're right. I apologize," said Edith. "Maggie?" Maggie continued to browse, although tears were brimming in her eyes.

"It's fine, Edith. But you're right, this is silly. Let's go home."

"No, no, please. My honesty is my Achilles' heel. Poor Liza came close to killing me more than a few times because of it."

"What would you say to her?" asked Maggie, still thinking about her legs. The truth was that she had noticed lately that they were not what they used to be, that there were spider veins trickling across the insides of her thighs; skinny purple highways of age. And her ankles, swollen by pregnancy, had never managed to fully deflate.

"About her weight. I was always suggesting this diet or that exercise." Edith shook her head. "I should have just let her be."

"It's hard to do that, as a parent," said Maggie. "Let them be, that is. My father, he was on me all of the time." She pulled a tan linen suit from the rack. "Oh wow, look at this. This should cover my cankles nicely, Edith, don't you think?"

"Maggie, I already apologized. Please don't make me feel any worse."

"Oh, I think I'll let you stew in your guilt for at least a few minutes more, Edith." Maggie winked at her, the sting of Edith's comment fading. They were just legs, after all.

"Fair enough," said Edith. "You should just ignore it anyway, Liza always did."

"I don't think so," said Maggie. "Liza was honest to a fault, too. Guess I know where she got it from." Edith smiled, looking through the clothes herself.

"Your father, what was he like?" she asked.

"What do you mean?"

"You said he was on you all of the time."

"He was a perfectionist," answered Maggie. "A 'B' was unacceptable, I had to have a 4.0. And second string on the soccer team, forget about it. I had to be scoring goals left and right." Maggie took a sheer, sand colored sweater off the rack and held it up to Edith. "Just your typical Tiger Dad, I guess."

"Did you resent him for it?" asked Edith, shaking her head at the sweater.

"At the time, no. But now, after everything that's happened, I do. It's like he walked off the field at halftime."

"Is that a sports analogy?" asked Edith. "I hate sports."

"Me too. I'm not sure why I chose it. I guess talking about soccer revived some old jock blood in me. I just mean that he clocked out early. Too early. His whole spiel was bullshit, if you ask me."

"How?"

"All of that time and effort he put into creating the perfect daughter and then, when I needed him most, he found a new family and rode off into the sunset." Maggie cleared her throat. Talking about her father made her uncomfortable. "I'm going to try on the suit. Edith, you try the dress."

"Are you kidding? It's too short for me. I'm an old lady."

"An old dancer lady. You still have your legs. From the knees down at least."

"I deserve that," Edith replied.

"You certainly do," said Maggie, heading towards the dressing room.

CHAPTER 14

Edith stood in the middle of the grocery store aisle, the shelves on either side closing in on her with their endless array of pre-packaged crap. Maggie hadn't looked pleased when she told her she was going to the store by herself, but that had only encouraged her. Edith wanted to be as far away from Maggie as possible after the way she had so carelessly insulted her that morning. And they had been getting along so well, Edith had thought, ever since their shopping trip a few days before. Until Maggie had ruined it, that was.

In the car, Edith's heart had raced. She hadn't been out alone since before their appointment with Dr. Bloom—before that even if you counted her hand. And there was her grip to contend with. But Edith didn't care—Maggie had had the nerve to call her boring, and so she was determined to shake things up. She'd left in a huff—to gather the ingredients for something. But now, no matter how hard she tried to summon what that something was, she could not. Her mind was blank.

Everything had gone well until Edith had walked into the store. It was her own fault, she knew—she had been feeling far too smug about her successful drive, so the Alzheimer's was showing her who was boss. Instead of gathering her ingredients, now she was hiding in the cookie and cracker aisle, attempting to collect herself for the drive home.

"Mrs. Brennan, is that you?" asked a voice behind her. She jumped, startled. "Forgive me, I have a way of sneaking up on people. I didn't mean to scare you." The woman blinked slowly at Edith, reminding Edith of a cartoon cow. "I'm Lois—I was a friend of Liza's. From the bookstore?"

"Yes, of course," Edith lied. She had never seen Lois before in her life. Or had she? "Hello."

"I'm so sorry about Liza," Lois whispered. "She was a true talent, and what happened to her was a shame. This town is not the same without her. I've been meaning to write you a note, to tell you just how much she's missed, but time just gets away from me." She sighed dramatically. "Still, that's no excuse. I'm glad I ran into you, though, so I could tell you in person." Edith stared at her, angry.

"Excuse me, Lois, but have a little respect for God's sake. Bringing up Liza next to the Oreos of all places, really. Shame on you." Lois recoiled, as though she'd been struck.

"I didn't mean to offend you, Mrs. Bren—"

"I'll be leaving now, thank you very much." Edith turned

on her heel and stormed out, her eyes glued to the Exit sign for direction. She was flustered and unusually warm; her chambray shirt felt like wool next to her skin.

There was her car, parked right in front. She opened the door and got in, her heart pounding. She breathed in and out, slowly, willing her pulse to follow. It was too much for one day, everything that had happened. The idiotic Lois had been the icing on the cake.

She couldn't drive home, that much was clear. She didn't care about her own life—death by car accident actually seemed like a tidy solution—but it was the possibility of taking some other poor soul down with her that wouldn't let her put the key in the ignition. She felt composed enough to make the short journey home, but then again she had felt like herself when she walked into the grocery store, too. That was perhaps the most frustrating thing about this disease. The minute you thought you were okay, you weren't.

"Goddamnit," she cursed aloud.

There was a knock at the window. Edith looked up, preparing to defend herself against a ticket. Instead, she found Maggie and Lucy wearing identical expressions of concern.

"What are you doing here?" Edith asked sharply, undercutting the unexpected wave of relief washing over her at the sight of them. Maggie mimicked rolling a window down.

"Just a minute," she mumbled, feeling silly. Instead of putting the key in the ignition, she opened the door, sending Maggie and Lucy stumbling backwards.

"Sorry, I'm sorry." Edith took a deep breath.

"Hi Edif," said Lucy. "You sad?"

"Me? No, I'm not sad, Lucy. I'm glad to see you."

"You are?" asked Maggie. "I'm sorry to stalk you, I just got worried."

"How'd you get here without a car?"

"Vinnie." Maggie turned to point him out, idling a few spaces over in his black Lincoln Town Car. He tipped the brim of his driver's cap in greeting. "I panicked when you weren't home soon enough, and didn't know who else to call."

"Well, that's embarrassing," muttered Edith.

"Sorry Edith. My anxiety got the better of me and I didn't know what else to do. I shouldn't have let you go alone in the first place."

"As if you could stop me!" said Edith. "You can go ahead and tell Vinnie to leave now."

"Sure. I'll drive us home. Come on, Lucy, let's go tell Vinnie goodbye."

Maggie returned moments later. "Okay, he's off," she said. "Said he looks forward to seeing you tomorrow night at Barbie's. Did you get what you needed?" She opened the back door and hustled Lucy into her car seat.

"No," answered Edith, getting out to circle to the passenger side. Maggie shut Lucy's door.

"Why not? They didn't have the ingredients?" She took the keys from Edith.

"I forgot what I came for," explained Edith quietly, getting in.

"Oh," said Maggie. Lucy began kicking the seat in front of her. Maggie knocked on the window and shook her finger at her, causing her to erupt into immediate tears. "I'm sorry, Edith. I know what you came for, if you'd like me to run in." Edith looked at her expectantly.

"Deviled eggs," Maggie explained. Lucy's pitch grew louder. "I can look up the recipe on my phone and run in if you don't mind babysitting Lucifer for a minute."

"No, it's okay. I need to go home."

"You're sure?"

"I'm sure."

"We going home?" asked Lucy, her face covered in tears and snot.

"Yes," replied Edith, pulling a tissue from her pocket to wipe Lucy's nose.

"Good," Lucy answered.

"I'm not really sure what happened this morning," said Maggie, once they were on the road. "But if I did something to offend you, I apologize."

"You're not sure what you did?" asked Edith, with a haughty laugh.

"No, I can't say that I am. We were talking about your book one minute and then the next you wanted to set me on fire."

"Maggie, don't play dumb. Really, it doesn't suit you. You're very bright for a housecleaner."

"Alright Edith, take it easy," said Maggie angrily. "There's no need to get nasty."

"I should say the same to you," Edith shot back.

"For fuck's sake, Edith, stop being ridiculous. Tell me what you think I did."

"Fuck," repeated Lucy.

"You told me I was boring, Maggie. That my stories were tiresome. Do you know how that makes me feel?"

"Edith, what in the world are you talking about? I did no such thing."

"You absolutely did. Hinting that we should get to my New York days, as though everything prior was irrelevant. It's my story, you know. Nothing is irrelevant. And you don't get to rewrite it!" Edith was shaking.

"Whoa, slow down. That's not what I said at all, Edith. I merely asked you about how you got to New York in the first place. Literally, that is the question I asked you."

"But out of nowhere, you asked it. Right in the middle of something else. I could tell you were bored! I could tell!" Maggie pulled into the driveway with a screech, pressing too firmly on the gas in her agitation. She parked and took a deep breath. In the backseat, Lucy began to yell, ruffled by their disagreement.

"Let's get Lucy out and settled, and then we can continue our conversation inside. Okay?"

Upstairs, Maggie turned on a cartoon and gave her daughter a sippy cup full of milk. Edith was losing steam, beginning to wonder if she had misinterpreted Maggie after all. Their earlier exchange, clear as day in her mind just moments before, was beginning to fade out, like a dream sequence in a bad movie.

"Come, let's go to the porch," said Maggie, leading the way through the sliding glass door and into the sunshine.

"Edith, I want you to know that I by no means meant to

imply that your childhood was boring. I'm sorry if I came off that way."

"Thank you. I accept your apology." Edith shielded her eyes with her left hand. It was as bright as the surface of the sun.

"I would never try to rewrite your story. It's yours. Trust me, I get that. I was just in the moment. You were talking about dancing, remember? New York came to my mind. That was all." Edith unclenched her fists.

"That was all?"

"Yes. Scout's honor."

"I think maybe my medication may be making me paranoid," said Edith.

"Could be," said Maggie. "Or it was just a simple misunderstanding. You're sensitive about your own story, I can certainly understand that." Edith nodded, grateful for the empathy.

"It's just that there was so much before New York, before I fell in love and got married and became a mother. There was a me before all of that, and I don't want to forget about her."

"Sure," said Maggie. "I didn't mean to rush you. Shoot, I have a hard time remembering that time in my own life and it was only, what, less than three years ago?"

"You do?"

"Of course. When I think about those days, before I became a mother, it's like I'm watching a film about somebody else. Not that I mind, I like motherhood for the most part, but the idea that thirty-whatever years of existence can just be rendered inconsequential is pretty depressing."

Maggie waved to Lucy, who had left her perch to ogle them through the screen.

"I promise to let you set the pace here, Edith. No more jumping ahead."

"Okay," replied Edith. "Thank you." Next door, a pool party was getting under way, its accompanying shrieks and splashes filling the warm air.

"Youth," explained Maggie.

"There's youth and then there are people like these." Edith stood up to peer over the trees. "Look at those women, all of their bits hanging out. There's no mystery anymore." Maggie stood up to join her.

"But come on, Edith. Everything is—pliant. Why not show it off? God knows it doesn't last." A pair of breasts barely contained by a fuchsia triangle bikini top glistened in the sun.

"Today was terrifying," Edith admitted.

"At the store?" Maggie asked.

"I felt so alone," said Edith softly. Tentatively, Maggie gave a slight squeeze to Edith's hand.

"You're not alone, Edith," she said, as the impending twilight turned the sky pink all around them.

Edith nodded, squeezing back.

EDITH SURVEYED HERSELF in the mirror. She was wearing the dress from her shopping excursion with Maggie. She looked elegant, she thought.

She slipped her feet into her shoes—a pair of gold flats that Maggie had insisted she purchase as well—and smiled.

She hadn't felt this fancy in years—decades maybe. It felt nice.

She grabbed her purse and made her way up the stairs, where Maggie was giving the babysitter explicit instructions. About what, Edith wasn't sure, since Lucy was sound asleep, but Edith could appreciate planning for the worst.

"So if she does wake up, which she won't, go downstairs with the sippy cup of milk in the fridge and— Wait, you know what? Just call me. I'll have my phone on."

The girl, Edith couldn't remember her name—something old-fashioned she thought—nodded at Maggie, looking bored. Edith hoped, along with her, she was sure, that Lucy would not wake up. Maggie ran the risk of imploding on the spot if so.

"Hi Edith," said Maggie, pausing to take a breath. "You look very pretty."

"Thank you, Maggie. You, too." She was wearing the suit, with a slinky silk top underneath, and her hair was up, away from her face for a change.

"Hello, Mrs. Brennan," said the babysitter.

"Hello," Edith replied, wracking her brain desperately for her name.

"This is Olive, Sam's daughter," Maggie reminded her.

"Ah, of course," said Edith. "Is Sam here?"

"No, he dropped her off. I'll take her home."

"He didn't stay to say hello?"

"No," answered Maggie, seeming uncomfortable. *So the date hadn't gone well*, thought Edith.

"Okay. Well, nice to see you, Olive. I think it's time to get going, don't you, Maggie?" Edith hated to be late.

"Right, of course. Olive, you're sure you're okay?" Olive nodded. "My list is on the table, with every possible number you could need, even though my phone will be on and—"

"Maggie, please," interrupted Edith. "She's got it."

"Okay, okay. Good night, Olive." Maggie shrugged apologetically and led the way down the stairs, with Edith at her heels.

"Thanks for dragging me out of there," Maggie said, once they were on their way. The apricot sky ushered a warm breeze through the open windows. "I'm just a wreck, leaving Lucy at night for the first time."

"I understand." Edith wanted to stick her hand out the window, to feel the breeze press against her palm, but feared she would look ridiculous. "That's your baby. It was always hard for me to leave Liza, too, at this age. Poor John used to get so frustrated with me. He was a social creature, liked to go out."

"You've told me nothing about him, you know. Your husband. Except that he was a set designer."

"John was wonderful. Just the kindest, most affable man on the planet. I have no idea what he saw in an old curmudgeon like me."

"You're not a curmudgeon."

"Maggie, come now." Maggie gave a small smirk.

"Well, maybe a little."

"I loved him very much. And he was such a good father

to Liza, with the patience of a saint. Six foot five, too. Handsome. Liza had his height. And his mouth. That big smile."

"Liza had a beautiful smile," added Maggie. "Lit up her whole face."

"Yes, John, too. A reassuring smile."

They had met on Christmas Eve, at a holiday party one of her fellow dancers was throwing. What show had she been in then? Edith closed her eyes, trying to remember what she had been wearing; how her hair had been styled. For the longest time, she had been able to recall both, bookmarking the night in her memory as the beginning of the rest of her life; the beginning of after. Now, it was harder—blurry.

"We met at a party," she told Maggie. "He was sitting on the couch, practically taking up the whole thing; it was a small couch—none of us dancers had any money, you know—drinking a hot toddy in a suit that was too small for him. They were always too small for him, because he was such a big man," Edith explained. "Somehow, I ended up sitting next to him, and that was that."

"It was that easy?" asked Maggie, laughing. "What I wouldn't give for that easy."

"Meeting him was easy, yes, but you know, believing in him—in us—was harder."

"How so?"

"Oh, well, you know—I had a past; a life before John. It's never so easy to trust your instincts. Your mistakes, they can haunt you."

"Tell me about it," said Maggie.

On their left rose the imposing wrought-iron gates of Barbie's estate that swung open to allow her invited guests in and up the enormous drive to her home. Maggie gave an appreciative whistle and pulled in, following the tea lights twinkling along its impressive stretch.

Vinnie stood in front of them, next to a slim, harried man-boy with a giant clipboard in his arms and an even bigger headset strapped to his narrow head.

"And you are?" he asked Maggie, in a comically nasal voice as she pulled up.

"Hi Vinnie," called Edith, ignoring the man-boy. "It's us."

"Oh hi, Mrs. Brennan. How are ya?" He stuck his head in through Maggie's window, plastering her against the seat. "I'm the bodyguard tonight," he explained, rolling his eyes. "And this shrimp is her nephew. Barbie loves a show."

"Like mother, like daughter," said Edith. Vinnie grinned.

"Exactly. Go on through. And have fun."

"Thanks, Vinnie."

Esther always disappeared at this event—the senior belle of the ball—leaving Edith on an uncomfortable bar stool, nursing a white wine spritzer and sushi that she could never bring herself to try. In past years, Liza would stick mostly by her side, but inevitably her fans would approach, turning her into someone else.

The difference between her daughter and Liza—Adored Author—had always shocked Edith, even scared her a little bit, but she had come to realize that it was a necessary evil of her career. And Liza thrived on it, at least initially. In the days and weeks after one of her book events, however, she would inevitably tumble from that high—down, down, down into her own self-created pit of despair. Edith was supposed to be the excavator—that's what mothers were supposed to do, wasn't it?—but she was a terrible fit for the position. She'd never had the patience.

"Look at this place," murmured Maggie, pulling up and putting the car in park for the valet to handle. He opened Edith's door for her with a practiced flourish. She took his hand and stood facing the mansion's enormous gray weathered wood and white shuttered window expanse; the inviting porch that wrapped around its perimeter with its rocking chairs and linen cushioned couches; a giant swing swaying slightly from its most recent inhabitant's departure.

"Jesus," whispered Maggie, joining her. "How many people live here? There's got to be, what, sixty rooms or something?"

"Just Barbie, her husband, Esther and her grandson," answered Edith. "Oh, and a chef. And a housekeeper."

On either side of them, guests in varying shades of cream; the women, with glimpses of shiny gold and silver at their feet, around their wrists and necks and dangling from their ears, flitted up the stairs and into the swell of music and conversation just beyond the house's massive front door. Maggie took Edith's arm.

"You ready?"

"As I'll ever be," replied Edith.

They proceeded through the door, into a backyard with tents and lights strung about like fairies on the wind. Waiters and waitresses in polo shirts and shorts circled around small herds of chic guests huddled in gossip, offering tiny servings of food.

"What does Barbie do again?" asked Maggie, her mouth agape.

"Something with real estate," answered Edith, scanning the crowd for Esther. A waitress approached, offering them two flutes of bubbly champagne.

"Oh yes, thank you," said Maggie. "Edith?"

She nodded, and Maggie secured them both a glass.

"Here, let's go set up shop at that table over there," Maggie suggested, guiding Edith's elbow gently. She stopped suddenly, en route. "Unless you want to make the rounds, of course. Please don't feel obligated to babysit me."

"Are you kidding? I'm terrible at these sorts of things." They set their glasses down on the off-white tablecloth.

"Do you want me to find you a bar stool?" asked Maggie, her eyes darting around for one.

"Maggie, please, I'm fine. It feels nice to stand up. Better view anyway. Just relax."

"Sorry. I have no idea what to do with myself." She took a sip, shaking her head. "Do you realize, Edith, that I am never alone? Even if Lucy's asleep, she's still there."

"You don't have to tell me," said Edith. "I lived with my daughter until she was practically sixty."

"Touché, Edith."

"Girls!" Esther's voice boomed behind them.

They both turned to greet her as she approached, in all of her off-white and gold, caftan'd glory. The gauzy fabric floated around her like a cloud of smoke as she swished her way towards them, bangled arms outstretched. "I'm so glad you're here."

Three waiters approached with bar stools, setting them down and offering the ladies a hand up before leaving as quickly as they had appeared.

"Where did they come from?" asked Edith.

"They follow me around like lapdogs all night. It's a tough life." She placed both hands on the table, revealing a gold manicure and a giant diamond ring. "Don't worry, it's fake," she assured them. "An expensive fake, but a fake nonetheless. So, how are we? Enjoying the party?"

"What a scene, Esther!" exclaimed Maggie. "You weren't kidding."

"Barbie knows how to throw a party, that's for sure. Did you get any food yet?" She glanced at Edith's glass. "Good for you, Edith. It's great to see you kicking back." She turned her head to the left ever so slightly, and the same waiters reappeared, this time with myriad plates of hors d'oeuvres.

"How did you do that?" asked Maggie, clapping her hands in delight and looking exactly like Lucy in the process, Edith thought.

"Magic," explained Esther, her eyes twinkling. "Help yourselves. Mi casa, su casa. You know something, Edith? I miss Liza tonight. She was always such a hoot at this thing, holding court as one of the resident celebrities."

Edith nodded, feeling a little dizzy. The champagne had gone straight to her head, which wasn't entirely unpleasant. She plucked a doll-sized piece of bruschetta off the plate in front of her.

"But you would never know she was a celebrity. So humble, she was." Esther put her hand over Edith's free one. "Just like her mother."

"Edith!" a voice cried behind them, an exact echo of Esther's. Edith turned to greet Barbie, fighting the urge to gasp at her latest face-lift, which made her appear as though she was encased in saran wrap from the neck up.

"Hello Barbie. You look lovely."

"Oh good, I'll let my surgeon know. You, too, Edith. And I'm so sorry about Liza. She was a pip." Esther shot her a look. "What, Ma? I wanted to tell her. And you must be the new girl," said Barbie, moving on to Maggie.

"Yes, more or less. I'm Maggie. Thank you for having me, Barbie. This party is spectacular."

"My pleasure, and thank you. It's just a little party I throw every year." She attempted to wink, but it came off as more of a twitch. "Why are your glasses empty?" Again, the waiters swooped in, each with a replacement glass for Edith and Maggie.

"Thanks, boys."

"You look like a dreamboat, Barb," said Esther, patting her daughter's arm lovingly. Edith watched, with an ache in her heart that spread to her stomach.

"Shelley!" screamed Barbie. "I've got to jet, girls. You all look fabulous. And Maggie, nice to meet you."

"Nice to meet you, too," replied Maggie, as she waddled off in her stilettos, click clacking across the tiled deck.

"I should go say hello to Miriam," said Esther, grunting slightly as she dismounted from her stool. "This night may just kill me. Remember, Edith, if I go, you get the emerald broach." Again, the waiter appeared magically, to escort Esther across the lawn. "Maggie, Sam is here, you know. Looking very handsome, I might add. And Edith, eat something, for God's sake. You look three sheets to the wind already."

Esther was right—she was. Edith squinted, enjoying the way the sparkling strung lights and lit votives blurred into a happy haze.

"Edith, I'm going to get us some real food," said Maggie. Edith stopped squinting, and looked at her. "Okay? Esther's right, we need to eat. You especially. Any requests?"

"A little of everything, please," she replied. "Except sushi."

"You got it. Stay here, okay?" Edith gazed down at the space separating the rung from the bar stool on which she perched and the grass below.

"I'm not going anywhere. Don't worry."

Maggie walked quickly towards one of the buffet tables that stretched along the left side of the lawn. Edith took a shrimp from Esther's discarded plate and dipped it into its accompanying dab of cocktail sauce. She ate it slowly, thinking about the party the following year. Would she be too sick to attend? A wandering, old lady version of her former self, with nothing in between her ears but air?

Working with Maggie gave Edith a sense of control where there normally was none, that was the best part about it. With Maggie's help, her life was real; it had happened. There would be proof.

"Okay, so I got us starter plates," interrupted Maggie, setting them down in front of Edith with a loud clatter. "We'll start with these, and then I'll go back for round two." Maggie deposited some silverware in front of Edith and hoisted herself up onto her bar stool.

"I had a son," declared Edith. Maggie spread her napkin across her lap.

"Do what now?" she asked, distracted by a small mound of caviar that she had procured for herself.

"A son. I had one out of wedlock when I was sixteen." Edith unfurled her own napkin. It felt good to say it out loud.

"You had a son, Edith?" Maggie slumped a little against the low back of the seat, testing the idea out loud.

"I gave him up for adoption." She looked down into her lap, her vulnerability plain.

"My God, Edith," said Maggie, not knowing what to say. "Was it your decision?"

"I was sixteen at the time, so it wasn't really up to me. But I knew that I didn't want to be a mother. And his father, well—I hardly knew him. He never even knew I was pregnant. Please Maggie, eat."

"You want me to eat now? With this news? Give me a minute, Edith."

"He was the cousin of an acquaintance," Edith explained. "In town for the summer. Looking back, I'm not sure why I agreed to sleep with him in the first place, other than the fact that he was very attractive and I was woefully misinformed. And naïve."

"Sounds about right."

"My parents were mortified, and did what everyone did

back then—sent me away to live with my aunt in Cincinnati until the baby came. Aunt Celeste."

"Celeste!" The name Edith had called Maggie when she fell.

"I'm sure everyone knew regardless," replied Edith, "although we told anyone who asked that I had left to study ballet."

Edith reflected for a moment, thinking of Celeste, who hadn't been too happy to have her, but took her in nevertheless. Single, and considered a spinster by Edith's mother and most likely everyone else including herself, she had worked in a hat store, shadowing a milliner.

Edith could still see her hats, perched on their little stands like exotic birds throughout her small apartment. Towards the end of her pregnancy, when Edith was as swollen as a hot air balloon in the summer heat and too uncomfortable to leave the house, she had given them names. Clara had been her favorite—a sharp navy blue number with a feather that swept over its front.

"Jesus, Edith," said Maggie. "This is unexpected." She took a gulp of her champagne.

"I know. But I wanted to tell you. To tell somebody."

"You never told anybody?"

"No one. Just my parents and Celeste, and of course the adoptive parents knew."

"But why?" asked Maggie.

"What was the point of telling anyone? I wanted to start over. No tracks."

"No tracks," repeated Maggie, shaking her head.

"I want to find him, Maggie. Just to see him. To see if he's okay. Before I forget he even existed."

Maggie nodded, looking out at the crowd, flitting around the white lights like moths in the night sky.

"Okay," she agreed. "We can do that."

"Good," said Edith, relieved. She was ravenous suddenly, as though food would fill the void where her secret had once resided. She drove her fork through the plate of food Maggie had prepared for her, bulldozing an enormous bite into her mouth.

"Edith, I'm flabbergasted," said Maggie, her own plate untouched. "I've always wanted to have a reason to use that word, and here it is. Now I know what you meant by a life before New York." Edith grunted her ascent. She couldn't get the food into her mouth fast enough.

"Shame on me for trying to rush you. But who knew?" Maggie shook her head. "I need to eat something. I'm dangerously close to drunk." She took a bite.

"Liza never knew?" she asked, after she had swallowed.

"No. But in retrospect, I wish I had told her."

"Really?"

"Maybe if I had shared more of myself, she would have shared more of her life with me. She didn't even trust me enough to tell me she was a lesbian for God's sake."

"I wouldn't be too sure, Edith. She was close-lipped about it with me, too. She was very private. At least with her own business."

"What does that mean?"

"What?"

"Her own business?"

"Oh, nothing. Just a turn of phrase."

"No, I can tell you meant something by it."

"It's nothing, forget it," pleaded Maggie.

"Maggie."

"The insomniac detective idea, that was mine," she blurted out.

"Come again?"

"The idea for her book about the detective. That was my idea. From a short story I wrote." Maggie shrugged. "Liza took it. Oh God, I can't believe I'm telling you this. Who cares now, anyway? It's all so pointless. I drank too much, forget it," Maggie rambled.

"That was your idea?" asked Edith.

"Yes."

"Well, it was a very good one."

"Thanks."

"I'm sorry she did that to you. But it's not a surprise."

"You mentioned that at lunch with Esther the other day."

"Did you have plans to tell that story yourself?" asked Edith.

"Maybe. But probably not," Maggie answered. "I was very angry about it for a long time, but hearing you talk about it at lunch, it shifted something in me. I don't think it was about the detective at all, actually. My anger, that is. More that she took something without asking."

"Something you valued," added Edith. "She let you down."

"Yes, exactly."

"I'm sorry on her behalf," said Edith.

"Don't be. It's all so silly now. So inconsequential considering how everything turned out. I wish I could have had the chance to talk it out with her. In person." A waiter appeared to clean their plates away and offer them more to drink.

"No, thank you," said Maggie.

"Me, either," said Edith.

He nodded and walked away, leaving them in silence.

"It's so hard now, with her gone. You think of all of the ways you could have done more to make her stay," said Maggie.

"I know," agreed Edith.

Night had taken over as they talked, Edith noticed suddenly. The moon peeked out from the clouds, shining down on the festivities. The band struck up an old Motown song.

"Maggie, I think I need to go home," said Edith.

"Me, too. Let's go." Maggie took her arm.

"That detective book, that was my favorite of Liza's," said Edith, as they parted the sea of off-white.

"Yeah?" asked Maggie.

"Yes."

"Thank you, Edith."

Maggie helped her down the front steps, towards the valet.

CHAPTER 15

Morning," mumbled Maggie. She was sitting at the dining room table in her sunglasses when Edith walked in, seemingly none the worse for wear despite matching Maggie glass for champagne glass the night before. She looked like she always looked, Maggie noticed, like she had been ironed from head to toe, hair included.

"Good morning," Edith replied. Maggie felt awkward in the wake of Edith's confession. Hers, too, for that matter. She was terrible at intimacy. After sex, she would spring out of bed, usually to scour the sink. Lingering didn't agree with her. She was better when she had a purpose.

Lucy sat across from her, eating her waffle with gusto, syrup dribbling down her chin. Under normal circumstances, Maggie would refuse such a treat for breakfast, but this morning she had no fight in her. Her head felt like a bowling ball atop her neck. She took a big sip of her coffee, accidentally slurping it in the process.

Edith sat down next to Lucy with her own cup.

"What a party," she said.

"I drank too much," Maggie admitted.

"Me too. Took me far too long to get out of bed this morning." Maggie regarded her carefully. She wasn't behaving like someone who had revealed a huge secret less than twelve hours earlier. It occurred to Maggie suddenly that Edith could have forgotten that she revealed it at all.

"So today, when we meet, I want to tell you more about my son," said Edith calmly.

"Right," answered Maggie. She took off her sunglasses. "Of course." So she did remember.

"I have some photos. I'll bring them," Edith added.

"Photos? On your phone?" asked Lucy, perking up. "I want to see." She held out her sticky hands.

"No, no. Not for you, Lucy. And not on her phone."

Lucy's face crumpled. "But I want to see!" she demanded, and began to scream.

"That's okay, Maggie. Lucy can see them now. As long as she cleans up first. I can't have syrup on my pictures," said Edith.

"Okay! I clean!" Lucy agreed, jumping down from her chair.

"Alright, let's unstick you. Edith, you're sure?" asked Maggie.

"Anything is better than that scream, isn't it? Should we get started now?"

"Get started with what? Writing? With Lucy around?"

"I just—well, I'd like to if you're able."

"Uh, okay. Sure." Maggie did not feel able at all, but she would. She had powered through worse. "Lucy, come here." She removed her pajamas, which were covered in syrup, and carried her to the sink. "Hands first," she commanded. "Now face." Lucy waited patiently as Maggie washed her, excited to be included.

"Okay Luce, I'll go get you some clothes. And I'll get my notebook and tape recorder. Edi—" But Edith had gone downstairs already, to retrieve her memories.

"Never mind, Lucy, come with me."

Downstairs, she clothed her daughter and grabbed her notebook and tape recorder, pausing briefly in front of the mirror to frown at the bags under her eyes. When she turned around, Edith was standing in front of her, a manila envelope tight in her grasp.

"Geez Edith, when you mean business, you mean business," said Maggie. "Here, or—"

"Let's go back upstairs so I can spread them out," said Edith, slightly out of breath.

The three of them trotted dutifully up the stairs.

"Lucy, have a seat on the couch, next to me," said Edith. "Maggie—"

"I'll sit on the other side of you." It was exciting, she decided, the possibility of seeing a teenage Edith. It almost took away her headache. Almost.

"Okay, here we are." Edith unclasped the envelope and slid out what looked to be a dozen black and white photos, their edges slightly brown with age.

"Where are you, Edif?" asked Lucy, staring expectantly at the first one.

"Here I am, Lucy. Right here." Edith pointed, but Maggie would have known her anywhere. That same wry smile and elegant posture; her spindly limbs.

"That's you?" asked Lucy. "But you're little!"

"Yes. I was little once. A long time ago." She looked at Maggie. "I'm sixteen here. Right before I met him."

"You're beautiful, Edith."

"Thank you." She took the photo off the top of the pile and placed it to the side. "And here he is. Just look at him. He was something, I'll give him that."

"Like a young Frank Sinatra," said Maggie. Skinny and tall, with eyes that sparkled, he dared the camera with his smile.

"He was my friend Ruthie's cousin, visiting for the summer," explained Edith. "From Chicago. His name was Anthony. The girls went wild for him, as you can probably imagine. A real tough guy. And he set his sights on me. It was so intoxicating, to be singled out like that, let me tell you. I felt like a princess."

"You never forget the first time a guy makes you feel like that," said Maggie.

"You don't," agreed Edith. "My parents wouldn't let me date, so we had to see each other secretly. It was all very exciting."

"I'm going to play," announced Lucy.

"Am I boring you?" asked Edith.

"Yes." She jumped up, leaving them to it.

"Lucy, that's not a nice thing to say," chided Maggie.

"It's fine. Better this way. Easier to talk. I had never had sex before Anthony, had barely even kissed a boy," Edith continued. "As pure as driven snow. But he had. Boy, he had. And he somehow convinced me, I'm embarrassed to admit, that if I jumped up and down afterward, I wouldn't get pregnant."

"You bought it?" asked Maggie.

"Hook, line and sinker." Maggie peered again at Anthony's face.

"I probably would have, too. I was a late bloomer, though."

"You were?" asked Edith.

"Yeah. Wasn't comfortable in my skin until college. And by then, well, I knew that jumping up and down wasn't a viable form of birth control. Just barely, though."

"Well, I learned the hard way," said Edith. "He left at the end of the summer, and soon I started to gain weight with no warning. Never had the morning sickness, though. With him or Liza. Did you? With Lucy?"

"Oh yeah, morning, noon and night. Taking breaks from scrubbing toilets to barf, that was a blast, let me tell you. I couldn't go five minutes without a Saltine for the first five months." Maggie grimaced, remembering the feel of the cold porcelain on her forehead. "It was horrible. Lucky you, Edith."

"I know. Don't know how I avoided it. They say it's genetic. Anyway, my dance instructor was the first to worry;

my energy was low and my leotards tight, and she suggested I make an appointment with my doctor. My pediatrician of course; I didn't even have a proper gynecologist at that point. Dr. Pritchard his name was. I must have put two and two together, because I made the appointment by myself and went to see him alone, without my mother. He confirmed the news, and told me I was about four months along. It was shocking really, like a death sentence almost."

"What did you do? Who did you tell first?" asked Maggie.

"Eventually, I couldn't hide it anymore. I didn't want to go to my friends; I knew even the closest ones would talk, so I had to go to my mother. She slapped me, straight across the face when I told her. But I couldn't hold it against her. It was a different time. Pregnancy out of wedlock had all of these connotations." Edith paused. "It wasn't like today, when no one gives it a second thought."

"I wouldn't say I didn't give it a second thought, Edith," replied Maggie defensively. "It's a big deal. A much bigger deal at sixteen than thirty-five of course, but still."

People always seemed to assume how Maggie had felt when her pregnancy test had come back positive—as though at her age with no other prospects, it had been a no-brainer. It hadn't been. She'd made an appointment for an abortion, fully intending to go through with it, but had changed her mind in the waiting room, not able to shake the idea that it was her only chance to have a child. Edith shrugged an apology before continuing.

"My mother was very angry with me. Called me a tramp."

"What did your father say?"

"She didn't tell him until all of the plans were made with my aunt Celeste. Until I was on the bus, practically. He just shook his head, told me to be safe and that he'd see me in a few months. And that was that."

"That was it?"

"That was it. He was a man of few words anyway, much less in the presence of a disgraced daughter."

"Like my father. About himself at least."

"But are any of us open about our pasts, as parents?" asked Edith. "Do our children even care?"

"I think so," said Maggie.

"You share your history with Lucy?" asked Edith.

"No. But she's two and a half."

"Two and a half; fourteen; twenty—same thing. It's rare for a child to be anything but completely self-involved. Unless of course they blame you for their problems. Then they want to know everything," said Edith. "But where was I?"

"You were boarding the bus," said Maggie. She had never asked her mother or her father about their lives before her, Edith was right.

"Ah yes, the bus to Cincinnati. So off I went, my dress straining around my expanding middle, to Aunt Celeste," continued Edith. "Celeste worked in a milliner's shop—left at eight and returned when it was dark. She was less than thrilled to be playing hostess, but I can't say that I blame her. I tried my best to keep to myself; be a good guest, clean up, cook, but really we were ships passing most of the time. I don't have any photos of her, though I wish I did. She hated having her picture taken."

Maggie had barely had the time to acknowledge her pregnancy, she'd been in such a panic to make money and turn her single girl apartment into a baby-suitable home. Occasionally, she would take a photo of herself in front of her bathroom mirror, to document her growing bump, but for the most part she raced around like a madwoman preparing. Now, looking at those pictures—the terrible lighting; her self-conscious smile partly obscured by the camera's reflection in the mirror—her heart ached. She should have slowed down, she thought. Enjoyed it more.

"You were never tempted to find Anthony and let him know?" she asked, thinking of Lyle.

"Oh God no," said Edith. "He wouldn't have wanted anything to do with me. I was smart enough to know that, at least. Celeste connected me to an adoption agency, and through them the new parents."

"Did you ever, you know, consider keeping the baby?"

"No, I was so disconnected from him. I had been conditioned to be ashamed of myself, and he was just an extension of that. Sad, really, but I knew my job was to deliver him, hand him off and get on the bus back home."

"That must have been so hard. You were so young, Edith."

"It's true that the first moments after his birth were hard and so— What's the right word—"

"Disconcerting?" volunteered Maggie.

"Yes, that's a good word. Disconcerting. I had been pregnant, and then I wasn't. Plus, the hormones. My God, the hormones."

Maggie nodded sympathetically. She had given birth

alone, holding the hand of a nurse. It was the most untethered she had ever felt, in that delivery room and the weeks immediately thereafter.

"It wasn't until much later, when I had a proper family of my own—when I had Liza—that I wondered where he was."

"I'm sure. It must have brought everything back to the surface for you."

"It did," agreed Edith. "But in the rush of new motherhood, I let it go again. Until he found me, that is."

"He found you?" Maggie clapped her hand over her mouth. "How?"

"Old records, he said. He called while I was making dinner for Liza, one winter evening. I remember that it was winter because I was making tomato soup. And while I was flipping her grilled cheese to go along with it, the phone rang. As clear as day I remember it." Edith took a deep breath.

"My goodness, this feels like I'm running a marathon. I apologize if I'm going too fast."

"You're not going too fast, Edith. That's what the recorder is for."

"Okay, good. Thank you, Maggie. I can't thank you enough for this. I— It feels so empowering, to get this out. To try and find him. Gives me a purpose."

"Me, too, Edith."

"So the phone rang, and I picked it up, and there he was."

"How did he introduce himself?" asked Maggie.

"He asked if he could speak to Edith Moore. That had been my maiden name. Right away, I knew it was him. Whatever you want to call it—maternal instinct maybe?—I knew."

"Was anyone in the kitchen with you to hear?"

"Thankfully I was alone, but I remember burning the grilled cheese because I hid in the pantry to take the call and lost all track of time. He told me his name was Arthur Geller, and that he hoped I didn't mind, but he was curious to meet me."

"What did you say?"

"I could barely form a sentence, but I could smell the sandwich burning on the stove, so I asked him for his number. I wrote it down on the notepad I usually made my grocery list on. I told him I'd call him back. And then Liza walked in, complaining about the smell, and I had to pretend as though nothing had ever happened."

"Incredible," said Maggie, thinking of all of the emotional pretending she did with Lucy. Acting happy when she was sad; energized when she was exhausted; capable when she was completely overwhelmed. It was an essential motherhood requirement.

"I am so thirsty," said Edith. "Maggie, would you mind—"

"Not at all. Lemonade? Water? Juice box?"

"Some lemonade would be lovely, thanks." Edith took a deep breath. "I'm speaking so quickly, it's like I'm forgetting to breathe."

"For God's sake, Edith, don't do that. I'm not going anywhere."

"I know. I'm just afraid—well, you know."

"I know. I'll be right back."

As Maggie poured the lemonade into an ice-filled glass, she thought about Lyle. With the way the world was now, the easily accessible internet pictures and records, and the incontestable way his daughter looked like him, it would feasibly only take his curiosity and a few Google searches to locate Maggie and through her, a photo of Lucy. Or worse, the other way around—Lucy's curiosity getting the better of her and her doing the searching instead. As much as she didn't want to, she had to do the right thing and let him know. What he did with the information was up to him.

"We can stop now, if you're tired, Edith," said Maggie, crossing the threshold of the porch to find Edith with her eyes closed. "Pick it up tomorrow."

"No, let's keep going—as far as we can."

"Okay, sure. Whatever you want." Edith stared at her, blankly. "Oh, you left off at the burned sandwich."

"Oh yes, the grilled cheese. Days passed, and I thought about Arthur all of the time. His phone call had piqued my curiosity—a curiosity I hadn't even known existed, mind you. Who was he? What had his life been like? Did he look like me or share any of my interests? Liza had her me-like moments, but for the most part she was a carbon replica of her father. Here, here's a photo of John. See? Doesn't he look like Liza?"

"He really does," agreed Maggie.

"So I decided to call him—Arthur—back the next afternoon," she continued. "John was at work, and Liza was at school, and so it was my only opportunity. I poured myself a bourbon and dialed his number. We forged a plan. I was to meet him at a coffee shop near Penn Station the next Tuesday—Tuesday because it's always been my lucky day.

Once John and Liza were out of the house, I would walk to the train station and make my way into the city for a few hours. It was all set."

"You must have been so nervous," said Maggie.

"I was. And excited. And scared. It was an electrifying couple of days."

"And still, no one noticed?"

"John asked me why I was so jittery, I think, but that was just in passing. Mostly I was able to play it close to the vest. And then, Tuesday came, and I was just a mess. No outfit was right, my hair was dreadful—you name it, and it was a problem. I had to force myself out of the house." She took a sip of her lemonade. "I took the short walk to the station, my heart racing all the while, playing out the various scenarios of what could happen in my head. What if he wanted something from me, like money for instance?"

"Or a kidney," added Maggie.

"Exactly. There was so much to consider. I bought my ticket regardless, and stood on the platform with the other commuters, as inconspicuous as they come. Never in my life before or since had I felt so small and unimportant. Here I was, with my heart beating out of my chest, and no one noticed. It was like I didn't exist.

"The train whistle signaled its approach. A chariot straight to my past, I thought. And thinking of it that way weakened my resolve to follow through. Why was I churning up the past when I had a perfectly good present and a hopeful future? What would meeting him gain for either of us? He thought he wanted to know me, but did he really? And who was I to ask that of him in return, when I had given up the chance to know him so many years before? It all seemed like such a mistake suddenly, as the train pulled in."

"You didn't—"

"I did. I convinced myself of all those things, and didn't get on the train. It went on its way, and I stood there for several minutes more, hoping I'd done the right thing and that he'd give up on me quickly in that coffee shop and go on with his day; his life. And that's what I did—I went on with it."

"He never called again?" Edith shook her head.

"No, and I respect that. But I've always regretted my decision. To let him down like that, again." She sighed. "Do you think he's still alive?" Maggie had considered that possibility already, or worse, that he was alive and would refuse to meet Edith altogether.

"How old would he be now?" asked Maggie.

"I did the math," said Edith, opening her notebook. "I wrote it down. Where is it? Ah, here. Sixty-six." She shook her head in disbelief. "An old woman with an old son."

"I'll start looking for him tonight," said Maggie. She switched off the tape recorder. "We'll find him, Edith, don't worry."

"I hope so. Or maybe I don't hope so. What if he hates me?" Maggie didn't know what to say. It was a distinct possibility.

"You must be tired, Edith. Let me help you down to your bed. Here, I'll get the photos."

"Who knew confessing could be so draining? I sympathize with the Catholics." She stood up and wobbled a bit, but Maggie caught her thin arm, which felt as fragile as an uncooked spaghetti noodle in her grasp.

Maggie followed her closely down the stairs—it was too narrow to continue side by side. At the bottom, she restaked her claim and led her to her bed, where Edith sat gratefully, looking down at her sandal-clad feet with a frown.

"Let me get those for you," said Maggie.

"Thank you, Liza," Edith murmured, lying back on the bed with her eyes closed. Maggie covered her with her blanket and closed the door.

She grabbed her laptop from her room and returned to Lucy. She had to email Lyle, before she changed her mind. If she was learning anything from Edith, it was that life was short. Things could change in an instant; she could be dead tomorrow for all she knew.

Quickly, as her daughter played with her blocks, stacking them one on top of the other with deliberate care, she began.

Lyle,

Hi. Long time, no speak. I hope all is well in Portland.

There's no easy way to say (or write) this, so I'll just go for it: you have a daughter. With me. Her name is Lucy; she is two and a half, and she is wonderful.

I discovered that I was pregnant shortly after you left. I'm sorry I didn't reach out to you then, but we were over and starting new lives. Perhaps it was selfish of me to assume that you were in no way keen on fatherhood, but I think we can both agree that to say I had a good hunch would certainly be an understatement. After all, we danced our dance for a long time. I know, or I knew, you well.

At any rate, I want you to know now, because Lucy is asking about her father, and I don't want to lie to her. I want to tell her the truth, whatever that may be according to and depending on your reaction to this news. Please know that I in no way expect you to assume any sort of responsibility here—my life would certainly be less complicated if you opted out, actually—but I wanted to give you the choice.

Feel free to either email me back or call. My number is the same.

                                                            M

Maggie didn't reread it, there was no need to edit her words. It was the truth, and that was that.

"Luce, I'm coming to play with you," she announced, and pressed send.

CHAPTER 16

Edith sat at the porch table, her photos in a neat pile in front of her. She pulled out the lone photo she had of her and Esther, dressed to the nines at some after-party, she supposed. So slim, like paper dolls in their fitted jackets and sharp hats, Esther in the fox stole that she had always kept under lock and key, in a steamer trunk at the foot of her bed. Edith had hated it, hadn't seen the appeal of wearing roadkill around one's neck, but Esther had considered it her most prized possession. Edith traced her own face delicately with her ring finger, thinking that she really had been quite lovely then.

She pulled out a photo of John, hoping that seeing his face would distract her from the irritation she had building towards Maggie, who was late for their session. It helped quell the fire somewhat, seeing his kind face, Liza's face, smiling at her.

She had taken the photo with their first camera, not too soon before Liza was born. She remembered standing on the other side of the lens, swollen and happy, filled to bursting with joy and optimism. She had loved being pregnant then—her situation couldn't have been more different than the first time around, and she had made sure to be grateful for that. He was wonderful, her John. A good, kind man with the most beautiful, strong hands. Hands that could build anything, and they did.

She slid the photo back into the pile and returned to being annoyed. Maybe Lucy wasn't going down for her nap, but even so, Maggie should have the decency to give her a heads-up. She could hear them downstairs, in Lucy's room—their voices a distant rumble. Edith would just go downstairs and inquire politely about the holdup. She realized that her version of polite often was not received as such, but she would try her best.

Edith stood up and began her journey down the stairs, only to turn around and gather her photos from the table. She would bring them inside. You never knew—a giant gust of wind could blow in out of nowhere, rendering the physical manifestation of her memories as scattered as the abstract.

Inside, she settled everything carefully on the kitchen counter before taking a deep breath and heading down the stairs. It was quiet now. Perhaps Maggie had gotten Lucy to sleep after all and was on her way up to the porch. She froze for a moment, until Lucy's giggle erupted, followed by Maggie's. Anger bubbled inside of Edith, and she resumed her march. The nerve of Maggie, wasting her time like this. She wrenched open the door roughly.

Inside, it was dark, and Edith felt ashamed. Lucy was napping. She had misheard; one of the faulty synapses of her brain was misfiring again. Suddenly, a bright light shone directly into her face, making it impossible to see.

"Edif, spotlight!" yelled Lucy, erupting into a fit of giggles.

"Lucy, be careful, honey," Maggie warned her, as Edith stumbled back, landing with a soft thud against the wall.

"Edith, are you okay?" asked Maggie, getting up from the floor. "Sorry, we're getting a bit carried away here. We're in the middle of a spotlight war."

"Spotlight war!" shrieked Lucy happily.

Maggie crossed to the window and opened the blinds, flooding the room with sunlight. Edith stayed where she was, against the wall.

"Well, I'm glad the two of you are having the time of your lives," she replied coldly. "Meanwhile, I'm upstairs waiting for you, like a fool."

Maggie tilted her head, seeming to sense trouble.

"If you have a standing appointment with someone, the least you can do is tell them ahead of time that you're not going to make it," continued Edith, gaining steam. "I have things to do, too, you know."

Lucy dropped her flashlight and it rolled backwards across the wooden floor, coming to a stop against the foot of her crib.

"Mommy?" she asked.

"I'm sorry, Edith," Maggie said again, picking Lucy up. Edith was coiled and tense, like a cobra.

"I'm not sure what you're so upset about, Edith. We already met today. This morning." Lucy, looking to her mother and back at Edith, began to cry. Maggie picked her up, holding her close and shushing her.

"It's okay, honey, just a misunderstanding. Don't cry."

"We most certainly did not," she replied, although she wasn't sure suddenly.

"I'm sorry, Edith, but we did. You told me all about Arthur. Remember?" Maggie explained, sounding nonchalant.

Edith looked around the room, trying to get her bearings. Something about what Maggie was telling her was ringing true. Lucy turned around in Maggie's arms, facing Edith with tear-streaked cheeks.

"Scary," she said to Edith.

Edith glanced at Maggie guiltily and then turned as gracefully as she could on her heel and walked the short distance back to her room.

Safe inside, she shut the door and removed all of the pillows except one from her bed, placing them carefully on the chair by her bureau. She sat on the coverlet and traced its faint pattern. Quietly, she began to cry, the tears rolling down her cheeks as she lay back, sliding her hands underneath her hips.

She could make all of the lists she wanted and still one day none of them would register. What would happen then? Maggie certainly couldn't handle that kind of care, and why should she? Edith pulled her hands out from under her and placed them over her wet eyes and cheeks.

If Liza hadn't killed herself, if she didn't know firsthand how cowardly a resolution that was for those left behind, she would do it herself. Although really, who was she leaving behind? Esther? She would go on just fine. And to be honest, Maggie—when it was all said and done—would probably breathe a sigh of relief. Even so, she couldn't. Being the one that had discovered Liza after the fact would forever prevent her from inflicting that kind of helpless sorrow on someone else. And what if, God forbid, it was Lucy who found her? Edith shifted to her side and stared at the wall, wishing for a window.

It had been a morning like any other, really. Liza had been in one of her moods for a while, but was finally showing signs of life again—getting dressed in proper clothes, writing, taking her trips into the city. She was like that: up, up, up with ideas and plans and shopping and redecorating, and then, the inevitable plummet back to earth where she would stew in her unhappiness for days, weeks or months, depending.

That time, Edith remembered, Liza's melancholy had been at least slightly warranted—her latest novel was tanking, and there was nothing she could do about it.

"They hate me, Ma," she had mumbled to Edith when she was in the thick of it, lying on the couch upstairs in the dark, a half drunk bottle of wine on the coffee table in front of her.

"Oh Liza, don't be silly, no one hates you," Edith had

replied, avoiding the topic. The truth was that the book was not up to par, she had read it herself, but she knew better than to say so. The problem was that she couldn't lie, was genetically predisposed to honesty whether the situation called for it or not, so she said nothing of importance about it at all.

Liza of course knew this—knew her mother's noncommittal responses were her way of agreeing with her—but didn't really want to know. And so they had both been stuck in the quicksand of Liza's deflated ego.

But it wasn't just a matter of ego of course, it was Liza's disease that was at the root of all of the fluctuations in her and Edith's life—made all the worse by her refusal to medicate or seek therapy with any sort of regularity. Edith had tried to keep her on her meds in the beginning, but it was no use. Liza was a grown woman and would do what she pleased; she had made that clear on countless occasions.

Ever since Edith had gotten lost on the beach, Liza had insisted on accompanying her on her morning walks, which irritated Edith to no end. She missed her freedom, but Liza held firm. And so, every morning, Edith had her coffee at the kitchen table and waited for Liza, who, good mood or not, would leave her writing and lumber up the stairs without a word, fix herself a to-go cup and wave her mother on as she followed behind, desperate to get it over with.

That morning, Edith had waited for Liza, but instead of the familiar creak of the stairs as she made her way to her mother, there was only silence. Edith had sat for five minutes after she had finished her coffee—she knew because she had watched the clock—and then she had washed her mug and gone looking for her daughter, mad as hell. Liza knew how important her walk was to Edith, especially then, in the wake of her diagnosis, and now she was sleeping on the job.

Edith had knocked twice on Liza's bedroom door, hard and sharp—a knock that meant business. When there was no answer, Edith had entered to find her bed neatly made with no Liza in it, which meant that she was writing. Edith had felt relieved then. Writing meant that Liza was feeling better—was making her way back up through the fog.

Relieved or not, she was still angry. Liza needed to write to feel like herself, but Edith needed her walk for the same reasons. Through the door to the porch and down the stone path Edith had marched, muttering to herself about Liza's selfishness as the sun crept higher in the sky.

At the door of the guesthouse, she knocked again, waiting for the *Yes?* from Liza and trying to keep her irritation in check. She didn't want a fight, she just wanted a walk. The *yes* had never come, of course, thought Edith now, still lying on her side. And still, naïve, self-centered person who she was, she hadn't experienced even a moment of concern. She'd figured that Liza was swept up in whatever story she was telling, and had gone right in.

The foot of the daybed faced the door, and when Edith immediately noticed that Liza was not in fact sitting at her desk as she had imagined, her eyes went there. The back of Liza's head peeked over the top of a pillow.

"Liza!" yelled Edith, her vow to stay even-keeled obliterated. "Liza, you know I need this walk," she had barked from the doorway. When she hadn't moved in response, Edith, finally, had experienced her first flutter of fear, deep in her belly.

"Liza?" she called again, this time timid. She had pushed off from the door, forcing herself to approach the bed.

Liza lay underneath her quilt as Edith stood over her, examining her face; a face that she knew as well as her own.

"Liza?" she asked again. She placed a trembling hand on her cheek. It was cold to the touch. Trembling, she pulled the blanket back and put her hand on her daughter's chest, also cold beneath the fabric of her top.

Now there was a knock on the door, jolting Edith back into the present. Every detail of that morning was so vivid, so real. How could her brain hold on to it so clearly, but forget how to make deviled eggs? Where was the rationale?

"Edith?" Esther had arrived to take Edith to hand therapy, and her voice bore through the wood like a drill.

"Come in," Edith replied, her voice shaky.

"Well, aren't you a sight for sore eyes," she remarked, entering in a cloud of Shalimar. Today she was wearing her denim muumuu, the one with the rhinestone buttons down the lapel. "Scoot over," she demanded, and hoisted herself into bed beside her. "You down here feeling sorry for yourself?"

"Maybe," answered Edith.

"I know it's hard, darling," replied Esther, searching for Edith's hand with her own, and lacing her fingers through hers.

"How do you know?" demanded Edith.

"My Irving. The Alzheimer's. You know he had it, too."

"How come you don't have it? Why did I get such a raw deal?" asked Edith.

"And how do you know I don't?"

"You do?" Edith asked hopefully.

"No. At least not yet. But don't worry, I have plenty of other things. Sciatica is no walk in the park, let me tell you."

Edith gave her wrist a gentle pinch.

"Listen, we have each other. And we've lived good lives. Not without heartache naturally, but good lives. What does your doctor say?"

"She says it's slow moving, which I guess is good news."

"You guess? Of course it's good news. Gives you time to complete this book project with Maggie. That's a great idea, by the way, Edith. Good for her, good for you—good all around."

"I don't know if I'm going to make it through my story, Esther."

"So, you'll do what you can. Maggie's a smart girl. She certainly can't assume it's all going to be easy."

"No, she doesn't," confirmed Edith.

"This disease is completely out of your control, Edith. You go as far as you can, and if you need someone to fill in the blanks, you know where to find me." Esther squeezed her hand. "It'll be fun for me to relive the old days. Let me help, already."

"Esther?"

"Yes?"

"Before New York something happened to me. Some-thing big."

"I like big. Go on."

And so, Edith did.

CHAPTER 17

Maggie closed Lucy's door softly behind her, just in time to see Esther doing the same with Edith's. *Is everything okay?* Maggie's raised eyebrow asked. *No*, Esther replied, via the raising of her own. She ascended the stairs with Maggie behind her, her denim caftan billowing in her face like a tent as she climbed.

"You got any Scotch?" Esther asked, sitting down with a loud sigh. "This day requires a stiff drink at—" She glanced at the clock on the microwave. "What time is it?" Maggie's eyes followed hers. "I can't see a damn thing."

"It's two o'clock," answered Maggie.

"That's acceptable. Do you have any? And what about iced tea? Do you have that?" Maggie turned to rummage through the cabinets. One by one, she opened their doors.

"I don't see any Scotch. Let me check the ones below." She knelt. "Ah, here's something. Oh, just whiskey. And vermouth." Esther made a face.

"No, that won't do. What about vodka? Check the freezer."

"Jackpot," Maggie called, triumphant. "And no iced tea, but we do have lemonade. Will that suffice?"

"That'll be just swell," said Esther. "Just swell. Load it up with ice, too, will you?"

"So," said Esther as Maggie slid a cold glass in front of her and sat down.

"So," said Maggie. They clinked glasses.

"Sour," commented Esther, wincing as she took her first sip. "But perfect. Thanks."

"How was she?" asked Maggie.

"She was sad. Embarrassed about her mistake. I told her she had nothing to be embarrassed about. Why should she? It's not her fault." Maggie nodded. "If she's lucky enough to know that she's even made a mistake to begin with, she's ahead of the game. Soon, that won't be the case, you know. You do know what's in store for her, don't you, Maggie?"

"As much as I can know based on what the doctor told us and reading about it. I'm sure I'm not prepared."

"You're not. I certainly wasn't, with my husband." Esther shook her head. "In a way, it's probably better that you didn't know Edith at all before this, so that you don't have to mourn her as she goes. That's what it's like, taking care of someone with Alzheimer's—you're mourning their loss even while they're right in front of you, usually yelling nonsense in your face or not recognizing you at all. You've looked into a home nurse, haven't you?" Maggie shook her head.

"I have some names. Remind me." Esther took a big gulp of her drink. "That's good. Straight to my head, thank God." She looked around the room, befuddled. "Where's the girl?"

"The girl?" asked Maggie, confused.

"Your girl?"

"Oh Lucy? I just put her down for a nap."

"Oh good. Listen, I'm starving and I bet you are, too."

"No, I'm fine, I'll just cobble something together here. You go out to lunch, Esther, really. Don't cancel your plans because of me."

"Plans? What plans? Taking Edith to therapy and lunch was my plan. Now that she's down for the count, you're the next best thing. Plus, you need a proper lunch—put some meat on those bones."

"Esther, please. Go ahead. I'll make myself a sandwich or something."

"Don't be ridiculous. I'll have Vinnie run you into town, and you can pick us up some hamburgers at Monroe's. It's not just a vodka lemonade at two in the afternoon kind of day, it's a hamburger day, too. And onion rings." She rubbed her hands together.

"You know where Monroe's is, don't you? Right on the main drag. I'd send Vinnie alone, but he's a terrible orderer. Performance anxiety. Have him drive you, get some fresh air—it'll be good for you."

"But what if they wake up? I—"

"They won't wake up. At least I know Edith won't. She's exhausted. Does Lucy make half hour naps a habit?"

"No. She's usually out until three or so."

"So? What's the problem? If she wakes up, I'll entertain her until you get back. Now get me a piece of paper and I'll write down my order. Don't screw it up, I don't want to be disappointed."

"I won't," promised Maggie. It would be nice to get out of the house, alone and very slightly drunk. Maybe she would buy herself something frivolous. On her way to the stairs, with Esther's order in hand, Esther called to her.

"Maggie?" She turned around to find Esther at the top of the stairs.

"Yes?"

"I know about Edith's son, by the way. She told me, just now. I want to help you find him. Time is of the essence, you know."

"I know," said Maggie.

"Can you imagine finding him, only to have Edith not remember why she was looking for him in the first place?" Esther shook her head. "We have to move quickly. Anyway, we'll talk about it when you're back. Go on. I'm going to take a brief siesta on the couch. Oh, don't look so alarmed. One ear will be open for Lucy."

"Thanks, Esther."

"Don't mention it. And for God's sake, don't forget the onion rings."

"THANKS, VINNIE," SAID Maggie, as she closed the door of his Town Car. She felt like a celebrity, being driven into town for burgers by her private chauffeur. "I'll be back in a minute."

"Take your time, I'm just going to park over there and read the paper." He pointed to a spot in the near distance, just past Siggy's.

"Did Esther put you up to this?"

"Put me up to what?" He gave her a smile and tipped his hat slightly before pulling away.

After ordering, she took a seat to wait, noticing that the place was practically deserted. In weeks prior, when she and Lucy had driven or walked by, there had always been a line of impossibly tan and thin people texting or corralling rambunctious kids spiraling out the door—down the block even. Now, it was just her and one other patron—an older man tucking into a basket of greasy goodness by the front window. Somehow, it had turned into September.

Maggie had of course known that Labor Day would signal a mass exodus, but the reality hadn't set in for her yet. She had noticed that the rental house behind them had been blissfully quiet for a week or two—twilight magical and still instead of pierced by pop music and pool splashing—but what that meant for the town at large; for the year-rounders; for her, hadn't occurred to her yet. Maggie was used to Manhattan, the city that never slept, not even for a second. Everywhere you looked, every place you went, there were people at all hours of the night and day—going, going, going. It was still hard to believe that wasn't her life anymore.

The streets were empty, too, now—no strolling couples or well-fed dogs with shiny coats; no children dressed like adults in replicas of their parents' expensive clothing. Maggie wondered which stores closed up shop completely for the winter, and which ones soldiered on for the sake of the locals. *What did Sam do?* she wondered.

"Number three," the counter girl called. Maggie retrieved her order, thanked her and left. Outside, it felt eerie, like the preface to a zombie invasion.

She hadn't told Edith yet, but she had found Arthur on the first try—staring back at her from the computer screen with a wide smile, sandwiched between what she assumed was his wife and daughter. He looked like any other older man, she supposed, with the exception of the fact that he had Edith's eyes and slender frame. Not a male version of his mother by any means, but she was there, without question. All she knew at this point was that he lived in Beacon, New York, and had retired, as revealed by his daughter's Facebook page. *Mazels on your retirement, Daddy!* the caption had read.

She had planned on telling Edith that evening—of showing her her son on her laptop; letting her have a few moments alone with his photo before they decided to proceed. Although she hadn't found his email address, she had found his daughter's very easily. They would go through her to get to him—that was Maggie's plan. But maybe it was best to hold off, wait a day or two, considering what had just happened.

"Hi Maggie."

Maggie looked up, out of her daydream, to find Sam

standing in front of her. He was tan and smiling, at ease like this wasn't an awkward run-in at all. Maggie tried her best to absorb his attitude, even though what she really wanted was to disappear into the sidewalk in a cloud of blue smoke.

"Hi Sam."

"Burger run?" he asked.

"What?"

He pointed to her bag.

"Oh this? Yes. Burgers for me and Esther. It's a red meat kind of day."

What did a *red meat kind of day* entail exactly? Maggie wondered as the words tumbled out of her mouth. Was it true that vodka had no odor? She hoped so, but closed her mouth tightly, just in case.

"I wanted to come say hello to you the other night when I dropped Olive off, but lost my nerve," he confessed.

"Your nerve?"

"Yeah, I didn't want you to think I had the wrong idea."

"Wrong idea about what?"

"About us. I know you're not interested."

"Not interested? What would make you think that?"

"I dunno. Body language, I guess?"

"What are you talking about?" asked Maggie, confused.

"On the walk home, you didn't even look at me." He laughed nervously. "Jesus, I sound like such a weenie."

"Sam, I took my clothes off in front of you."

"That's true. But I didn't get the impression that that was a sexual thing." He laughed again. "There I go again, weenie city."

"You don't sound like a weenie. Well, maybe a little. And it wasn't, you're right. But I wouldn't say that I wasn't interested. I—I had a lot on my mind, I guess. That swim, it stirred up a lot of stuff for me."

"Yeah?"

"Yeah. You could have called, you know. Just to see if I was okay," said Maggie.

"You're right. I could have. I should have. I was just sure that you would rather I didn't."

"Well, maybe you were wrong. Although I probably inadvertently gave you that impression. My track record at conveying interest isn't the greatest."

"You're a hard to get kind of woman?" Sam asked.

"No. Just impossibly strange." Sam smiled. A great smile, Maggie thought. Genuine.

"You looked very pretty the other night at Barbie's. From a distance, at least. And Olive said that Lucy was a dream. Didn't wake up once."

"Olive was a godsend. I needed a night out desperately. With my octogenarian girlfriends, that is."

"The Golden Girls."

"Yes, that's about what it's come to."

"Want to try it again?" asked Sam suddenly.

"Try what?"

"A date. Olive can babysit and we'll leave the house. We can bring bathing suits just in case. Unless I'm too young?"

"What?"

"I'll be eighty soon enough, Maggie. In thirty-something years or so," he teased.

"Age *is* just a number," she agreed. "Okay, Sam. Let's try again."

"Great, I'll call you."

"I've heard that before."

"No, I will. I always wanted to."

"Sounds good," said Maggie.

She waved goodbye, not quite believing that this, whatever it was between her and Sam, was still alive. A few steps ahead was Vinnie; the Town Car was idling.

"Sorry about the wait," she offered, climbing inside.

"No problem," replied Vinnie. "I owe Esther twenty bucks, though."

"Really, why?" asked Maggie, alarmed that her dawdling was going to cost him actual money.

"I said the two o' youse was done, but she said I was nuts. Guess she was right."

"As usual, huh?"

"You got it, miss."

CHAPTER 18

Edith stared into the bathroom mirror, feeling fragile and small.

"Edith Brennan," she whispered. She was Edith Brennan. She lived with Maggie and Lucy. She had had a daughter, Liza, but now she was dead. Her best friend was Esther. She had had a son who called himself Arthur. *Good*, she thought. *Very good*.

She looked down, eyeing her crooked fingers reproachfully. They looked like witch's fingers now, minus the green pallor. Beneath the skin, her knuckles were as round as bowling balls.

Upstairs she heard Lucy, having breakfast. Bang, bang, went her little orange plastic cup against the table. And then Maggie, her tone stern. "*No!*" Lucy yelled back. She was just starting to exercise her opinion, that one, and boy did she have one. About everything.

Liza had been like that. No to dresses; no to carrots; no to shoes; no to books; no to hugs. She was that way all of her life, thought Edith. Had to think she was in charge or else all bets were off. Like mother, like daughter.

"Arthur Geller." She said his name out loud, settling on the image she had created for him in her mind. He was of medium height, and slim, with slightly squinty brown eyes like her own and generous eyebrows, also like her own. He had a Roman nose and a strong chin, like his father, though he concealed it with a well-groomed beard. And he wore glasses—the kind with the invisible frames like that broad-caster on CNN wore. Serious glasses. Arthur Geller was se-rious. Serious but kind. Edith knew that everything else was pure speculation, but of that she was sure. She had heard it in his voice.

She didn't know if he had a family, but she hoped so. Was he gay, too? Or bipolar? She had often wondered if her genes were responsible for the way that Liza was—dormant in her, only to be reborn through her daughter. If Arthur was either, then certainly that had to be the case, right? After all, John had been as straight as the day was long, and as even-keeled.

Edith got dressed, pulling on her uniform, washing her face and brushing her teeth. As she ran her brush through her hair, she regarded her face in the mirror again with grate-ful resignation. Her face was wrinkled and tired, but it was her face. And to be able to recognize it without hesitation was a gift now, plain and simple.

"Hello girls," she said, once she had reached the top of the stairs. Lucy and Maggie looked up from the table with the same expression. They were glad to see her, Edith could tell.

"Hi Edif," greeted Lucy. "I have a pancake," she explained, holding up the crescent moon remains of her breakfast.

"That looks delicious, Lucy." Maggie lifted her mug of coffee in greeting.

"Morning, Edith. Can I get you anything?"

"No thanks. I have something for you, though. More photos." She laid them on the table in front of Maggie.

"Who dis?" asked Lucy. Maggie held the photos up and away from her.

"Let's clean you off and get down from the table before we look at them, okay?"

"Okay," agreed Lucy.

"See how much easier things are when you're agreeable?" Maggie pointed out.

"Pictures!" Lucy demanded, ignoring her. As Edith slid her bread into the toaster, the two of them made their way over to the couch.

"Who dis?" asked Lucy again.

"Oh, my goodness, I think that's Edith and Esther!" Maggie exclaimed. "Look at them. So beautiful."

"When they was little?" asked Lucy.

"Yes, little. Edith, this one is amazing. How old are you here?"

"Twenty, I think? That was at a wrap party for one of the shows we did, I can't remember which. Esther will know, I'm sure."

"You look amazing. So glamorous!"

"Oh yes, that was all Esther. She took all of our clothes to her cousin, a tailor on the Lower East Side. Even the cheapest things look expensive if they're tailored correctly." Edith looked down at her toast. She couldn't remember what to do with it.

"And this is Liza! Baby Liza. I'd recognize that face anywhere."

"Liza?" echoed Lucy.

"Yes, Lu. Liza. It's the same face, Edith. Exactly the same."

Edith continued to stare at her toast, trying desperately to summon her reason for making it. She poked it tentatively. She didn't want to ruin the morning, a morning when her memory had seemed ironclad just moments before, by admitting to Maggie that she had forgotten how to prepare toast. Quickly, she threw it in the garbage.

"Hey Luce, why don't you play with your dollies. I'm going to talk to Edith for a minute, okay?"

"No," countered Lucy. "You play."

"No, I'm not going to play right now. I'm going to talk to Edith. You play with your dolls." Lucy shrieked and threw herself on the floor, writhing in protest as Maggie walked away.

"Sorry," she said to Edith. "She should wear herself out in a minute or two." Lucy's shrieking got louder. "Or not."

"She's two," said Edith. "What can you do?"

"So Edith, I found him," said Maggie, as the screaming subsided.

"Found who?"

"Arthur."

Edith's eyes widened. "You did? Where?"

"On the computer. Through his daughter's Facebook account."

"He has a daughter?"

"Yes, and a wife. And I think a son, but I'm not one hundred percent sure on that one."

"For some reason I thought he would be harder to find," said Edith.

"Would you like to see him?"

"Yes," answered Edith, not quite sure she meant it.

Maggie got up to retrieve her computer from the couch as Edith considered calling the whole thing off. Then, her stomach growled, reminding her of the toast incident, and she remembered why she couldn't.

Maggie returned, pulling her chair close to Edith's before sitting down. With a slight thud, she set her laptop on the table and opened it. In seconds, a photo appeared on the screen. Edith leaned in for a closer look.

"You know what, I'm going to take Lucy downstairs to get dressed. You take your time with it. There are two photos of him actually—you just have to scroll through his daughter's, like so. Lots of her, obviously. And the maybe brother I was telling you about." Maggie's voice sounded very far away, despite the fact that her head was hovering inches from Edith's own. Edith nodded as she walked away.

There he was—Arthur. Smiling back at her and not at all looking like whom she had imagined. Instead of tall, he was of average height—just barely topping out over his wife and daughter. Not particularly thin, but not fat, either. And there were shades of Liza in his face, too—his jaw and gaze. For the first time, Edith realized that her daughter had actually looked like her, because Arthur certainly did. All of those years and times when John had told her so and she had brushed him off—he had been right. There was a rising in Edith's chest, like a chunk of ice detaching from a glacier.

She had been right about two things, however—he did have a beard, and his smile seemed genuine, but a little forced, as though his face wasn't accustomed to it. *Serious and kind.*

She studied his daughter, trying to figure out her age. It was hard nowadays, with everyone so healthy and slathering expensive moisturizers all over themselves, to know, but Edith's guess was mid-thirties. She had her father's same smile, but a playfulness in her eyes that looked like her mother. The mother was pretty, in a suburban way, with hair a little too coiffed and highlighted for Edith's taste. She was mid-laugh in the photo. A good balance for Arthur, Edith thought, even though of course she didn't know him at all.

There was so much she wanted to ask him, and yet she knew how unfair that would be. Even if he agreed to meet her, opening up to her would no doubt take a considerable amount of time—time she wasn't sure she had. She wondered again if she should do it at all. This whole thing was very selfish of her. What did he owe her—the birth mother who had abandoned him not once, but twice? Nothing.

Maggie and Lucy clomped back up the stairs, signaling their return.

"Edif, look at my boots!" commanded Lucy. Edith turned to see her in striped purple and turquoise tights, pink rain boots and a green T-shirt.

"Oh Lucy, you look terrific," said Edith. "You're ready for anything in that outfit." Lucy nodded happily and ran off to her animals.

"I gave up," Maggie declared, returning to her seat with a defeated sigh. "She can wear whatever the hell she wants."

"Better to pick your battles," murmured Edith, turning back to the screen.

"So? You okay?" asked Maggie. "He looks like Liza, no? And his daughter is pretty. The wife looks nice, too. Here, let me find the guy I think is his son."

"Maggie, I don't know about this anymore," said Edith.

"What do you mean?"

"I mean, I don't think this is such a good idea. I abandoned him. Twice. I should leave him alone."

"But Edith, isn't that his decision? You reach out with an email, and he makes the call about whether or not to respond. Think about the questions he must have."

"But that's just it. By the time we meet, who knows if I'll even have any answers? Who knows if I'll even remember who I am, much less him? And then what does our reunion become?"

"We'll tell him that in the email, Edith. We'll tell him why you're reaching out now, and why your time is limited."

"Oh no, that's too much. Why should he pity me? No."

"Edith, you keep making this all about you. It's about him and what he may need, too. If he does have questions that he's wanted to ask you for years and years, aren't you doing him a favor by letting him know that the time is now? And if he wants nothing to do with you, he wants nothing to do with you. He doesn't answer your email or he does and he says thanks, but no thanks. At least you know you tried."

"I can't—I can't do this. I should leave it alone." Edith began to get up from her chair. First, her own daughter didn't care enough about her to stick it out, and then him? It would hurt too much, to have to stomach his rejection, too. She couldn't bare it.

"Edith, no. You can't. You have to go through with this. For yourself." Maggie took her hand and pulled her slightly, back down. "I know it's scary, and that it puts you in a very vulnerable position, but I'm telling you that it's the right thing to do. He should know that you're out here, wondering about him. He should know that you care. Really, before it's too late." Urging Edith to face her fear made Maggie think of her own.

"Did you know that Lucy's father has no idea she even exists?" she blurted out.

"What?" asked Edith. "Why not?"

"There was no point in telling him. Not in an Anthony way obviously—we were together, more or less, for years— but when I got pregnant, he was on his way out of New York. By the time I knew about Lucy, he was hundreds of miles away forever. I considered it his parting gift, and that was it. I never thought about the fact that Lucy had a right to know. Never even crossed my mind until a month or two ago, and that's only because she asked. And because of you."

"Me?" asked Edith.

"Yes. Lucy's opportunity to know her father has nothing to do with me."

"I don't understand," said Edith.

"I don't quite, either, Edith." Maggie rubbed her temples. "But something about being out here with you and learning about your journey has shed light on my own. You say that you abandoned Arthur, but I don't think that's fair. You wanted him to have a better life, a life you knew you couldn't give him. And he did, from the looks of it. He really did."

"But I left him at a coffee shop, waiting for me like a fool. It wasn't right."

"Maybe not," said Maggie. "But the timing was wrong. You weren't ready. You had a family of your own to contend with, a daughter who occupied all of your heart."

"So now she's dead and I reach out to him? It's selfish of me."

"No, it's not. This could be his last chance to know you, Edith. Admitting that to yourself, and to him for that matter, is the opposite of selfish. Like me, with Lucy. Lying to her about Lyle is selfish. Giving him the chance to be involved in her life, whether I'm on board or not, isn't. I can see that now."

"So you're going to tell him about Lucy?"

"I told him. Sent an email just the other day. What he chooses to do with the information is completely up to him, but I have to at least give him the option of becoming involved. As much as I want to lie to her and tell her he's dead or on the other end of an anonymous vial of sperm, I can't. I have to be honest. With Lucy, with Lyle, with me."

"I need more time," said Edith.

"Edith, you know that you don't have time. You know that."

"I'm scared," she admitted.

"I know. But I think you should do it. And if it doesn't work out the way you want it to, I'm here. Esther's here. We'll get through it together."

"But I have no idea what to say. You're the writer. Will you help me?"

"I'm the writer?" Maggie asked. "Yes, I'm the writer," she answered herself. "Of course, Edith. I'll help you."

Hello. I hope this email finds you well. I realize you don't know me, so please let me introduce myself. My name is Edith Moore Brennan. I am eighty-two years old, and live in Sag Harbor, New York. I am looking for your father. My apologies for involving you in this search, but unfortunately I was unable to procure any of his direct contact information.

To make a long story short, I gave birth to your father when I was sixteen years old. I gave him up for adoption because I was in no way prepared for motherhood myself. I've always been confident in that decision, and now, so pleased to know that he has a beautiful family of his own.

Many years ago, your father contacted me, and although I initially agreed to meet with him, I'm afraid that ultimately I let him down. I'd like to apologize to him for that, and also to ask if I could meet with him now. You see, I have recently been diagnosed with Alzheimer's, and worry that my time and possible value to him are limited. Today, I could answer any questions he may have, but as for tomorrow, I can't be sure.

Thank you very much for your time. You seem like a lovely young woman, and I wish you all of the best.

Sincerely,

Edith Moore Brennan

CHAPTER 19

Underneath the cabinets, you need to wipe them down with a cloth. Spiderwebs," Maggie explained impatiently.

"Sí," answered the housekeeper.

"Rosa, right?" Rosa nodded in response.

"Okay, Rosa. You need to like, really wipe them away." Maggie got down on her knees to show her. "Obliterate them," she continued, looking up at her. "I clean, too, Rosa. Or I used to. Apartments in Manhattan." Rosa stared at her, not understanding or just choosing not to answer, Maggie couldn't be sure. "I'm watching you," she added.

Rosa's eyes widened, signaling her comprehension. Maggie was sure she would tell all of her friends about this exchange later, the crazy new white lady in the dead author's old house.

"Okay, good," said Maggie, standing up. "And the bath-rooms, too—you have to scrub the tiles. Each one, indi-vidually."

"Sí," answered Rosa. "Can I get back to work now?"

"Yes, yes of course," answered Maggie. She wasn't sure what had happened. She had planned to forge an alliance with Rosa, but a need to upstage her had risen up in Maggie in-stead. She was so anxious lately, waiting for a reply from Lyle that had yet to arrive in her inbox. It infuriated her, the fact that he couldn't so much as type three sentences in response.

"Hey Rosa," she called. She turned around to face Maggie with a sigh. "I'm sorry. Ignore me. Well, not about the spider-webs. But the other stuff. I'm going through a thing."

"It's okay, miss."

"Okay. Good. Thank you, Rosa. Lucy, let's go," she called to her daughter, who was playing in her room.

"Where we going?" she asked suspiciously.

"For a walk."

Maggie grabbed her keys, a sippy cup and some Cheerios for Lucy, and headed out, Lucy close at her heels. On the porch, she took a deep breath in, swallowing the sky.

"Jump in," she instructed her daughter. She climbed into the stroller, hands up to receive her moving snack. Moments later, they were on the road. The air felt different, Maggie noticed. Crisper. Cleaner. Fall was coming.

That morning, she'd been working on Edith's story, tran-scribing her memories, when without warning, she'd veered off-track, into the recesses of her own brain. Initially, she'd tried to fight it, but soon she found herself pulling up a blank document, the words pouring out, her fingers flying over the keyboard like they belonged to someone else. It both exhilarated and scared her, that kind of open access to her past. Working with Edith, seeing her so desperately try to cling to her own history, had pulverized Maggie's resolve to avoid her own.

For so long, she hadn't allowed herself to think of her parents; herself as their child. There were painful memories that made sense now, in terms of the choices she had made, like why she had abandoned her ambition when her father left. She had cut off her own nose to spite her face, or however the saying went. Sure, he had instilled the value in her initially, but her drive was her own; it belonged to her. To give that up in an attempt to spite him had been silly; childish. She should reconnect with it on her own terms, she had been thinking. And maybe him, too. She just had to figure out what those terms were exactly.

"Hey!" she heard behind her. "Hey, Maggie!" She turned around to find Sam on his bike, barreling towards them.

"Hey," she replied, self-conscious about the fact that she hadn't even bothered to look in the mirror before she left. He disembarked from his bike, smiling goofily beneath his helmet.

"Where are you guys headed?" he asked.

"Just the beach."

"It's a beautiful day, huh? First day in a long time I'm not sweating like a pig."

"Yes," agreed Maggie. "Fall is coming."

"May I join you?" asked Sam. "I can just walk my bike."

"But aren't we seeing each other tonight?"

"What? Too much?" he asked, looking hurt.

"No, no. Let's go."

"You sure?"

"Mom, let's go!" commanded Lucy.

"Aye-aye, captain!" replied Sam.

They began to walk.

"So how are you?" he asked.

"Good," Maggie lied. "Well, actually, not so good. A little anxious, actually."

"How come?"

"I'm not sure. Well, that's not true. I—I started writing again. My own stuff, this morning."

"That's good news, isn't it?" asked Sam, his shoulder brushing hers slightly, sending a pleasant tingle down her spine.

"I guess so. I don't know. I'm not like, *writing* writing. It's personal stuff. Memories from when I was a kid. Not my style at all. It's disconcerting, actually."

"Why disconcerting? Don't writers always mine their personal lives?"

"Maybe. I don't know. I never did before."

"Maybe it's being out here, the salty air. It's loosening everything up," said Sam.

"I don't know about that." They made a right, towards the water. "I probably shouldn't tell you this, but Edith has Alzheimer's."

"I know," said Sam.

"You know?" Maggie stopped walking. "How?"

"It's a small town. Word travels."

"Esther?" she asked.

"Yeah."

Maggie resumed walking. "It would break her heart if she knew."

"Well, nobody here has the bad sense to bring it up with her. She'll never have to know."

"Except maybe that guy—what's his name? Murray?"

Sam laughed. "The King of Sag Harbor?" he replied. "No way. Edith could eat him for lunch, he knows that."

"Oh okay, good."

"Here, let me park my bike at the rack," said Sam. "No need to drag it through the sand." Maggie watched him lock it up, impressed by the ease with which he handled it, the way his forearms flexed.

"Mommy, I get out!" yelled Lucy.

"But Luce, you're not in your bathing suit. You'll get sand everywhere."

"Moooom!" she screamed.

"Fine. Go." She undid the Velcro of her sneakers and lifted her up and out of the stroller. "Stay away from the water!" she called after her. "I'm learning to pick my battles," she said to Sam.

"An essential parenting strategy," he confirmed.

"You think the stroller is safe here?" she asked. "I don't really feel like pushing it through the sand, either." Sam looked up and down the deserted beach.

"I do," he replied. "How's it going with Edith, speaking of?" he asked, as they began to follow Lucy.

"She's asked me to write her memoir, so to speak. She relays her memories and I compile them for her."

"That's really cool," said Sam. "And good of you."

Maggie shrugged. "I enjoy it, actually. It's good for both of us."

"So her memories are triggering your own?"

"I guess so." Maggie bent down to pick up a seashell. "Fully intact. That never happens. Lucy!" she yelled. Lucy turned around and ran back to them, her curls springing with each step.

"Look at this," Maggie said, extending the shell to Lucy. "Isn't it beautiful?" She held it up, examining its pearly pink interior in the late morning sun.

"Booteeful," Lucy agreed. She patted it as though it were a puppy and took off again, running just ahead of them.

"Yes, I suppose that's what's happening," she continued. "But it's making me think about things I don't like to think about."

"Like what?" asked Sam.

"Like my childhood. Why I am the way I am."

"And what way are you?"

"Weird. Unambitious. Defensive."

"What an attractive pedigree," said Sam with a laugh. "You don't seem like those things to me."

"You know a lot of college-educated cleaning ladies?"

"You know a lot of philosopher toy store owners? Life just presents itself sometimes, Maggie. You have to move with the current, or you drown. I don't know if I'd call that un-ambitious."

"Do you always employ water metaphors at the beach?" Maggie asked.

"Where else would I employ them?"

Maggie glanced at her watch. "Lucy, come back! We have to go. Lunch!" she called. They waited for her to pass before pivoting themselves.

"How much longer until your triathlon?" Maggie asked.

"It was yesterday."

"Yesterday! You doof. Why didn't you tell me?"

"You didn't seem all that interested when I told you in the first place."

"But still! You could have at least mentioned it."

"Yeah, but that would have meant a text just to mention it. It's not like we had a dialogue going already. Or I would have had to bait you with small talk and then been like, 'Oh, by the way, I'm doing that triathlon thing today.' Too complicated. Better to wait until after the fact. Believe me, I thought about it."

"It certainly seems so." He had thought about her when she wasn't around. That pleased Maggie. "So you survived?"

"I did. Can't believe it."

"That's amazing, Sam. Really. I know it meant a lot to you, to finish. Congratulations."

"Thanks."

"What the hell are you doing out for a bike ride the day after?" asked Maggie.

"Hoping to run into you." They'd come to the place they

had started, their respective vehicles waiting for them patiently. A seagull perched on top of the stroller, staring at them.

"You're good," said Maggie. "No really, how are your legs moving?"

"Not easily," he admitted. "But they say you should move around the day after, just to keep them from turning into slabs of concrete." Maggie shook her head in disbelief. "Don't worry, after this I'm going home to soak in an Epsom bath for six hours."

"I'm exhausted," Lucy declared, climbing back into her stroller.

"So I'll see you tonight? After your bath?" asked Maggie.

"I'll bring Olive by at eight. Drop her off and pick you up."

"See you then," she said over her shoulder as she wheeled Lucy home.

"EDITH, REMEMBER THOSE impromptu dance parties we used to have, in our apartment?" Esther asked jovially, reaching for a slice of pineapple from the platter she had brought over. Her bangles—a mix of yellow and rose gold, with silver in between—clattered and clinked together over the sleeve of her sweater. "God, we had so much energy. We'd dance all day and then come home to dance some more. Remember?"

"Yes, of course," answered Edith. "Some of my happiest moments."

"And who was it, Carol, who used to do those splits? Right in the middle of everything? Like it was nothing?"

"Yes, Carol," said Edith. "With the red hair. Such a show-off, that one. What was that song we loved? By Rosemary Clooney? Something 'My House'," Edith continued.

"'Come On-a My House'!" Esther shrieked. "Exactly. Maggie, do you have that song? The 'My House' song?"

Two beaming faces stared at her expectantly, as though the concept of Maggie owning a song that had preceded her birth by several decades was entirely plausible.

"You know, I don't, but I'm sure I can easily download it. Wait, let me go in and get my computer."

"Yes, *download* it," Edith commanded, handling the term awkwardly.

"Do whatever you have to do," urged Esther.

Maggie opened her laptop and searched for it, finding it easily. Before returning to Edith and Esther, she checked her email just in case, and there it was. An email from Arthur Geller. She clicked it, only to have the dreaded color wheel of doom pop up, as her tired old machine dug deep.

"Oh, for fuck's sake," Maggie whispered, grateful that Edith and Esther seemed to be happily preoccupied outside. Finally, it appeared.

Dear Edith, blah blah blah, Maggie skimmed. And then, the jackpot: *I would like to meet you, too.*

"Maggie, let's go already! What's the holdup?" Esther bellowed.

"Coming!" Maggie yelled back, wanting Lucy to wake up from her nap. She was so happy suddenly, so moved by Arthur's unexpected graciousness; his understanding of how badly Edith needed this closure now, that all she wanted in the world was to hug her daughter.

"Did you find it?" asked Edith.

"I did. But there's something else."

"What? What else? What could possibly be more important than a little Rosemary Clooney?" asked Esther, oblivious.

"Did he?" whispered Edith.

"Did who?" asked Esther, looking from Edith to Maggie and then back again.

"He did," Maggie replied. She set her computer down on the table facing Edith and opened it.

"Who is he?" asked Esther. "Oh, my God, of course! What a dolt I am. Arthur."

"Where are my glasses? I need my reading glasses," said Edith, patting her empty pockets nervously.

"They're around your neck, for God's sake," said Esther. She reached out to pluck at the delicate strand of lapis lazuli beads from which they hung.

"I'm scared," Edith said quietly. Esther clasped Edith's hands in between her own.

"It's okay, Edith, there's nothing to be scared of. It's good news," said Maggie.

"It is?" Edith squeaked.

"Go on, put your glasses on and read it, Edith," urged Esther.

"You have to press a letter on the keyboard to bring the screen back up," said Maggie.

"Which letter?" asked Esther.

"Any letter."

"Any letter? We don't want to break it. You better come over here and show us."

"No really, Esther, you can't break it," replied Maggie, irritation creeping in. "Just press any letter."

"I'll press A for Arthur," said Edith, pecking it quickly and then rearing back, as though something was going to explode. The screen lit up, illuminating their faces.

Maggie looked out beyond the porch, to the tree branches just starting to lose some of their leaves. Soon their plumage would turn yellow, orange, and they'd have to move their sessions inside. If their sessions were even still happening by then. There was no way of knowing. Maggie would miss them, when they were gone.

"He wants to see me," whispered Edith.

"Isn't it wonderful?" asked Maggie. "The best possible outcome."

"Should we take a road trip?" asked Esther, clapping her hands in delight. "Vinnie can drive us. We'll pack snacks, maybe a bottle of champagne—the whole nine yards. When should we go? Next week?"

"Esther, wait," said Edith. "I haven't even answered him yet."

"Fair enough, but time is of the essence here, Edith. No use pussyfooting around. We need to move, and fast." She looked to Maggie. "You agree with me, right, Maggie?"

"Yes, but let's give Edith just a moment. You and I can sort through the logistics later."

"You're right, good idea. Absolutely. Edith, it's wonderful news. What an opportunity."

"I think I'm happy," said Edith. "But I haven't felt happy in so long. Since Liza died. It seems wrong now, to be happy at all. Ever."

"I don't think Liza would have wanted that for you," said Esther.

"But the way she went. How can any mother be happy ever again when their child kills themselves? How do you move past that guilt?" Edith asked. "Now I feel guilty that I even went looking for him in the first place."

"Why?" asked Maggie.

"One child dies, just go find the other one," Edith explained.

"It's not like that and you know it, Edith," said Maggie. "We talked about it before, remember? It's much more complicated."

"For all you know, you would be on this quest even with Liza still here," said Esther. "Alzheimer's would have had you in its grip regardless. Maybe you would have told her about Arthur; asked her to help you. You never would have even known Maggie if Liza hadn't died, after all."

"I don't think I would have told Liza." Edith glanced at Maggie. "It very well could have ended up in a story of hers without my permission. She was my daughter, and I loved her very much, but I was wary of that."

"You know, I'm over it," Maggie said to Edith.

"Over what?" asked Esther.

"How'd you get over it?" asked Edith.

"I was never going to do anything with that detective on my own. Liza was right."

"About what?" asked Esther again.

"The insomniac detective was my idea," Maggie answered.

"That book that made a trillion dollars?" Esther whistled.

"In the end it was just an empty idea for me," said Maggie. "You can't copyright an idea, you have to turn it into a thing, something tangible, to truly claim it. I never did that. Liza did, though—she was good at it. Bestseller good. It wasn't about the detective anyway, my anger. And I'm writing again, so—it's okay. I'm okay."

"You're writing again?" asked Edith.

"Sort of. Gradually."

"That's wonderful, Maggie."

"But what about Arthur?" Esther asked. "It's okay to be scared, Edith, but this other stuff—you're just kidding yourself. Making up excuses. Set up a date and time already."

"Yes, Edith. You should," agreed Maggie.

"You think so?" asked Edith.

"We do," said Esther.

"You don't think it's a mistake?"

"We don't," answered Maggie.

"If it's a disaster, I'm coming for you both."

"Deal," said Esther. "Hey Maggie, can you play that song already?"

Maggie reached for the computer and pressed play. As the music wafted out of the speaker, Edith and Esther both began to sway in their chairs, moving their hands in time to the beat, and perfectly together as well, as though they had rehearsed. Singing blissfully, they could have been twenty-one again, Maggie thought, dancing in their Hell's Kitchen apartment—their nylons, the ones with the lines drawn up the back, hanging over the radiator.

She raised her phone and snapped a photo, neither of them noticing in their revelry. She would show it to Edith later, when things were not as happy, to remind her of her smile.

"How was your afternoon?" asked Sam, sitting across from her at the quaint seafood restaurant he had chosen for their date. Fishing nets drooped from the wood paneled walls, along with life preservers and plastic fish replicas. Red and white checked tablecloths covered the tables, and red lanterns, lit from within by candles, glowed all around them— the restaurant's sole customers.

"Not bad," replied Maggie, feeling flustered from her mad dash to put Lucy to sleep and make herself remotely presentable. "What about you?"

"Good, mostly. A little overwhelmed with Olive at the moment, but good."

"Really? Why?"

"She just started her sophomore year of high school, you know? She's fifteen. It's a lot."

"Fifteen. That's a brutal time to be a girl."

"No kidding, not to mention the father of said girl. Maggie, sometimes she is so mean to me that I come close to tears."

"Sad tears or rage tears?"

"A little bit of both, actually."

"Sometimes Lucy makes me cry, and she's only two and a half. I understand."

"Here you go, miss," said the waitress, interrupting with Maggie's glass of wine.

"To the completion of your triathlon," she announced. Sam joined her with his own bottle of beer.

"And the hopeful regaining of feeling in my legs." He shook his head with a wry smile. "Any day now. That makes this my second celebratory dinner. Olive and I had pizza and ice cream cake in the kitchen last night, and she tolerated me for over two hours. It was perfect."

"Well, you earned it. Seriously, I'm not sure that I can even jog to the bathroom from here. Congratulations." She raised her glass again. "How does it feel, having done it?"

"Optimistic."

"That's a great way to feel," said Maggie.

"It is." He took a sip of his beer. "You know, I've been thinking about what we were talking about today, on the beach."

"Oh yeah?"

Sam broke a piece off the tiny French baguette on the table and buttered it carefully.

"Your writing and all. Your memories resurfacing. I think it's a good thing. That it's meant to be, maybe the reason you're here," he continued.

"How do you mean?"

"I mean, here you are, caring for a woman who's losing her memories, and yours come back. It makes perfect sense."

"Is that the philosophy talking?" Maggie asked, not disagreeing.

"Maybe."

"I wonder if Liza—if she knew that something like this would happen. The other day, I thought to myself, maybe that was why she chose me in the first place," said Maggie. "That that was the real reason my writing never took off, because I was avoiding so much."

"That's interesting," said Sam. He plunged a hunk of his lobster into a white dipping bowl of butter and extended it to Maggie. "She knew that about you?"

"Thanks," she said, taking it from his outstretched hand. "Yeah, she did. She was always trying to get me to open up about my parents and the whole college to cleaning lady trajectory. 'Write what you know,' she would say. But it never appealed to me before. I didn't see the point in dwelling in what was over and done with. Now, with Edith, I'm seeing things a little differently."

"I bet," said Sam. "But about Liza's intentions, I don't know. Suicide is a pretty selfish decision. I'm not sure she would have had the foresight to think of anyone else."

"I guess that's a valid point," agreed Maggie. "I wish she had left a note. Some sort of explanation, you know?"

"I know," agreed Sam. "Although I bet if there was one, you'd wish there wasn't."

"What do you mean?"

"I think it's probably more interesting to fill in the blanks yourself."

"To create her story ourselves," added Maggie.

"Something like that," said Sam.

"Today I accosted our poor housekeeper," said Maggie. "She thinks I'm nuts."

"I wanted to ask you about that. Why did you decide to make that—"

"My career?" finished Maggie. "I dunno. I'm good at it and it paid well. And the solitude of it, I enjoyed that."

"But what about getting into other people's grime?" asked Sam. "That didn't turn you off?"

"Not really. Seeing how someone presents themself to the outside world versus how they behave privately, it can be fascinating. I used to have this client, she was as rich as they come—a pied–à–terre in Paris, a giant place out here in the Hamptons somewhere, a closet as big as my apartment, filled with shit you see in magazines. She gleamed like marble she was so waxed, plucked and stretched." Maggie pushed her plate away, finished with her meal. "Her penthouse was clean as a whistle, but her personal bathroom was like something you'd find in a tenement. Barf everywhere, because of course she threw up all of her food. Hair clogging every drain, toothpaste smeared on the sink. It was shocking. But a real porthole into her soul, I think. You'd have never known."

"You never wanted to write about that?" asked Sam, untying his bib and laying it on top of his plate—the lobster's white flag of ultimate surrender.

"It felt wrong to me at the time, like I was betraying some sort of maid code."

"You wouldn't have to be literal about it. Change her to a him or something, New York to Los Angeles. You're the writer, you can do what you want."

"But it's someone else's story."

"So what? She invited you into it. You're just borrowing."

"Borrowing implies giving it back," said Maggie.

"It comes back one way or another," said Sam. *That was the truest thing she had ever heard*, Maggie thought. She gazed at him across the table, his face bathed in candlelight, and felt butterflies of affection flutter in her belly.

"Hey, if you were going on a road trip with two old ladies and a two-year-old, what would you bring?" Maggie asked.

"Valium," Sam answered, without missing a beat.

Maggie laughed. A real laugh, with her head thrown back.

"You want to get out of here?" she asked giddily, heeding the tickle of those feather-light wings.

"YOUR PLACE IS so homey," Maggie said, wandering through the living room. Books and antique wooden toys filled an entire wall. Another claimed black and white photos of Olive.

"Baby Olive, toddler Olive, kid Olive, preteen Olive, teen Olive," said Maggie, standing before it. Sam handed her a glass of red wine.

"It's crazy, isn't it? How they grow?"

"Yes," agreed Maggie. "Sometimes I look at Lucy and can't believe it. Little still, but so big."

"Tell me about it."

"She looks like you," said Maggie.

"You think?" Sam looked closer. "The eyes, for sure. Maybe the face shape. But really, she's her mother."

"She lives here?" asked Maggie. "In Sag Harbor?"

"We're not quite sure where she is."

"What?"

"She took off with her trainer. Two years ago." He laughed. "I don't know why I'm laughing. It's not funny."

"Sam, that's horrible. She just left Olive? Just like that?"

"Yeah. I know, it's awful. Olive has had a tough time."

"Obviously," said Maggie. "She left her at thirteen?" He nodded. "Jesus." Maggie had been twenty-two when her father had chosen a new life, but thirteen was a different ballgame. Olive hadn't even been a fully formed person yet. She peered closer at the photos, looking for clues of unhappiness. There was a sadness to Olive's smile, a slight downturn at the corners of her mouth. It reminded Maggie of her own.

"Well, I wasn't totally innocent. The marriage hadn't been working for a while, but I refused to go to therapy or you know, do anything proactive about it."

"Still," said Maggie.

"Yeah. It sucks." They continued to stare at the wall in awkward silence.

"What's the story with Lucy's dad?"

Maggie turned and made her way to the couch. "He's out of the picture, too. From conception, though. Lucy never knew him."

"That doesn't sound exactly easy, either," said Sam.

"No, but it was my decision. He never knew about her."

"One night stand gone wrong?"

"No, more like years long pseudo-relationship gone

wrong. He moved to Portland, but Lucy was his parting gift. Unbeknownst to him, of course."

"You ever think about telling him now that Lucy will probably wonder herself?"

"I emailed him last week to tell him, actually." Maggie drained her glass. "Haven't heard a peep back."

"A week ago?" asked Sam, incredulous. "Maybe he's out of the country."

"Last time I checked there was internet access everywhere." She shook her head. "But you know what? It doesn't matter. I did the right thing by Lucy in telling him. What he does with the information is on him."

"You're not angry?"

"No, I am. Even I couldn't have imagined him to be so self-involved. But honestly, life without him suits me just fine. I'd rather have Luce all to myself anyway."

"Yeah. You may not feel that way when she's older," said Sam. "I'd love to hand Olive off once in a while. Or push her overboard. Either one." They both laughed, empty glasses balanced against their stomachs as they melted into his plush couch, which smelled vaguely of popcorn.

"He'll answer," said Sam.

"How can you be so sure?" asked Maggie. "You can't even find your ex-wife. People are assholes."

"Was Liza an asshole?"

"Liza?" Maggie held up her glass. "You have any more?" Sam got up to retrieve the bottle from the kitchen.

"It's complicated with mental illness," she said when he returned. "On one hand, she was an asshole most of the time, but on the other hand she couldn't help it. Wasn't always easy to remember that."

"How was she an asshole?"

"She prided herself on being honest, but a lot of times her honesty was just, you know, mean. Once she told me that my job made me a loser. And that I'd have much better luck dating in New York if I lost ten pounds."

"What the fuck?" asked Sam.

"See? You're getting angry. But if you knew Liza, if you knew what she grappled with, you couldn't take it personally. For longer than five minutes at least." She took a sip, feeling a little dizzy in the dimly lit room. She'd come here with the intention of having sex, and now it was the furthest thing from her mind.

"And let's face it, a lot of the time she was right," she continued. "Cleaning apartments for a living did sort of make me a loser in the grand scheme of things."

"But what did she know about your past? What may have brought you to that choice in the first place? And ten pounds, come on. You're gorgeous." Maggie blushed.

"She asked me about my past but I wouldn't tell her anything. And when we first met, I had ten pounds to lose. She was right. So I did." Maggie laughed. "That was the problem. She was right a lot."

"What does a lesbian care about being attractive to men?"

"You know, Liza never told Edith."

"Told her what?" asked Sam.

"That she was a lesbian."

"You're kidding me," said Sam. "That's sad—that she was

out in every sense of the word to the outside world, but not to her own mother. You would have thought Liza had no reservations about who she was."

"Well, obviously she did," said Maggie. "She killed herself."

"She must have been terribly depressed beforehand," said Sam.

"I wouldn't know. We hadn't spoken in years."

"Why? She became too much for you? Too much honesty?"

"Never a good quality in a friend," said Maggie. "God forbid they tell you the truth." Sam laughed. "No, it was something silly."

"Silly like what?"

"You ask a lot of questions, Sam— Oh, my God, I don't even know your last name."

"Gold. Sam Gold."

"Maggie Sheets." She sat up and extended her hand for him to shake it, but he pulled her towards him instead.

"I haven't done this in a long time," she whispered as he kissed her neck.

"Done what? Kiss?" He placed his lips on hers. They were surprisingly soft. She kissed back, responding to the increasing insistence of his mouth, but she didn't like it. Maggie hated kissing, actually. Tongue kissing anyway. It was too wet. Reminded her of mopping the floor.

"Is everything okay?" asked Sam, pulling back.

"Sure, yes, fine," said Maggie, allowing herself to be kissed again. All day long she braided hair, changed clothes, wiped a bottom, prepared food, swept up crumbs and scrubbed tiny plastic dishes. A mom body: property of Lucy. To be a different kind of body, the kind of body that a man might want to touch, was laughable to Maggie.

She tried her best to let go, to be swept up in her attraction to Sam—she was attracted to him, she was sure—but she couldn't do it.

"Hey Maggie, is everything okay?" Sam asked.

"I'm sorry, Sam. I know this is going to sound highly suspicious, but it's not you, it's me."

"Oh Jesus," he said, rolling his eyes and sitting up as though she had caught on fire. "Maggie, please."

"I mean it. This is the first time I've been with anyone since I got pregnant. Everything about my body belongs to Lucy now—I can't remember what it felt like when it was mine." Sam sat back against the couch with a heavy sigh. "And it's not just my body, either. My mind, as well."

"Who does that belong to?" asked Sam.

"Don't be condescending," chided Maggie.

"I'm not. Well, maybe a little. Typical male sexual frustration. I'm sorry."

"I thought I was ready for this—I'm certainly attracted to you—but focusing on this, on us doing this, is impossible."

"Listen, there's part of me that understands where you're coming from, but you know, it's not exactly good for the ole ego, regardless of your explanation." Maggie began to argue, but he cut her off.

"Let's just pretend this part didn't happen. We came back here, we had a nice talk, we got to know each other better and I took you home. Can we do that?"

"Sure," answered Maggie. "You okay to drive?"

"My buzz is long gone. C'mon, let's go."

MAGGIE LAY IN bed, staring at the ceiling.

All the signs had been there that she was ready to have sex, but when they'd begun, she'd felt as wooden as the antique marionette puppet propped up on one of his bookshelves.

All of that touching and rocking and hugging of Lucy had done her in, it seemed. There was nothing extra to give. Or receive, for that matter. And once her brain had clamped down on her disinterest, it had begun to race. Had she ever really enjoyed sex at all? she'd wondered as Sam kissed her neck. What was wrong with her?

Penetration had always felt good, but not for the reasons it should, she thought. Not for the shared intimacy of the act. She never, not with any of her partners, viewed it as a means to a deeper bond. It was more of a physical necessity, an animalistic itch that had to be scratched. Very rarely was there a release for Maggie. Of any kind, really.

There was so much screwed up about her, Maggie thought. Why couldn't she just have been a normal person who went to college, got a good job, had meaningful sex while gazing into her partner's eyes, saw her parents on holidays, got married and had a kid or two? But what was normal anyway? Her parents had tried their best given their means—she knew that even as she blamed them for her own inadequacies.

She tried every day to be a good mom, to be her best self for Lucy. Edith said she had done the same, with Liza. And she had been thinking lately, that her father had done his best, too, without a partner he could depend on; a partner that went in and out like an AM transistor radio, even when she was sitting across the table from them. There but not there.

Love to Edith was honesty. Love to Maggie was patience. Love to her own mother had been kindness. On the rare occasions she'd had the energy to give it, she'd been very kind to Maggie. And love to her father had been discipline. She didn't fault him for that. And she supposed, if she took her own hurt feelings out of the equation, she couldn't fault him for being so quick to seek solace in someone else, once the burden of his marriage had been lifted. The hurt of him abandoning her, though, that would take a long time to heal. But maybe not forever, as she had once thought.

Maggie flipped over onto her stomach and buried her face in the mattress, putting the blanket up and over her head.

CHAPTER 20

"Who wants a bagel?" asked Esther, riffling through her enormous bag on the floor of the ridiculous, in Edith's opinion, limousine she had managed to acquire for their three-hour trip. Vinnie sat up front, separated from them by a glass partition that Esther raised and lowered with wild abandon.

"I'll take one," said Maggie. "Lucy, want to split a bagel with me?"

"No," answered Lucy, glued to the iPad, also courtesy of Esther.

"Ryan has two of these things, so I borrowed one," she'd explained, handing it to an enchanted Lucy. Edith watched Maggie regard the exchange in horror, but to take it from

Lucy after she knew it existed would mean certain death for all of them. Today, technology would win.

Maggie shrugged her shoulders now, an hour and a half later.

"More for me," she said in response to Lucy's refusal. "Edith?"

"No thank you," answered Edith. Her stomach was in knots, anticipating Arthur.

"You have to eat, Edith," Esther chided. "Here." She shoved a bagel with cream cheese at her. "Just a bite or two."

Edith took it, just to shut her up, and looked out the window. The green leaves were going, replaced by pops of pinkish red and orange.

"Vinnie, what's the time check?" asked Esther, lowering the partition yet again.

"We have an hour to go," he answered, as patient as a saint. Edith gazed down at the bagel in her hands. It might as well have been a bag of worms as far as her appetite was concerned.

"Edith, you okay?" asked Esther. "You sure you don't want one of us to go in there with you to break the ice?"

"No Esther, I don't," she growled.

"Esther, really, stop asking her," said Maggie. "We'll walk her to the door, meet the family and then the three of us will leave and go get lunch somewhere. Maybe go to the museum. Then we'll come back in two hours and pick her up. Right Edith?" Edith nodded.

"Fine, fine, whatever you like, Edith. This is your day.

I'm just so curious. But I promise, I'll be good. Cool as a cucumber."

Maggie exchanged a glance with Edith as she carefully retrieved the iPad from a now sleeping Lucy's grasp.

"What? I can do cool."

VINNIE PULLED UP to a two story, white brick house with gray shutters and a gray door. In the front yard, a huge oak tree extended its branches in greeting, and a rope swing, old and frayed by time, hung from one of them. It was a nice house, thought Edith. A happy family lived here. She put her hand to the window.

"Well, here we are," said Esther. "Very sweet, this house. A nice Jewish family lives here, I can tell."

"How do you know they're Jewish?" asked Maggie, nudging Lucy awake.

"Arthur Geller is a Christian name?" Esther frowned into the mirror or her compact as she reapplied her orange, too orange Edith thought, lipstick. "Besides, I can see the mezuzah from here."

"All the way from here?" asked Maggie.

"Jew sonar," explained Esther, flipping her compact shut. "Edith, you need some lipstick or something. Here, use mine."

"No thank you," replied Edith. "I'll use my own." She riffled through her purse with trembling hands. She could barely speak she was so nervous.

"Here, let me help you," offered Esther. Carefully, she painted Edith's lips, as Edith sat with her eyes closed.

"She coloring her lips?" asked Lucy, fascinated.

"Yep," answered Maggie. "Isn't it pretty?"

"Yep," agreed Lucy.

"Okay, now here—blot with this tissue," instructed Esther. "Let me just straighten your blouse. There we go." She sat back, appraising her work. "You look fantastic, Edith."

"Yes, very elegant," agreed Maggie.

"Booteeful," added Lucy.

"Thank you," Edith replied.

"Okay girls," said Esther. She rapped on the partition and within moments, Vinnie was opening Edith's door. She took his outstretched hand and stood on the sidewalk, waiting, as the others followed.

"We all here?" asked Esther, taking attendance. "Alright Edith, you lead the way."

Edith tried to walk, but her feet were frozen to the spot. This was a mistake. They should just turn around and get back in the car, and go back to their lives. She should have left well enough alone and not bothered this poor man. She should—

"Hello!" called a voice. The front door had opened, revealing the young woman from the Faceplant or whatever it was called. She was pretty, Edith thought. "Edith?"

"Come on now, Edith, off you go," urged Esther.

"Edif, you want to hold my hand?" asked Lucy, looking up at her earnestly.

"I'd like that, Lucy, thank you," Edith answered.

Together, with Esther and Maggie bringing up the rear, they approached the house.

EDITH SAT ACROSS from Arthur in the sitting room. It was a formal room, with not much in it besides the gray couch with two red chairs facing it, one of which she perched on. There was a rectangular glass coffee table between them, on which sat a vase of sunflowers. A yellow and white patterned rug spread out on the floor beneath her. Through the windows behind him, the perfectly blue sky framed his head as though he was a photo, and not the real thing.

The real thing. Her real son, in the flesh before her. Edith's legs were crossed, her dangling foot vibrating. His eyes were so much hers that she touched her own to make sure they were still there. And he was slim, like her, too.

"So."

"So!" echoed Edith, her voice shaking, too.

"I look like you," offered Arthur, reading her mind. "Same eyes."

"You really do. But you have your father's nose and chin."

"I do?"

"Oh yes."

She hadn't thought about Anthony in decades, but the resemblance brought him back, smiling at her that first time she had met him, like he had plans for her.

"How are you?" asked Arthur.

"Me?" Edith pointed to herself even though there was no one else in the room. His daughter and wife were in the kitchen, quiet as mice. "I'm nervous," she admitted.

"God, me, too," said Arthur. "I—Well, I had imagined for so long what you looked like. It's surreal now, to actually see you."

"I know," agreed Edith. "You're very handsome," she added.

"And you, you're like a swan," said Arthur.

"A swan!" Edith laughed. "That's a nice thing to say to an old lady."

"It's true."

"Arthur, I'm sorry, about everything," she blurted out.

"What's to be sorry for? I had a great life, Edith. My parents were wonderful people. Are wonderful people, I should say. I only lost my father a year ago. My mother is still with us—living by herself in Florida; refusing to budge." He threw up his hands. "What can I do? Anyway, that's not the point. The point is, don't be sorry."

"But that day in New York. That was wrong of me, to leave you high and dry like that. I should never have told you I was coming."

"It's okay, Edith. I forgave you a long time ago for that. It was a lot to ask of you."

"No, no it wasn't, Arthur. It was a cup of coffee. And I'm not sure what went wrong with me. Certainly, hearing your voice—knowing you were alive and well, and that you sounded like a nice young man—that lifted me up. It really did."

"It's funny. I had the opposite reaction," said Arthur. "Knowing that you were alive and well and happy, with a new family of your own, made me sad. And a little angry I suppose. But that was an unhappy time in my life, really. I thought that somehow, seeing you would provide me with some grand answer to everything."

"I feel terrible, leaving you in the lurch like that."

"Don't. Really. In the end, it was probably the best thing you could have done, not showing up."

"Abandoning you for the second time," added Edith. "I fully intended to come, Arthur, not that that matters much to your side of things. Got myself to the train station and everything; bought the ticket. But then when the train pulled in, I panicked. I couldn't get on. I was scared."

"I waited for hours," confessed Arthur. "Staring out the window of the coffee shop for whom, I didn't know. Every woman that walked in, I would brace myself." He laughed unconvincingly. "It was like that children's book, where the baby bird goes around asking pigs and cows if they're his mother. Do you know that book?" Edith shook her head. She didn't. "Doesn't matter. In the end, it all came out in the wash." He shrugged his shoulders, a gesture that reminded her exactly of Liza.

"I'm so sorry about Liza," he said suddenly, reading her mind.

"Liza?" Edith asked, surprised.

"Yes, your daughter. I read about her death in the *New York Times.*"

"Oh. Yes. Thank you. You were a fan of her work?"

"Well, yes, she was a wonderful writer." Arthur gave her an apologetic half-grin. "But Liza and I—we were friends."

"I'm sorry, what?" she asked, sure that she had heard wrong.

"We were friends," he repeated. "We lost touch sadly, but

we were close for a good twenty-year run or so. She was an incredible person." Edith folded her arms in front of her chest, shielding herself against the shock of his words.

"I debated about whether or not I should tell you today, but I thought it might be nice for you to know." He paused, taking in Edith's stature. "Or not."

"Liza Brennan? My Liza?"

"Yes. Your Liza. I broached the topic of her telling you many times, but she always refused. Said she didn't want to upset you. Said that if you'd gone to the trouble of keeping me a secret for her entire life, why not just keep up the charade? She was adamant about the fact that my birth was part of your journey, and that since you had always respected hers, she would respect yours."

"She said that?"

"Word for word."

"She said that I respected her journey? What does that even mean?" asked Edith, wrinkling her nose at what she considered new age jargon crap.

"Who she was, I guess?" answered Arthur. Edith considered his interpretation.

"I always thought that I was too pushy with Liza, too intrusive with my opinions."

"It seems you must have let her be on some level," said Arthur.

Edith unfolded her arms, thinking. It was true that she had never discouraged her daughter from being herself. When she hadn't wanted to play with dolls, Edith had bought her

Lincoln Logs. When Liza had refused to wear a dress, Edith had sewed her pants because there were no suitable ones for little girls in the stores. And of course, there was the typewriter. Even Liza's trips into the city on the weekends as a teenager Edith had supported, arguing passionately with John on her daughter's behalf. "She's an artist, she needs the city," she had explained, and eventually he had caved.

A great sense of relief washed over Edith, causing her to catch her breath. She had done many things wrong, as a mother, but she had also done a thing or two right. And Liza had been grateful. The proof was here, in Arthur's living room.

"Are you okay?" asked Arthur. "I'm sorry if I've upset you, Edith. My wife told me to keep my mouth shut, asked what the point was, but I felt like you should know."

"No, I'm okay. Shocked, but okay. Can you tell me more about the two of you? How did you even meet in the first place?"

"After that afternoon—"

"When I stood you up?"

"Yes, that one. After that afternoon, I fought and fought the urge to call you the next day, to give you a piece of my mind, until finally I gave in. I called, and it rang and rang until finally, someone picked up."

"Liza."

"Indeed. I almost hung up, but Liza being Liza—she asked me who I was; why I was calling." Edith had never gotten many phone calls of her own; she could understand Liza's curiosity.

"I didn't tell her right away, but something about her voice, I don't know, she reeled me in."

"She was like that," Edith agreed. "Made you feel like the only person in the world, when she was at her best."

"Exactly. Even as a teenager. Beyond her years. We ended up meeting for coffee in the city, and before I knew it I was spilling my guts to her. Completely inappropriate, I know."

"Yes, she loved the city. Even as a tiny girl, when we would take day trips in as a family." Arthur nodded.

"When she was there for college, I was working. We would meet all of the time. I adored her. Eventually, our friendship trumped my need to meet you." Edith made a face.

"Not in a nasty way, Edith. More in the sense that I had gotten to know this fantastic extension of you—my half-sister, whatever you want to call it—and that was enough."

"What kind of person did you think Liza was?" Edith asked.

"An eccentric, funny, wonderful one. She had a wisdom about the world that was beyond her years. But there was a certain sadness to her, as well, in the way she saw the world. She was quite lonely, I think. Relationships, hetero ones anyway, seemed to baffle her."

"Did she tell you she was gay?" Edith asked.

"Not outright."

"The same with me," said Edith. "She never told me herself, never talked about it with me. But then, I never asked."

"I only knew because she brought a date to my wedding. Didn't call her a date, but I knew."

"She was at your wedding?"

"She was. And she brought a woman, although of course I can't remember her name. She seemed so happy with her. Vulnerable in a way I had never seen her before. She presented such a tough façade, you know."

"Yes, I know," said Edith, thinking of herself.

"But after that, we lost touch," Arthur continued. "I had moved here to settle down; she was still in the city, just beginning her writing career. Our lives became too different, I think. But I thought of her often. Thought of calling you when I read about her death—coming full circle—but couldn't get up the nerve. And then, your email arrived. It was such a nice surprise."

"Were you alike?"

"Liza and I?" Arthur asked. "In some ways, yes. In other ways, no. In most ways no, actually. Her emotional range—it was something."

"That's one way of putting it," agreed Edith. "She wasn't well, you know."

"I know." He shrugged. "Although, I have to say that I mostly saw her when she was up. That was when she was at her most social."

"No one could work a room like Liza," said Edith.

"Did she get that from you?" asked Arthur.

"Me? God no. Socializing has never been my forte. Too shy. And cynical. And judgmental, I suppose. I was better at it when I was young of course, but what wasn't I better at when I was young?"

"Touché," agreed Arthur.

"Did you worry about her at all, Arthur?"

"Of course. She was so fragile, underneath that tough exterior. But every time I tried to help, she pushed me away."

"You know, she killed herself."

"No. Oh no." Arthur lowered his gaze to the floor. "That's terrible, Edith. I'm so sorry."

"Is that what you mean by fragile?" Edith asked. "Did you think that was something that could happen to her?"

"I suppose. In the back of my mind. Is that a terrible thing to admit? It feels like a terrible thing to admit."

"I don't know." Edith set her drink on a coaster. "I wish she would have told me that she was feeling so desperate." Edith shook her head. "What an idiot I was."

"No Edith, you can't blame yourself."

"But I do, in a lot of ways. For the mother I was, and wasn't. Maybe things would have turned out differently for her if I had been another kind of person altogether. Maternal and nurturing instead of—instead of me." To her great embarrassment, tears began to well in her eyes. "There was too much of a separation between us, and that was my fault. If I had been more vocal and less territorial, maybe she would have felt the freedom to open up, too. About you, about being a lesbian, about feeling so alone that death was the only viable option." She began to sob. Arthur got up from the couch and crossed to her, kneeling at her side.

"Look at me, blubbering away!" Edith wiped her eyes. "Today was supposed to be about you, for God's sake. This is ridiculous." He patted her knee.

"Edith, you did the best you could. Unfortunately, we can't change who we are just because we're parents."

Edith wiped her eyes, trying to compose herself. "I wish I could have seen you and Liza together," she said.

"I do have one photo," said Arthur. "From my wedding."

"You do?"

"Here, let me see if I can find it in our album." He stood up. "Of course, I have no idea where it is, but my wife will. Sheila?" he called. She popped her highlighted head around the corner, looking very much like one of the sunflowers in the vase on the table in front of her, Edith thought. Her face was perfectly round.

"Yes?" she answered.

"Do you by any chance know where our wedding album is? I wanted to show Edith a photo."

"Not of—?" Sheila asked, the rest of her body snaking out from around the other side of the wall as she joined them.

"Yes, of Liza," Arthur answered. "I told her."

"Good lord, Arthur." Edith examined the rug. She didn't want to get involved.

"Sheila, honestly. She's okay. She wanted to know."

"Arthur, really." Sheila sighed heavily. "Fine, I'll go get it." Arthur sat back down on the couch with a forced smile.

"You are okay with this, right, Edith? It hasn't been too much today, meeting me and then this news?"

"I may be old, but I'm not dead yet. Bombshells are good for me. Keeps the blood flowing," said Edith, not sure if that was entirely true.

She felt a little dizzy. She wanted to believe it so badly, on this, a good day. A day where she knew who she and Arthur were; a day when she could look at a photo of her daughter and know who she was, too. The urgency not to take a day like this for granted weighed on her heavily, even as she was grateful for it.

"Do you mind me asking what my father was like?" asked Arthur, no doubt feeling the urgency, as well, Edith realized.

"His name was Anthony Clark," she volunteered. "Handsome, mysterious, confident. He was from Cincinnati, only visiting for the summer."

"A stud?" asked Arthur, a smile playing across his lips.

"Yes," said Edith. "A stud. We dated for a month or two and then, well—"

"Me," finished Arthur.

"Yes, but by the time I knew you existed, he was long gone."

"He never knew?" asked Arthur.

"No. There was no point. We barely knew one another." She paused. "And it's a good thing, too, because he was Catholic. Only reason I know is because he wore a silver cross around his neck. God forbid, his parents may have made us get married."

"He was Catholic?" Arthur gestured towards the mantel, towards a photo of his family in which he and his son were wearing yarmulkes. "I'm Jewish."

"Me, too," said Edith. "Technically, anyway."

"L'chaim," offered Arthur.

Edith smiled, feeling a little better now; less like her head was a balloon floating away from her body.

"Here we are," announced Sheila, returning with a very large white square tucked under her arm. She slid it onto the table.

"Edith, I just want to thank you for coming here today," she said. "It means so much to Arthur."

"Oh, you're welcome," replied Edith. "It means a great deal to me, too." Sheila left the room. Edith and Arthur stared at the album as though they expected it to open itself.

"Ah okay, here we go. I'll just find it for us." Arthur picked it up. His hands were long and slim, his fingers tapered.

Just like mine, Edith thought, feeling woozy again.

"Here we are," he said, sliding the open book across the table to Edith. She lost her grasp as she picked it up with her right hand, forgetting that it was weak. The album fell to the floor with a thud.

"Oh God, I'm such a klutz!" she cried out. "I'm so sorry."

"It's no problem, Edith. This album has been around for thirty-eight years and withstood the grubby paws of two kids. It can certainly handle a little tumble." He knelt to retrieve it and placed it, open to the photo he had spoken of, directly in Edith's lap.

The balloon feeling was back. She took a deep breath and looked down, right into Liza's smiling eyes. Her heart, it swelled in her chest like it was being inflated by a bike pump. She missed her so much.

She was so young here, in this picture. Totally unaware of what would be. Her daughter. She was beautiful, Edith thought. Beautiful in her complexity. The introvert and the extrovert fighting each other always, mired in the darkness that lurked at her core. Edith brought the album closer to her face, to get a better look. Freckles spread across the bridge of Liza's nose like stardust.

Next to her, to Edith's disbelief even as she sat in his living room having just learned of their friendship, was Arthur. Her son. Her daughter and her son. Together without her ever having been the wiser.

In the photo, his arm was around Liza, his hand squeezing her shoulder. They looked alike, Edith realized. The eyes. Her eyes. A young Arthur beamed at the camera, seeming to be caught mid-laugh. They both looked so happy. Without her.

She was mad suddenly. Mad at Liza for keeping this from her. Ultimately, it would have brought Edith joy, their friendship, even if she balked at it initially. The journey business was a load of horseshit. Liza had wanted to have one up on Edith; emotional artillery in her arsenal for her next novel, the one she would write when Edith was dead and gone.

"Lovely," said Edith, closing it with a resounding thwack. It was mean and calculating of Liza, that's what it was. Her choice to keep Arthur a secret had nothing to do with respect, she was sure of it suddenly.

Outside, Vinnie pulled into the driveway. Edith watched through the window as the back door of the car opened and Lucy tumbled out, her face smeared with ketchup. She skipped across the yard, with Maggie and Esther trailing close behind.

"My ride is here," said Edith.

"Edith, would you like to have the photo?" Arthur asked.

"Oh no, I couldn't, it's part of your wedding album."

"No, really, have it." He pulled the plastic back and peeled it from its place. "Here." Edith took it.

"You're sure?" she asked.

"Positive."

"Thank you," she said, looking down at it again.

"Can we stay in touch?" asked Arthur. "Meet again? I can come out to Sag Harbor next time."

"Sure," replied Edith. For all she knew, she'd forget about this morning in a week; forget that she had met him at all; forget the roller coaster of emotions she had just ridden. At the stoop, Maggie lifted Lucy up to ring the doorbell.

"Arthur, there's a chance, you know, that the next time you contact me I won't remember who you are. Or that we even met today, for that matter," said Edith quickly as Sheila answered the door, ushering in the chaos.

"I know, Edith," said Arthur.

"I want you to know that I think you're a kind, very decent man," she continued, truly meaning it. None of this was his fault. "I'm grateful, too, that you let me back in, back here to meet you. You didn't have to do that."

"Edith, it was as much for me as it was for you."

"You have a lovely home and a lovely wife and family. And even though I have no right to be, I'm proud of you."

"Edif!" yelled Lucy. "I got French fries!"

"Thank you, Edith," said Arthur. Edith smiled at him before turning to Lucy, a lump in her throat.

"Lucy, you lucky duck!" she replied.

"Are we ready?" asked Maggie. "Everything okay?"

"Yes, fine," said Edith. "We had a nice time. Thank you, Arthur," she said. "And Sheila."

"Our pleasure." Sheila reached out to pull Edith into an awkward hug.

"What a beautiful home you have," said Esther appreciatively. "Very clean. Maggie, isn't it clean?"

"Yes, very."

Edith slid the photo into her purse and made her way out.

"Look at this!" demanded Edith, shoving the photo into Esther's hand once they were back on the highway and Lucy had fallen asleep.

"Is that Liza?" Esther asked, squinting. "I don't have my glasses."

"Maggie!" yelled Edith.

"Yes?" She turned from the window, startled by the shrillness of Edith's tone.

"Look at this photo." Edith snatched it from Esther and handed it to her.

"Oh wow, it's Liza," said Maggie, staring at it. "Who's she with?"

"What do you mean, who is she with? That's Arthur!"

"Edith, please, could you keep your voice down? I don't want Lucy to wake up," said Maggie before she could process the news. "Wait, what?"

"That's Liza at Arthur's wedding," explained Edith.

"Edith, what are you talking about, Liza at Arthur's wedding?" asked Esther, shooting a look of alarm at Maggie.

"Find your damn glasses in that suitcase of a bag and have a look, Esther. See for yourself. They were friends, can you believe it?"

"Who were friends?" Esther pulled her glasses case out of the bag and fumbled to get them on as quickly as she could.

"Liza and Arthur!" said Edith. "Maggie, show her."

"Holy cow, would you look at that?" said Esther, holding the photo just inches from her bespectacled gaze. "Edith, I don't believe it."

"Neither did I, let me tell you," said Edith, satisfied to have impressed her point at last.

"But how?" asked Maggie. "How did they even meet in the first place?"

"Exactly what I asked," said Edith. "After I stood him up, he called the house, looking for me. Liza being Liza—well, she befriended him."

"I don't believe it," Esther repeated. "This had been going on for how long?"

"Twenty-something years, apparently," answered Edith.

"So let me get this straight," said Maggie. "Somehow Liza got Arthur to tell her about you? And then they became friends, and she never told you that she had met him?"

"Never so much as alluded to the fact," confirmed Edith. Oh, she was mad. So mad, just thinking about it.

"But why?" asked Esther.

"Arthur fed me some crap about her respecting my secret,

about not wanting to upset me, but I know better. She wanted to one-up me. It was payback." Edith's whole body began to tremble, her voice, too. Esther reached around her, attempting to quell the vibration of Edith's frustration with a hug.

"No, don't, Esther. I don't want to be touched."

"Edith?" asked Maggie.

"What?"

"Why do you think that's the case?"

"What do you mean, why? She was getting back at me, for being a bad mother." Saying those words out loud, admitting that her worst fear had been realized, made it hard for Edith to catch her breath. She bent over, struggling for air. Esther pounded on the partition, signaling to Vinnie.

"Vinnie, do we have a paper bag in here? Anything?"

"There should be one in the first aid kit, next to the cooler," he called over his shoulder.

Maggie unlatched her belt and grabbed the kit, releasing its clasp with trembling hands of her own. A shower of Band-Aids rained down upon her lap as she pulled it out.

"Mommy, is Edif okay?" asked Lucy, concerned.

"Yes, she's fine. Just tired. Go back to the iPad, honey."

"Okay," Lucy agreed, easily transfixed by its colorful screen.

"Here it is. Edith, take this. Breathe into this," Maggie commanded her, kneeling on the floor in front of her in the limo. "That's right, in and out." Edith complied, the bag inflating and deflating as she composed herself.

"Here Edith, have some water," said Esther, when she sat

back up, as pale as a ghost. She lifted the small plastic bottle to Edith's mouth.

"Thank you," whispered Edith, after she had taken a grateful sip.

"Edith, are you okay?" asked Maggie.

"I'm beside myself," she answered quietly. "Completely beside myself."

"Can I ask you something?" said Maggie.

"Yes."

"Why are you choosing to believe the worst?"

"What do you mean? It's as plain as day," answered Edith, getting worked up again.

"Maggie, really, maybe we should just let this go for now," warned Esther.

"No, I don't want to let this go, Esther," said Edith. "I can't let anything go anymore, not when so much is at stake. Go on, Maggie, say what you want to say."

"I don't think you were a bad mother, Edith. And I know that Liza didn't, either. The idea that she would want to one-up you, it's not based in reality."

"How do you know that? Liza told you that I was a good mother?"

"Not in so many words, no," answered Maggie.

Edith shook her head. "You see?" she said. "So it is reality."

"She didn't have to is what I'm saying, Edith. The proof was in the way she loved you. She took you in, didn't she? When you needed help? And here she had this piece of your history, obviously a very painful and complicated piece, but she respected the boundary that you yourself had set up. That's not the way a daughter who's been let down by her mother behaves. I don't know so much about love, but it sure sounds like that to me."

"I agree," said Esther. "This business about Liza wanting to have one over on you, that's not the relationship you had. You had your issues, sure, every parent and child does, but the love you shared was real. There was no mother prouder of her daughter. No mother that believed in her daughter more. Liza knew that, I'm sure of it." Edith looked down into her lap, the kindness of their words like a salve.

"But she kept so much from me. She was afraid of me, of my judgments."

"I don't think so," said Maggie. "You kept so much from her, too, after all. Were you afraid of Liza?"

"No."

"So why then?" asked Maggie.

"I wanted something for myself," said Edith. "A piece of myself that belonged only to me."

"Maybe she felt that way about her sexuality," said Esther. "Maybe she was more like you than you ever imagined."

"Maybe, Edith, it had nothing to do with you," continued Maggie. "Just like Arthur. It had nothing to do with Liza. She understood that. And what's more, she kept it out of her writing, too. She didn't do that with me, or with her father, but with you, it was different. It was a respect that transcended everything else."

"She loved you the most, don't you see?" asked Esther.

"Then why did she leave me?" asked Edith. She hadn't realized she was crying, but her face was wet. Esther handed her a tissue but she waved it away.

"She was sick," said Maggie. "There's nothing you could have done to fix that."

"I miss her," Edith sobbed. "I wish she had held on. There was so much left to say. So much left to do."

"I know," said Maggie, leaning forward to pull Edith close.

CHAPTER 21

Lucy, let's go," urged Maggie. Lucy faced her defiantly, naked from the waist down and sucking the last remnants from a juice box, its empty insides groaning in protest.

"No!" she yelled back.

"Lucy, I know you have to go, honey. Let's try the potty."

"No!" she yelled again, dropping the juice box on the floor and running into the kitchen.

Maggie put her weary head in her hands, praying for patience. It wasn't even yet noon, and she wished the day was over already. It had begun with Edith insisting on going for a walk by herself, sans shoes, in fifty-degree weather. The amount of cajoling it had taken to get her back into the house had drained her completely. Potty training on top of it—it was too much.

In the kitchen, Lucy calmly went about reorganizing the Tupperware cabinet as a steady stream of urine puddled on the wood floor beneath her. Maggie sighed heavily. Her phone skittered across the counter, propelled by a vibrating ring. Grabbing some paper towels, Maggie answered it, not bothering to check who was calling.

"Hello?" She swabbed the floor as she answered.

"Maggie?" That voice. She sat back on her heels. "Hello?"

"Lyle," she replied, her mouth as dry as the Sahara. Lucy sorted through myriad plastic tops like a twenty-something at a sample sale.

"Hello." He cleared his throat. "How are you?"

"Fine. Just fine." Lucy looked up, concerned by the tone of Maggie's voice.

"It's okay, honey, here," said Maggie, handing her a red lid that had rolled out of her grasp. "I'm just going to stand over here by the window, okay?"

"Is that her?"

"Lyle, why are you whispering?"

"Shit, I don't know, Maggie. What do you expect me to do? This is weird as hell for me."

"I take it you got my email."

"Yes, I got your email," he hissed. "Great way to tell somebody they're a father after the fact, by the way. I hope it wasn't too much of a strain, typing out all of those words, Maggie. Why not just text an emoji?"

"Alright Lyle, take it easy. The fact of the matter is that I could have gone her whole life not having told you at all."

"Oh, that's rich, Maggie. Great example to set."

"Listen Lyle, what do you want to do? I told you for Lucy's sake. Whatever you decide is up to you."

"So if I opt out and you tell her she has a deadbeat dad, it's the truth? You've backed me into a corner here, Maggie, and you know it."

"You know what? I'll just tell her you're dead. That's how I prefer to think of you, anyway."

"Come on, Maggie, I don't deserve that." He sighed loudly. "Sorry to be nasty. I'm just out of sorts. Which I'm sure you can understand. I mean, come on, Maggie."

"I get it. Honestly Lyle, if you opt out, my life will be easier. Like I said, this is about Lucy. I'm just giving you the option." Lyle's sigh rumbled through the phone's speaker like a gust of wind.

"What's she like?"

"She's terrific. Funny, smart, sweet, intuitive, beautiful. Strong-willed. Everything I want to be when I grow up."

"You sure she's mine?"

"Lyle."

"What? I'm kidding. Sort of."

"She's yours. She looks just like you."

"She does? Shit, no kidding." He sighed again. "As luck would have it, I'm in New York in two weeks for work. Maybe I could drive out and meet her? Where'd you say you were again? Sag Harbor?"

"Yes, Sag Harbor." Maggie felt nauseous. Where there had been two, now there would be three. Lucy would no longer be just hers, no matter what he decided. She walked over to the dining room table and sat down. "And yes, that would be fine," she continued.

"Okay. Okay, cool. But I'll just meet her as like, a friend, right?"

"What do you mean?"

"I mean, you won't tell her that I'm her dad or anything, will you?"

"Jesus Lyle, she's two and a half."

"So just a friend?"

"Of course just a friend. You have to be all-in—and I mean all-in—if you want her to know."

"Of course. Although what does all-in mean? Joint custody or something?"

"Oh God, no. Let's not get carried away, Lyle."

"Right," agreed Lyle. "Okay. One step at a time. I'll send you an email to coordinate everything."

"Okay."

"Okay," repeated Lyle. "Well, I guess that's it for now."

"I guess so."

"Okay. Bye."

"Bye."

Maggie hung up and put her head on the table. She wanted to cry, but exhaustion and uncertainty had scooped out her insides. A small and very warm hand grasped her leg.

"Mommy?" Maggie lifted her head and peeked out at Lucy, who was regarding her solemnly. She reached over to smooth her curls.

"Yes, honey?" What an angel, making sure that she was

okay. Wise beyond her years. They would weather this paternal storm together. Of course they would.

"I pooped my pants," she announced.

MAGGIE OPENED HER eyes, confused. Somehow, she had fallen asleep on the couch after putting Lucy down for her nap. A miracle, really, since her head had been churning since her conversation with Lyle. She guessed it had exhausted her, all of the catastrophizing she'd been doing since they spoke. She'd convinced herself that Lyle would fall in love with Lucy and demand joint custody; they'd have to go to court; she'd never win because of the judge's own mother issues; they'd wind up broke and homeless, Edith included. And all because she had to do "the right thing." Screw the right thing.

She looked at the clock. Not only was she unprepared for her daily meeting with Edith, but Edith was late, too. She was never late. Maggie stood up, feeling a shift of uncertainty in the pit of her stomach. Something was awry, she could feel it.

She went down the stairs, to Edith's room. The door was wide open, the bed empty and unmade. Shit, thought Maggie. Shit, shit, shit. She crossed the room to Edith's bathroom, fighting the image of her sprawled on the floor, her head bleeding from the impact, but Edith wasn't there, either. A deeper feeling of dread formed, coursing through Maggie's veins like blood.

She jogged to her own bedroom. Empty, too. Out through the sliding doors and to the guesthouse she went, hoping with every fiber of her being that she would find her there. Nothing. She ran to the pool, but its surface was as still as glass save for the leaves floating aimlessly through it. And the air, it was eerily silent.

She ran back to the house and into Lucy's bedroom. No Lucy. Panic set in. Maggie flew to the front door, scrambling into her flip-flops. What should she do? Where should she go? She ran to the car, her keys shaking in her hands like wind chimes.

Behind the wheel, her mind raced. They couldn't have gone far. She would find them, cajole Edith back into the car and escort them safely home. She knew Edith would be belligerent, that she could count on, but Maggie wouldn't yell. It was best to remain calm during an episode, she had read. But it was going to be so hard not to wring her neck, Maggie thought. So, so hard. She had taken Lucy. Her baby.

Slowly, she drove towards the beach, her eyes peeled for that crisp white bob and the orange stroller. Nothing, The street was empty. She screeched into the beach parking lot. Maggie was not religious, but she found herself praying. "Please God, let them be here," she whispered. She got out of the car, barely remembering to turn it off before she did so, and ran through the sand. Up ahead, she saw them. Her stomach seized. She ran.

"Edith!" she cried out. "Edith!"

She turned around, not looking like herself at all. Her hair stuck out from her head in tufts, and her shirt was misbuttoned, lopsided against her. Calm, Maggie reminded herself.

"Who are you?" Edith demanded, as Maggie jogged towards her.

"It's me, Maggie," she said, pushing past her to the front of the stroller. Inside, Lucy slept, a blanket arranged carefully around her. Maggie exhaled.

"What are you doing?" shrieked Edith, her eyes lifeless as marbles. "That's my baby. What are you doing?"

"Edith, I'm Maggie. And that's my daughter, Lucy. We live with you. Now, let's go home."

"It most certainly is not your baby! This is my Liza." Edith pushed the stroller through the wet sand, away from Maggie.

"Edith, come with me." She reached out to grab her arm.

"Get your hands off me!" screamed Edith, waking up Lucy. Lucy looked up at Maggie, confused.

"Mama?" she asked, still half-asleep.

Maggie had no idea what to do. To argue with Edith in her current state would be a losing battle, that was becoming clear. Playing along seemed like the easiest solution.

"Your baby is beautiful, Edith," she forced herself to say. "But it's cold out. Shouldn't we get her home? We don't want her to catch a cold, do we?"

"She has a blanket," said Edith. "She's fine. Now get away from us or I'll scream. I'll really scream!" She resumed her pushing, but now Lucy was fighting against the straps of her seat.

"Mama!" she yelled.

"Edith," Maggie pleaded, getting desperate now. "Edith, you have to let me take you home. Liza is hungry and you don't have any snacks."

"She doesn't need a snack!"

"I'm hungry!" Lucy cried out in defiance. "I do need a snack! I do! Edif! Let me go!"

"I didn't bring any with me," admitted Edith, her resolve loosening a bit as uncertainty finally, blessedly, crept in.

"It's okay, we'll just get in the car and go home. Plenty of snacks there." Lucy began to whimper. "Looks like it's going to rain, too," said Maggie. A cluster of gray, pillow-like clouds had gathered in the sky, covering the sun almost entirely. "You don't want Liza to get wet, do you?"

"You leave us alone or I'm going to call the police!" screamed Edith.

"That's it," mumbled Maggie angrily. "I can't do this anymore, Edith, I just can't. Sorry, I give up." She began to unlatch Lucy.

"What are you doing? Police! Police!" screamed Edith. She tried to pull Lucy from Maggie's arms.

"Edith, get off!" Maggie yelled, swatting at her spindly arms.

"Hey, hey," said a male voice Maggie recognized. Sam.

Maggie turned to him, with Lucy wrapped around her front and Edith at her back, as grateful as she had ever been. "Help," she said as quietly as she could. Sam's eyes darted from her to Lucy to Edith.

"Are you the police?" Edith asked, marching right up to him.

"Yes, I'm the police. I'm a policeman." Sam looked down at his T-shirt and running shorts; his sneakers. "What seems to be the problem here, miss?"

"This woman is taking my child!" Edith declared. "Arrest her."

"Your child?" he asked.

"Yes," replied Edith, although not as confidently as before.

"Are you sure?" Sam asked kindly. "This little girl is yours?" Edith looked from him to Lucy, who was clutching Maggie tightly.

"Isn't she?" asked Edith.

"I don't think so, Edith," said Sam, siphoning the fight out of her with the patient register of his voice. "I think this is Lucy, Maggie's daughter."

"She is?" Edith's voice was small. Sam nodded. "Can you take me home?" she asked suddenly, surrendering. The rain was coming faster; cold, fat drops splattering on the sand.

"Sure, I can do that." He took her arm.

"Thank you," Maggie mouthed, meaning it more than she ever had in her life. With her free hand, she grabbed the stroller. Pushing it through the rain and wet sand while holding Lucy was impossible. Instead, she dragged it behind her.

"Baby, are you okay?" she murmured into Lucy's ear. "I know that was scary."

"Mommy, why Edif so mad?" asked Lucy. "Why?"

"She's not mad, honey. She doesn't feel well, in her head."

"In her head?" asked Lucy.

How could she explain Alzheimer's to a toddler? Maggie wondered. How could she tell Lucy not to go anywhere alone with Edith, ever?

"Yes, in her head," she replied. She would worry about

that later. Now, she had to get them into the car and home, and Edith into bed. That was all she wanted in the world.

"WOW," SAID SAM, sitting next to Maggie on the couch. Once they had gotten Edith in the car, she had become mute in her exhaustion, falling asleep on the way home. Sam had carried her in, somehow, and together they had put her to bed as a stunned Lucy looked on.

A warm bath and snack for Lucy later, she was napping, too. Outside, the rain continued to fall.

"No kidding," said Maggie, as exhausted as she had ever been. Still in her wet clothes, she had wrapped herself in a blanket. "Sam, I don't know what I would have done without you today. I can't thank you enough."

"You're welcome," he replied, taking a sip of the tea she had made him. "I'm glad I was there."

"I completely lost it," said Maggie. "Like, lost it. Literally on the verge of a fist fight with an eighty-two-year-old woman with Alzheimer's." She covered her face with the blanket and drew her knees to her chest. "I tried, you know. I tried to be patient, I really did. I even played along with her, pretending that Lucy was Liza. But when Lucy started to panic, I just couldn't." Maggie sighed deeply. "I have to get better at this."

"Better at what?" asked Sam. "How patient can you be when somebody takes your kid hostage and is showing no signs of surrender? Come on, now."

"How did you just appear?" she asked him.

"I was out on a run," he said, shrugging. "Total coincidence."

"More like magic. What do I do when Edith wakes up?" asked Maggie. "What if she's still in it?"

"You think she will be?"

"I don't know. In the past, she goes to sleep and when she wakes up, it's like it never happened. She has no recollection."

"So it will probably be like that," said Sam.

"But what if it's not? I mean, eventually, if not today, this confusion is going to be Edith's permanent state. There will be no waking up."

"Can you call in some help? Get a nurse? You're going to have to, you know. Liza provided for that, didn't she?"

"She did. But I can't help feeling like I should be able to handle this on my own."

"No way, Maggie. You need licensed help. This disease is bigger than both of you. I'll stay with you today, until she wakes up." He looked down at his sweaty, wet clothes. "Or at least go home to shower and change and come back."

"You don't have to do that," said Maggie.

"I know I don't have to. I want to."

"I'm sorry about the other night," said Maggie. "That was so weird of me."

"It wasn't that weird," said Sam. "Disappointing for me maybe, but not weird."

"I really am attracted to you, Sam. I just, I'm so in my head lately. Everything is like this long, overwrought chain of past, present and future. The memories and my writing, and Edith and Liza and Lucy's father and my own parents—it's all swirling in there constantly. My libido doesn't stand a chance, I guess."

"It's okay, Maggie. Probably better that we stay in the friend zone now anyway. I have a tendency to rush into things; destroy potential with my own overthinking before I even get started."

"You do?"

"Let's just see what happens, okay?"

"Just like that? You're that easy?" asked Maggie.

"Sort of, yes."

Maggie pulled her hand out from under the blanket to grasp his. Outside, the rain continued to fall.

CHAPTER 22

"One leg at a time, not both, Lucy," instructed Maggie as she helped her shimmy into a pair of leggings that were clearly too small. Either her daughter had a growth spurt every two weeks or vanity sizing started early.

"Where we going?"

"Nowhere. Someone is coming here. To meet you."

"Who?"

"His name is Lyle."

Why she had told him about Lucy, she had no idea at this moment, a mere hour before he was due to arrive. What was a little white lie to Lucy? Dead, alive, donor sperm, whatever—he was bound to be a shitty dad. She should have saved her the heartache.

Sam disagreed with her—he thought she had done the right thing. Edith, too. Esther was on the fence.

"If it ain't broke, why fix it?" Esther had said.

"Lyle," Lucy repeated now. "He nice?"

"Yes, he's nice."

"Okay. I'm hungry. Let's eat." She took Maggie's hand. "Come on, Mommy."

At the kitchen table, Edith sat with Gloria, the nurse Maggie had hired part-time, shuffling cards. Nothing like the beach incident had happened in the two weeks since, but Edith was forgetting things more and more. Just that morning, Maggie had found her hairbrush in the freezer.

Edith had not reacted well to the news of the hire, as expected, but Maggie had explained that it was just a precaution; just in case.

"You took Lucy to the beach without me," she had told her. "You thought she was Liza."

"No, that didn't happen," Edith had said initially, but when Maggie's eyes didn't waver from her own, she had stopped talking; a silent concession.

Gloria was kind, solid and dependable. For now, she blended into the background, but Maggie knew that when the time came, she would rise to the occasion, ushering Edith out of her agitation with the experience and patience Maggie didn't have. It reassured Maggie, knowing she was there.

"Good morning, Edif!" Lucy shouted. She had forgiven Edith easily for her transgression. "What you doing?" She climbed up into a chair to survey her spread keenly. "Cards?"

"They make a great noise. Have a listen," said Edith. Lucy turned her head, placing her ear almost directly on top of the deck. "Move up just a little, Lucy. Okay, that's good."

"Cool!" Lucy exclaimed. "Sounds like a train."

"A train! How interesting. Let's do it again."

Maggie turned to face the refrigerator, grateful that Edith was lucid and helpful today. She had considered asking Gloria to shuttle her off somewhere for the visit, but decided against it. Having support nearby, even it wasn't quite reliable, felt necessary. It was a change for Maggie, asking for help, but it didn't make her feel weak, as she once had feared. She felt stronger instead—safe in a way she had never felt before. Like she was part of a family.

"Maggie, you've done the right thing here—now it's up to him," Sam had said to her the night before. They had driven to the beach after dinner, and were watching the moonlit waves crash on the shore from the comfort of his car.

"But how do you know it was the right thing to do?"

"Maggie, it's Ethics 101," he explained, taking her hand in his.

"But maybe I could have waited? Until she was eighteen or something?"

"You know, he could opt out altogether, making all of your worrying for naught. But I think if you had waited for eighteen, you would have regretted it. Hell hath no fury like a teenage girl scorned."

Downstairs, the doorbell rang. Maggie looked up, her eyes wide.

"Who's here?" demanded Lucy. "Is that Lyle?" Before Maggie could stop her, she was out of her chair and down the stairs.

"I can't open it!" she whined, struggling with the knob as Maggie rushed up behind her.

"Let me help you." Maggie turned it, pulling it back to reveal Esther.

"Mea culpa," Esther pleaded. "I know, I know, I wasn't invited, but I couldn't let you do this by yourself. And with Edith, who knows? Sure, she's fine now but in a half hour she could be wearing her underwear on her head." Maggie gave her a look. "What? It's true. And look, I brought donuts!" She held up the giant bag as a peace offering.

"Donuts!" Lucy exclaimed.

"Come in," Maggie offered, glad to see her as she opened the door. Esther was her family, too. Of course she should be here.

"Oh, thank you, Maggie. I promise I'll be good. I can't be the only one not to see him, for God's sake. My head would explode."

"Literally," added Maggie. "It would literally explode."

"Come on!" Lucy shrieked, trying to grab the bag. "Donuts!"

"This one is turning into quite the diva. You're gonna have your hands full with her."

"Like I don't already?"

"Hello?" Maggie froze, the only one to hear the soft greeting, as Esther and Lucy continued up the stairs. Collecting herself, she turned around.

"Hello Lyle."

In his too small plaid flannel and gray skinny jeans, with his blond stubble intact and curly hair pulled back from his face, he looked exactly the same. Skinnier maybe, but the same. And so much like Lucy that it took Maggie's breath away.

"Hi Maggie. Nice place."

"Thanks." She stared at him for a moment more. "Oh God, sorry. Come in." She opened the door and he walked past her, the smell of cigarettes pungent. All of that fuss about organic, locally sourced and grass-fed this and that and the guy still smoked. That was Lyle in a nutshell.

"So," he said, facing her. "I'm crazy nervous. Almost didn't come."

"Me, too," admitted Maggie. "I've pretty much convinced myself that this was all a huge mistake."

"It wasn't. I mean, I don't think it was. I'm glad to know. And meet her."

"Good. Okay, well, shall we?"

What if Lyle and I had never met? Maggie found herself thinking as she led the way up the stairs. What if she had funneled all of the energy she had wasted trying to convince him to care about her into someone who actually did? What if Lucy wasn't Lucy at all, but some alternative version of herself, produced with a partner who was actually present? No, despite all of the struggles, Maggie had no regrets. She was proud of her imperfect journey; proud to find herself in this moment.

"Hello there," greeted Esther. She waved her donut at them, powdering herself with sugar in the process.

"Hello. I'm Lyle."

"I'm Esther, and this is Edith and Gloria." Edith nodded curtly. "We're her bodyguards."

Lyle laughed nervously. Lucy approached him like a cat, weaving in and out from behind the furniture stealthily until she had reached Maggie's leg. Safe, she hid behind it, peeking out to examine their guest.

"And this is Lucy," said Maggie. Lyle looked down at her, registering her sameness. Maggie felt a stab of jealousy. It wasn't fair.

"Hi Lucy," he said quietly.

"Hello," she replied. "I'm almost free."

"Three? Cool. I'm forty-one."

"Forty-one! Yuck!"

"Yeah, I know." Lucy regarded him curiously. What Maggie would have given to be able to read her mind.

"Do you want to come see my Legos?"

"Sure, that sounds good." He looked to Maggie for her approval.

"Of course! Check them out," she said, trying her best to sound upbeat. She had hoped that the visit wouldn't go so well—that Lucy would have clung to her out of loyalty, somehow sensing him as a threat.

"Bye Mommy," said Lucy, tugging him down the stairs.

So much for that.

"Bye Luce."

She turned to face Esther, Edith and Gloria, who were all pretending not to be eavesdropping. Crossing to the table, she collapsed into a chair, reaching across to grab half of a chocolate glazed before shoving it into her mouth. As she chewed, they fidgeted with their own plates, Edith rearranging her crumbs and Esther dividing a Boston cream into quarters.

"Cut the shit, ladies, I know you were listening." None of them replied. "Oh, come on! We were standing right there. You had front row seats."

"Well, they do look alike," offered Edith. "No question about that."

"Physically yes," agreed Esther. "But Lucy's mannerisms are all her mother. The smile; her smarts; her curiosity. That's all Maggie."

"Lyle seems—" said Edith.

"Like a dud," finished Esther.

"A dud?" asked Maggie, feeling surprisingly defensive. "How so?"

"Like he thinks his shit doesn't stink," said Esther.

"Really Esther, can't you think of a nicer way to say that?" Edith wrinkled her nose.

"Oh Edith, really. We're all adults. You know what I mean. He just seems holier than thou. Wearing his hair in a bun? Give me a break.

"But it doesn't matter," Esther continued. "Together you made a beautiful child, and whether or not he chooses to be a part of her life is up to him. I'm sure he has some good qualities, or else you wouldn't have been with him, Maggie. God knows my Irving wasn't perfect."

"John either," agreed Edith. "You did the right thing, telling him. For Lucy's sake."

"And maybe for yours, too. Who knows? If he decides to step up, it could mean some time off for you every once in a while. And wouldn't that be nice?" asked Esther.

"Yes, it would be nice," said Maggie. "Of course he'd have to prove himself first."

"I regret not telling Liza about Arthur," Edith volunteered.

"You do?" asked Maggie.

"I wish I had shared that part of myself with her. A lot of those boundaries I set up as her mother, they backfired. Telling Lyle and Lucy is for the best, Maggie. These kinds of secrets, they don't stay secrets forever. Better to be ahead of them. And now you are."

"Mommy!!" yelled Lucy.

"I better go," said Maggie, as she pushed her chair back reluctantly.

"Go on," urged Esther.

"What's wrong? What is it?"

"Mommy, look!" said Lucy. "He's Esther!"

Lyle looked out at Maggie from underneath the treasures of Esther's latest donation to Lucy's dress-up pile: an enormous black sunhat complete with zebra striped sash paired with at least a dozen strands of wooden beads in different shades of gold, silver and turquoise, with a diaphanous lavender and gold scarf draped artfully around his shoulders.

"Esther, you've never looked better," said Maggie.

"Why, thank you. It's these new vitamins I'm taking."

"No, no, no," said Lucy. "It's the 'sessories."

"The what?" asked Lyle.

"Accessories," translated Maggie.

"Mommy, now I do you. Stay," Lucy commanded.

"How's Portland?" Maggie asked, as Lucy rummaged through her pile.

"Great," Lyle answered. She found him much more tolerable in drag. "Such a cool, open community of people, you know? The weather, the lifestyle, the cost of living—everything is cool. Don't know why I tortured myself in New York for so long." Maggie looked down at the floor. "No, of course I don't mean us," he stammered.

"Lyle, it's okay, please." Lucy climbed onto her mother's lap in order to drape a plastic lei of flowers around her neck. "I—we—kept our relationship, or whatever it was, alive for way too long."

"Hey, it wasn't just you, Maggie. It was me, too." Lucy returned with an armful of plastic bangles, which she slid onto Maggie's wrist one by one.

"Shhhhh!" said Lucy. Maggie turned to her in alarm. "Lucy, that's rude. We're having a conversation." She cocked her head, surveying her mother.

"Needs more. I be back."

"Well, thanks for taking some responsibility, Lyle. I appreciate that. And you know, it wasn't all bad."

"Not at all, Maggie. We had a lot of fun." He pulled the scarf from his neck, winding it around his arm instead. "Can I ask you, though—like, what were you thinking? Did you want to get pregnant?"

"No. I considered as abortion at first, but then I thought,

shouldn't I? This could be it, my only shot at motherhood,"
Maggie explained. "With my age and everything, you know?
And I didn't have the money to freeze eggs or anything obviously, so—" Lucy climbed on the bed behind Maggie to place
a maroon beret on her head. "I took the pregnancy as a sign."

"So why tell me now?" asked Lyle.

"Lucy started to wonder about other people's dads; to ask
questions. Not about hers yet, but just the concept in general. I didn't want to lie, I guess. And I met someone. It's not
anything yet, but it could be. Maybe." Maggie blushed.

"I get it," said Lyle as Lucy returned with a leopard velvet
scarf.

"Here Mommy, put this on." Maggie complied as Lucy
stood back watching. "Okay, looks good." She sighed with the
conviction of a job well done. "I'm hungry," she announced.

"I bet," said Maggie. "Styling is hard work."

"It is," Lucy agreed.

"Do you want to go ask Esther for a donut?"

"Donuts!" Lucy exclaimed, running for the door.

"Don't forget the magic words!" Maggie called after her.

"Maggie, how did you end up here?" asked Lyle. "If I may
ask?"

"Where? In Sag Harbor running a nursing home? Esther
doesn't live here, by the way. Or Gloria. She's the nurse. Just
part-time. It's just Edith, Lucy and me. Still odd, though, I
know."

"Yeah. Never pictured you as the Hamptons type."

"Edith is Liza's mother," Maggie explained. "Liza, she—
she committed suicide."

"Oh Jesus, I'm sorry. Wait, who was Liza again?" he asked.

"Remember? The author? I used to clean her apartment?"

"Oh yeah, the one who stole your idea. That detective thing. I thought you stopped talking to her after that."

"I did. For years. This—" Maggie swept her arm out "—this was a shock. She left me this, and Edith, in her will."

"Wow," said Lyle.

"Yeah," agreed Maggie.

"No," said Lyle. "Jesus. How awful. I'm so sorry. I remember her now. I met her once, at her book launch party. She hated me."

"She didn't hate you." Lyle raised his eyebrows at Maggie. "Okay, maybe a little."

"So this, this is her apology? For doing what she did, with your idea?"

"I'm not sure," said Maggie. "There was no note, so who knows. Regardless, I'm not angry about it anymore anyway. It was just an idea. Not my story to tell. She told it better, in the end."

"You're not still cleaning houses, are you?" he asked.

"No, not anymore."

"No more scrubbing the bathroom grout with an old toothbrush at three in the morning, either?"

"I didn't say that." She had done exactly that the night before, unable to sleep because of her nerves.

"So what's with the mom? Why the nurse?"

"She has Alzheimer's. Early stages."

Lyle whistled softly. "Heavy. My grandmother had Alzheimer's. It gets pretty gnarly, although I'm sure you know that." Maggie thought that a forty-something-year-old man should not be using the word *gnarly* under any circumstances, but she didn't say as much.

"I know. Hence the nurse," she said instead.

"Hey, are you writing again?" he asked.

"I am, actually. Nothing big or anything, just here and there."

"That's great, Maggie. You were good at it. And it made you happy."

"You think?" she asked.

"Definitely. You never did give yourself enough credit, Maggie."

"Maggie, do you guys want to eat or what?" Esther yelled down.

"You hungry?" she asked Lyle, unwinding her scarf.

"Yes, actually." He removed his hat.

The two of them removed their Lucy-approved accessories in silence, except for the occasional noise of wood and brass clanking together. It was so familiar and yet, not at all. Maggie had been another person entirely when she was with Lyle, she realized. Clinging to something less than she deserved.

"About Lucy," said Lyle, dropping his last strand of beads on top of the pile.

"Yes, what about Lucy?" Maggie braced herself.

"I—I don't know how I feel right now, if I'm being honest. She's a wonderful kid, and I do feel a particular kind of affection towards her obviously, but I just don't know." He removed the elastic from his hair and regathered it nervously.

"I'm not sure if it's fair to promise to be a part of her life at this point. I—I'm not sure I can keep up my end of the bargain."

"The bargain?" Maggie asked. She was angry, but she couldn't say why exactly. This was what she wanted, right? Him to just go away?

"That's not what I mean, sorry. I just need some time, to think about it. About how I can most efficiently fit into her life, in a way that's fair to everyone. Does that make sense? I'm not even sure what I'm saying, man. It's a lot."

"I know it's a lot, Lyle, I'm in it every day, twenty-four hours a day."

She took a deep breath. She was forgetting the facts. What had she expected?

"But you're right. You need to be sure before Lucy even has a remote notion. I get that."

"I appreciate it, Maggie. I really do."

"Good," she replied.

Let him take his time. There was no rush.

CHAPTER 23

I found her this morning, in the guesthouse," Maggie told Esther. "I went in there to write, and there she was, curled in a ball amongst Liza's books, fast asleep."

Up ahead, Edith and Lucy combed the shore for seashells; the muted blue water melting seamlessly into the gray horizon.

"What did she say when you woke her up?"

"She was looking for Liza's note, she said," replied Maggie.

"Poor thing," said Esther, shaking her head.

"What if there is one?" asked Maggie.

"One what?"

"A note, hidden somewhere. A secret to uncover when the time is right," answered Maggie.

"I doubt that," replied Esther. "What do you think Liza left, a novella explaining everything away?"

"Maybe. Maybe she owned up to some stuff."

"Maggie, you don't off yourself if you're in the mood to own up to stuff. What would be the point?"

"I don't know—closure for your loved ones?" asked Maggie.

"If Liza had cared about closure, she would have stuck around."

"Esther, you're being glib," said Maggie.

"Am I? I don't mean to be." Esther started walking again. "Why do you want a note? What kind of answers do you need?" she asked.

"I don't know. About the Arthur thing, maybe."

"You provided the answer to that, the other day in the limo. Shakespeare himself couldn't have written a better script."

"Sure, but I was winging it. I'd like to believe in the happy ending, but what do I know? She could have been keeping it to herself for all of the wrong reasons, just like Edith suggested."

"Maybe," said Esther. "But your version is better for Edith. Better for all of us, really. And you have the right to wing it, to side with the good. Liza left us no other choice but to improvise. Which I'm grateful for, actually. And you should be, too."

"Why?" asked Maggie.

"She may have taken a story from you, but you got to

finish hers. Put a silver lining on the dark cloud of her passing. Liza knew what she was doing when she picked you, Maggie. You've done good here, with Edith."

Maggie walked in further towards the water, gulping back tears and shivering slightly as it tickled her toes. Esther's praise reminded her of her father when it had been good between them, his and now her recognition like ice water in the desert. She wiped her eyes and turned back.

"Thank you, Esther," she said, taking her arm to guide her through the sand. "I needed to hear that. I still wish that there was some sort of closure from Liza herself, though. Is that so wrong?"

"Of course it's not wrong, honey. A little naïve maybe, but not wrong. In this case, though, the only closure you're going to get is the closure you create yourself. Suicide doesn't care about closure."

"I have been able to do that, actually," said Maggie. "I've forgiven Liza, for the book thing. And other things are starting to make sense somehow, out here. With all of you."

"See?" said Esther. "Who needs a note?"

"Mommy, Mommy!" Lucy yelled, running towards her at breakneck speed, her arm outstretched. "Edith found me a hermit crab! Can we keep him?" Maggie eyed the tiny speckled creature in her daughter's hand suspiciously.

"Please?"

"You'll take care of him?"

"Yes," Lucy answered earnestly.

"Sure, okay."

"Okay here, you hold him." She deposited him into Maggie's hand. "Edif, she said yes!" she shrieked, running back to her.

"Great," said Maggie.

"Don't worry, it'll be dead in a week. You can teach her a life lesson," said Esther.

"Do you think Edith has closure?" asked Maggie.

"I think so," answered Esther. "The Arthur thing, it relieved some of that burden she's been carrying around, don't you think?" Maggie nodded.

"You know, she has Liza's ashes," said Esther.

"Edith does?"

"Yes, in an urn on her bureau. You never noticed?"

"I so rarely go in there," answered Maggie. "No."

"The two of you, you should spread them somewhere that Liza would have liked. Together. Make it official."

"You think Edith would be open to that?" asked Maggie.

"Only way to find out is to ask. But yes, I do."

"But I didn't know her life out here. I don't have the first clue about where to spread her." Maggie shivered. "Spread her. Jesus."

"So ask Edith. Or hell, take her back into the city."

"No, not the city," said Maggie. "She belongs here. With us."

"Okay," agreed Esther.

"Will you come? Wherever we end up?" asked Maggie, as Edith and Lucy circled back towards them.

"I don't think so, honey. This is between you and Edith. But I'll watch Miss Lucy. Save you the trouble of a sitter."

"Okay," said Maggie. It wasn't like Esther to choose to miss out on anything, but she was right.

CHAPTER 24

Edith had had mixed feelings about the ashes when Maggie had approached her, but a little time had persuaded her to say yes. That and Maggie's eagerness. Maggie seemed to be uplifted by the idea; kept making passionate speeches about the importance of it for the two of them. Edith didn't agree, but Esther had warned her not to be selfish.

"You won't remember it the next day anyway, Edith," she had joked. "But Maggie will. And she needs it. So let her have it."

And so, Edith had. They had decided to do it underneath the sprawling oak tree next to the guesthouse; a tree that Edith remembered Liza lounging underneath in the warmer months. She couldn't be completely sure, what with her memory, but it sounded good, and seemed to satisfy Maggie.

Edith walked out to the porch, staring down into its now sparse canopy of leaves to the ground below. They'd considered the beach of course, but the truth was that Liza never strayed far from home. She had loved this house. She belonged here.

"Everything okay?" asked Gloria, joining her. Edith had gotten used to Gloria, quite liked her actually. She made Edith feel safe, which was something she needed to feel now. She didn't know whether she was coming or going anymore. Today was a good day, though. So far at least.

"Sure," she murmured back.

"Edith?" asked Maggie, joining them. "You ready?"

They passed through the living room, where Lucy played cars with Esther on the floor, down the stairs and into Edith's room.

"Can't forget the guest of honor," said Edith. She grabbed the gray urn, holding it close to her chest.

"You got it?" asked Maggie. "I can carry it if it's too heavy."

"I've got it," said Edith.

They walked through Maggie's room and out the doors, en route to the tree. Before she realized what was happening, Edith lost her footing. She wobbled precariously, and the urn slipped out of her unreliable grasp, smashing to the floor and shattering into dozens of pieces. All around them, Liza rose up, a cloud of dust.

Maggie and Edith stood, looking down at the mess, at Liza all over their shoes, not knowing what to do or say.

"Whoops," said Edith finally, breaking their stunned silence.

"Oh no, Edith," said Maggie. "What do we do now?"

"I don't know," answered Edith. "I can't believe that happened."

"Me, either." Maggie laughed. "But it did, so? What can we do? I'm sure Liza loved this porch, too."

"Yeah, you know, I was thinking that I probably made that business up about the tree anyway," said Edith. "Maybe I saw her there once."

"And she complained about the bugs for a half hour before getting up and going inside," said Maggie. "That sounds like the real Liza."

"Yes," agreed Edith.

"So, it's fitting that this happened."

"Perfect, really."

"Should we just do it here?" asked Maggie.

"Do what?" asked Edith.

"I don't know, eulogize her?"

The sky was so blue, Edith thought. The kind of blue that only autumn could claim. And the air—it was as crisp as an apple.

"If that's what you want," said Edith. "Although I think it's unnecessary, this whole thing, if I'm being honest."

"Why?"

"We've both let her go, haven't we? And out of that, we made this. The end."

"This?"

"Us. This new life."

"That's it?" asked Maggie. She shifted her feet, the dust sliding off her shoes and through the cracks of the porch.

"I think so," said Edith.

"Maybe you're right," said Maggie. "I don't know, I just thought something more formal would be nice."

"Say what you want to say, Maggie. Don't let me stop you."

"Here?"

"Sure, where else?"

"Well, okay." Maggie cleared her throat. "God, I forgot everything suddenly."

"Welcome to the club," said Edith.

"You know what? I don't think I need to do this, after all."

"You're sure?" asked Edith.

"I am. The accidental release of Liza was perfect. A metaphor, really. She would have appreciated it, I think," Maggie replied.

"Maggie, I want to thank you," said Edith. "You've been wonderful to me. I know I haven't been easy."

"You? You're a breeze." Maggie smiled at Edith.

"I mean it. Liza made the right choice, by choosing you." First Esther had said it, and now Edith. Maggie believed them, too. She had had so much healing to do herself, healing she hadn't even realized she needed. Edith's journey to forgiveness had become her own. Who knew if Liza had known that would happen, but Maggie chose to believe that she had, just an inkling at least. It was another happy ending that Maggie had the right to choose, as the chosen keeper of the narrative.

"I'm glad she chose me," Maggie said. "My life, it's better

out here. And Lucy's, too. Helping you with your memories has helped me with coming to terms with my own. You've been so brave."

"I'm not brave," said Edith. "What's brave about me?"

"Are you kidding? You're the bravest person I've ever met."

"You're brave, too, you know," said Edith.

"I am?" asked Maggie.

"Single motherhood? Starting over? Bravest things there are."

"Thanks, Edith." They were quiet suddenly, listening to a lone bird chirp. "This has turned into something else entirely, huh?" asked Maggie.

Edith shrugged.

"But I guess that's the point," continued Maggie. "Life goes on, after death."

"After heartbreak," said Edith.

"And disappointment," added Maggie. "If only Liza had known that."

Edith surveyed the porch; the dust and fragments amongst the brittle red, yellow and orange leaves.

"Should we pick up the pieces?" she asked.

"Sure," answered Maggie.

They began to fish them out, one by one, together.

About the author

About the book

Read on

Insights,
Interviews
& More . . .

Meet Zoe Fishman

Karen Shacham

ZOE FISHMAN is the author of *Driving Lessons*, *Saving Ruth* and *Balancing Acts*. Her books have been translated into German, Italian, Dutch and Polish. She's the recipient of many awards, including selection as one of Target's Breakout and Emerging Author Picks and a *New York Post* Pick. Zoe has also been featured on NBC's *Atlanta & Co.*, as well as in *Publishers Weekly* and the Huffington Post. She is currently at work on her next novel, as well as teaching writing at the Callanwolde Fine Arts Center. Zoe lives in Atlanta with her husband and two sons. ∼

Discovering Maggie

IT TOOK ME FOREVER to write
Inheriting Edith, or at least forever in
terms of my prior writing track record.
From the idea's inception to the fourth
rewrite, it was two years, give or take.
I became pregnant, had my second son,
balanced the work and motherhood
seesaw sometimes well and sometimes
not so well, my novel sputtering along
in starts and stops all the while. Edith
was always fully realized, I could write
her in my sleep for some reason,
probably because I felt like I understood
her from the start. It was Maggie who
eluded me. She wasn't me and, for better
or worse, so many of my previous
protagonists have been.

I turned my first draft into my editor
just before I gave birth, not really happy
with it but relieved to put it in someone
else's capable hands before mine were
inconceivably full. The first six weeks
passed in a haze of no sleep and breast
milk, my sweet three-year-old blessedly
delighted to be a big brother and
surprising me with his empathic
tenderness. He went to camp, my
husband went to work and it was just
the baby and me, doing what new
babies and their mothers do in the
heat of an Atlanta summer—getting
to know one another in air-conditioned
confinement.

When my brain was able, I would
fret over Maggie. Who was she? Was it
possible to make her three-dimensional
without the personal experience to ▶

back her up? Maybe she wasn't so dull, maybe it was me being too hard on myself. And then the letter from my very smart, very wise and very patient editor arrived, confirming my doubt, albeit in a very nice way. Maggie was a dud.

I continued to fret, although now it had blossomed into a full-blown panic. No matter how hard I tried, I just could not make her work. Was it writer's block or just utter exhaustion? Would I have to scrap Maggie altogether, create another protagonist from scratch? I certainly didn't want to, but as time crept on, I couldn't see any other feasible resolution.

Finally we were gifted with a somewhat breezy July morning. It was official: all of us could go to the park. We loaded what felt like our entire home into the car in preparation and took off. I felt like a mole, blinking against the light as it streamed through the trees, my breasts like giant, hot water balloons underneath my shirt. As we pulled up, I glanced at the clock on the dashboard, noting that it was time to feed. *You guys go ahead,* I said, hoisting myself up and out of my seat to grab the baby. With dutiful nods, they jogged towards the swings.

I adjusted myself and turned the radio to NPR, thinking I would zone out as I performed my motherly duty, a duty that was thankfully easier, practically enjoyable, the second time around. Suddenly, a writer came on—a woman—talking about how she didn't believe in writer's block; how sitting your butt down every day, whenever you could manage, and forcing out however many words you could, even if they were terrible, made writer's block obsolete. I wish I could remember who the writer was or what exactly she said verbatim, but I can't. All I know is that it was the most perfect thing I could hear—like a key in the ignition of my brain. It was miraculous really, so I owe a huge thank you to NPR—for so many things, but especially for that moment.

I exited the car with the baby, thinking about Maggie. At that point she was a writing student of Liza's: a thirty-something freelancer who was just lucky enough to be mentored by a bestselling author. She was lost but not in any tangible way. There was no why, she just was.

In the park, my family and I scurried along the dirt path, our eldest pointing out sticks and plants, squirrels and precarious surfaces from which to jump. Another boy appeared, a bit bigger than mine, setting the tone for play in the way that older kids do. In the shade of an enormous oak tree, his mother, a friendly woman who asked us about the baby, joined us and introduced us to her son.

We began to make the kind of parenting small talk you make when you're at a park: "Boy is it hot, where is he in school?", and in the case of summer in the South, "Do you belong ▶

Discovering Maggie *(continued)*

to a pool?" They did, she said, and then somehow she ended up telling us a story that turned another key: the key to Maggie, in as little as the maybe ten minutes it took her to tell it. Really, it was that fast.

She gave swim lessons in her spare time, she said, a fact that excited me because I grew up doing the same. We swapped war stories for a moment or two, and then she casually mentioned that she had been a very good swimmer as a kid, good enough to qualify for the Junior Olympics. "That's amazing," my husband and I replied, because it is amazing; to show that much promise so young.

She shrugged her shoulders. "Yeah," she said, "I guess." She paused before continuing. "But you know, I had the ultimate Tiger Mom. I came in fourth and she took me out of swimming forever. I never competed again." She was laughing, but her eyes were sad.

"Oh my God," I said, my jaw hanging open. "Why? Why would she do that?"

"Saving face," she explained. "Fourth was an embarrassment."

At that point, the conversation switched gears, one of the children needed us I'm sure, but I was deeply affected by her story. My goodness, the repercussions of such a thing! To be taught as a kid that if you weren't the best, you shouldn't even bother? That personal enjoyment was a nonissue? It blew my mind.

All day long I thought about her.

I thought about my own childhood; my own parents. I thought about myself as a parent and if I was inadvertently sending the wrong kinds of messages to my sons. I thought about Maggie. What had her parents been like? Were they the reason she was so complacent? Why?

I sat down to write early that next morning while the kids were asleep; tiny windows of insight opening in my brain as I reimagined her. Part of her problem was the whole former student of Liza's angle. It was too easy; too flat. How could Maggie gain insight into Liza in an unexpected way? I wondered, frowning at the dust bunnies clustered around the legs of my desk. I need to clean, I thought, sighing. Clean. Clean! Could Maggie have been Liza's house cleaner? Yes! I returned to my keyboard, typing at the speed of light. And if Maggie was Liza's housecleaner, why?

Why would a college-educated girl in her twenties, in New York City no less, become a housecleaner? Where was her ambition? Had she had a Tiger Parent who had stripped her of it? No, I thought at first. Well, maybe just a little Tiger. Tiger Light. And what was the other parent like? Like Liza, perhaps? Depressed as well, so that the disease was familiar to Maggie?

I wrote and wrote—nothing that would make it into the novel itself, but just a character sketch for myself. ▶

Discovering Maggie *(continued)*

Why Maggie was the way she was, and whether she was bothered by it or not. Because that was a huge part of Maggie's character, too, her level of self-awareness.

Once I had her figured out (at last!) the rest of the novel came together for me. Plot points had motivation; my characters' realizations felt authentic and hard-won; and even Edith, who I thought I had figured out from the get-go, became more compellingly complicated.

I was like a spider, reweaving the web of my story thanks to one unexpectedly motivating morning on an otherwise ordinary day. From nothing: something. Or in Maggie's case, someone. ⌒

Reading Group Guide

1. In a lot of ways, housecleaning is therapy for Maggie, even if she isn't fully cognizant of this. Are there any tasks in your own life that provide this sense of solace?

2. As parents, we blame ourselves for so much of our children's trouble. Edith is no exception, especially in the wake of Liza's suicide. Do you think we're culpable, or that people are just born the way they are, destined for their own story lines despite our best intentions?

3. Inheritance is such a complicated concept. Even if we are gifted with the good, it usually comes with a catch. If you were Maggie, would you have taken the house knowing that it came with Edith? Are you the kind of person that sees the glass as half full in this type of instance or half empty? If so, why? Is it a trait you've inherited or have you learned through experience?

4. Edith shares her secret with Maggie only when her memory of it is threatened. If you were to find yourself in Edith's shoes, is there something you would feel compelled to resolve? How would you go about resolving it?

5. Liza is bipolar, but chooses to forego her medication because it doesn't make her feel like herself, a common complaint about antidepressants in general. Have you or anyone you know been faced with such a dilemma?

6. Maggie wonders whether Liza's decision to bequeath her home to her is her way of apologizing for stealing her story line. What do you think? Was she sorry underneath the bravado of claiming artistic license? Why do you think Liza leaves the house and Edith to Maggie?

7. In the limo on the way home from Arthur's, Maggie tells Edith that Liza's decision to keep her friendship with Arthur a secret was not steeped in malicious intent, but instead a show of respect for her mother. Do you think Maggie's theory is correct? And do you think Maggie believes her own words or that it's merely to soothe Edith? Does it matter?

8. Maggie comes to realize that it wasn't about the "stupid detective" at all in terms of her anger towards Liza; that it wasn't anger at all really, but a deep-seated hurt at her betrayal of Maggie's trust. Have you ever experienced the same sort of realization in your own life? How were you able to get to the root of it?

9. There's so much about loss in this novel—Alzheimer's, suicide, Maggie's parents. Do you think that memory eases or intensifies the pain of loss?

10. Liza doesn't leave a note, but if she had, what do you suppose it would have said? ∾

Favorite Recent Reads

Astonish Me, Maggie Shipstead
We Are All Completely Beside Ourselves,
   Karen Joy Fowler
The Middlesteins, Jami Attenberg
Swamplandia, Karen Russell
Where'd You Go, Bernadette,
   Maria Semple
After Birth, Elisa Albert ∾

Have You Read?
More by Zoe Fishman

DRIVING LESSONS

Sarah has had her fill of the interminable hustle of the big city. When her husband, Josh, is offered a new job in suburban Virginia, it feels like the perfect chance to shift gears.

While Josh quickly adapts to their new life, Sarah discovers that time on her hands is a mixed blessing. Without her everyday urban struggles, who is she? And how can she explain to Josh, who assumed they were on the same page, her ambivalence about starting a family?

It doesn't help that the idea of getting behind the wheel—an absolute necessity of her new life—makes it hard for her to breathe. It's been almost twenty years since Sarah's driven, and just the thought of merging is enough to make her teeth chatter with anxiety. When she signs up for lessons, she begins to feel a bit more like her old self again, but she's still unsure of where she wants to go.

Then, a crisis involving her best friend, Mona, lands Sarah back in New York—a trip to the past filled with unexpected truths about herself, her dear friend and her seemingly perfect sister-in-law . . . and a surprise that will help her see the way ahead.

SAVING RUTH

When Ruth returns home to the South for the summer after her freshman year at college, a near tragedy pushes her to uncover family truths and take a good look at the woman she wants to become.

Growing up in Alabama, all Ruth Wasserman wanted was to be a blond Baptist cheerleader. But as a curly-haired Jew with a rampant sweet tooth and a smart mouth, this was an impossible dream. Not helping the situation was her older brother, David—a soccer star whose good looks, smarts and popularity reigned at school and at home. College provided an escape route and Ruth took it.

Now home for the summer, Ruth's back lifeguarding and coaching alongside David, and although the job is the same, nothing else is. She's a prisoner of her low self-esteem and unhealthy relationship with food, David is closed off and distant in a way he's never been before, and their parents are struggling with the reality of an empty nest. When a near drowning happens on their watch, a storm of repercussions forces Ruth and David to confront long-ignored truths about their town, their family and themselves.

With beauty, brains and a high-paying Wall Street position, Charlie was a woman who seemed to have it all—until she turned thirty and took stock of her life, or lack thereof. She left it all behind to pursue yoga, and now, two years later, she's looking to drum up business for her fledgling studio in Brooklyn. Attending her college's alumni night with fliers in tow, she reconnects with three former classmates whose post-graduation lives, like hers, haven't turned out like they'd hoped.

Romance book editor Sabine still longs to write the novel that's bottled up inside her. Once an up-and-coming photographer and Upper East Side social darling, Naomi is now a single mom who hasn't picked up her camera in years. And Bess, who dreamed of being a serious investigative journalist a la Christiane Amanpour, is stuck in a rut, writing snarky captions for a gossip mag. But at a weekly yoga class at Charlie's studio, the four friends, reunited ten years after college, will forge new bonds and take new chances—as they start over, fall in love, change their lives . . . and come face-to-face with haunting realities.

Discover great authors, exclusive offers, and more at hc.com.